Tragic Coincidence

A novel by

Geoff Kenure

Copyright © Geoff Kenure

ISBN: 978-1-917778-16-9

All rights reserved, including the right to reproduce this book, or portions thereof in any form. No part of this text may be reproduced, transmitted, downloaded, decompiled, reverse engineered, or stored, in any form or introduced into any information storage and retrieval system, in any form or by any means, whether electronic or mechanical without the express written permission of the author.

All characters in this book are entirely fictional and any resemblance to any person alive or dead is purely coincidental.

Also by this author

<u>Fiction</u>

Loyalty's Legacy (2025)

Non-Fiction

The Heydays of the Independent Probation officer in England and Wales 1950s – 1970s. (2018)

For

Kathy, Andrew and Ali.

'Faith, hope and love: and the greatest is love.'

1 Corinthians 13.13

Contents

Prologue

Part One - Reaction

Chapter 1	Death Knock
Chapter 2	Immediate Aftermath
Chapter 3	Distant Light
Chapter 4	Making Arrangements
Chapter 5	The Journey
Chapter 6	An Arrival

Part Two – Renaissance

Chapter 7	New Beginnings
Chapter 8	Incidental Consequence
Chapter 9	Day Off
Chapter 10	Social Christmas
Chapter 11	Historical Echo
Chapter 12	Sothern Sojourn
Chapter 13	Altered Landscape

Part Three – Reverberation

Chapter 14	New Perspective
Chapter 15	Significant Night
Chapter 16	Potential Repercussions
Chapter 17	What Now?
Chapter 18	Garnering Information
Chapter 19	Final Preparations
Chapter 20	Tragic Coincidence
	Post Script

Clackmore - circa 1963

Sketch from the papers of E Mathieson and to which he refers at page 156.

Key

1 Alistair & Morag's house
3 Dougie's house
5 Jetty Lodge
2 Ewan's house
4 Boat shed
6   To Newton

Prologue

A setting autumnal evening sun lit the solitary little croft house by the stream at the head of the bay, casting long shadows across the inland field. The only movement visible was made by grazing animals and fluttering birds until the door opened and figures emerged one carrying a woven shopping basket. Without noise, other than the crunch of feet on a loosely gravelled track, they made their way down to, and across, a narrow single track tarmac roadway and onto a small ribbon of grassy machair which skirted the top of the bay.

Turning to their right they moved along the machair keeping above the huge boulders of Torridonian stone, and as they did so they disturbed the grazing rabbits which scurried away to their burrows. The rocks and boulders preserved the machair from the twice-daily tidal attack of the sea, but even though the tide had probably just about reached its fullness, this particular attack was of a very muted kind.

It was one of those autumn days, indeed one of those very rare days irrespective of the season, when waves did not fling themselves against the rocks but merely lapped in almost friendly fashion. Reaching the end of the machair the figures turned to the left along the rocks which skirted the north side of the little bay. They jumped in a hopping dance from rock to rock until, on their left, they passed the extent of the tide and moved further on towards the headland. After a while they settled, each figure taking its own vantage point from which they could watch the gentle swell of the sea pass them and go on towards the shore. With the passing of each small wave the kelp and other sea flora lifted and fell with the sound of a gentle sigh.

Unspeaking the figures sat watching the calm viscous sea until one of them rose and bent to pick up a piece of driftwood and, taking a few paces forward, threw it gently onto the surface of the sea. Returning to the vacated seat the figure, with its companions, stared at the driftwood. After a while, apparently satisfied that it was being tidally borne seaward rather than landward, the same figure rose and lifted the woven bag and produced from within it a small solid object and dropping the woven bag moved to the edge of the sea. A lid was removed from the object and the main body of it was upended, causing a dust storm to be emitted and to fall onto the oily looking water. The figure returned, replaced the solid object in the bag and resumed sitting.

The figures stayed seated watching the point where the dust had settled on the sea and remained until it had apparently dissipated. In a while the figures, as if by mutual unspoken consent, rose and retraced their hoppity progress along the rocks until they gained the relative flatness of the machair again. Retracing their steps they again disturbed the grazing rabbits, for the figures had been so long about their business that the rabbits had felt safe to return. The figures re-crossed the tarmac and ascended the slight incline of the unmade track which led to the croft house.

With hardly a backward glance they went inside.

Part 1 - Reaction

Death Knock

How many things would we do differently if we were to know in advance that a life changing event was just around the next corner? A person on death row might be reasonably certain of the time of his execution but his choices as to what he might do on his last day will be constrained by his incarceration. Similarly, the person with a terminal illness is often constrained, in their last hours, by the ravages of their illness. But both of these souls, with a finite or very short lifespan before them, may choose to write or say things that they would like others to hear, occasionally in anger but more often with a view to 'putting things in order'.

But for the relatively healthy person, and in particular the relatively young – let us say under thirty five as that is halfway to three score years and ten – we often do not dwell on our own mortality or that of our contemporaries. In the absence of the onset of a serious unexpected illness we operate on the principle that death is for the elderly and not for us. We defer the consideration of our own demise, or that of a loved one, to a future 'to do list' that will not need addressing until we have at least passed middle age – and even that we assume is a long way off. In this general mind-set we have no concept of the likelihood of a traumatic life changing event being imminent and in the absence of that knowledge, we simply engage in the routines of our lives. And so it was with me that fateful morning in 1963.

The two little brass bells on the top of my wind-up alarm clock tinkled their wake-up call shortly after six thirty. I went to the bathroom to shave whilst Linda, my wife, went down and I could hear her raking out the fire and generally beginning the business of the day. By seven o'clock I was halfway through my bowl of Kellogg's cornflakes when Carole our daughter came into the kitchen looking half asleep, dragging her favourite blanket behind her. At five and a half years of age she had just started in the infants section of Cardinal Road School the previous September and, while she seemed to be managing to cope with it, she was nevertheless prone to become very tired and in need of her comfort blanket, at least in the privacy of home.

My job was in the accounts department of a company which specialised in air freight, most of which went through Heathrow airport, that rapidly expanding aeronautical terminus in those early years of the 1960's, and for obvious reasons our offices were located on an industrial estate not far away, in fact on Faggs Road just between Feltham and Hatton. Our own semi-detached house was in Boundaries Road, Feltham and all I had to do to get to work was to cycle to the end of my road and turn right and the offices of my place of employment were something like a mile and a half away, from door to door. Leaving home on my bike at about seven forty got me to my desk by eight.

About half past seven I reminded Linda that I was going to meet Billy after work for a couple of drinks and I would be late home for tea at about seven that evening. Linda was not a fan of Billy's and whilst I accepted and understood that, I retained a certain loyalty to him because of what he had done for me directly and also indirectly for Linda and Carole. Billy, was a mate from early schooldays and we were parted by the intervention of the Eleven Plus exam, which he passed and I did not. This exam separated us into two groups, the brainy ones who went on the more academic route to the Grammar school and the rest of us who went to Secondary Modern schools which had some basic academic work, but also taught practical skills like woodwork or metal work for the boys and the grandly titled 'Home Economics' or 'Domestic Science' for girls. So off Billy went to his Grammar school, and we were separated for some years until National Service, when, by an extraordinary accident of fate, we ended up in the same Army unit and we renewed our friendship.

Before conscription Billy had been working for his father for some time but was obviously glad to get away. It proved hard to get to understand what his father did, he owned a number of grocery shops and he occasionally imported some overseas products to add to the usual home produced fruit and vegetable staples. His business had thrived after the end of rationing in 1954, as people were keen to buy new and more exotic items not previously available except on the black market. Occasionally he imported some items by air, especially in the lead up to Christmas. Whatever the situation it was clear that the business made a healthy profit for Billy's dad. I believe that he had originally made his mark during the war when he was, in the parlance of the day, a quite successful 'spiv' and that would be the thing that 'straight as a die' Linda would have disliked. When the time for our demob was due I faced an uncertain future, because my secondary modern school education had not given me any significant employment skills, as I had proved poor at manual skills with wood and metal. After school and before National Service I had worked in local factories but never really adapted to that sort of work either. The Army, however, did something for me in that regard. I did general training and even got to take and pass my driving test, and later I was assigned to the regimental quartermaster's staff as a storeman. Minutely recording, as was the army way, every item of stores received and from whom, and every item dispensed and to whom. A kindly warrant officer noted that I had an aptitude for figures and arranged for me to get some basic training in book keeping. I have always been fascinated by numbers and the work appealed to me and I soon became proficient.

When my time in the Army was coming to an end I began to think about how I could organise my life. One thing was very clear, that Linda and I, sweethearts since secondary school, would get married. She had done domestic science at school and was now working in the canteen of a big local factory. I had been careful to save as much as I could of my Army pay as I was neither a drinker nor a smoker. But what I was going to do for work was the question that not only exercised me but also Linda in her letters to me. This is where Billy came in.

Through occasionally importing fruit and vegetables by air, Billy's dad knew Mr Stewart, the manager at Air Freight & Trading Ltd., so at Billy's suggestion my name was given to him. Now Mr Stewart had seen military service during the war and co-incidentally in the same regiment as that to which I had been assigned at the end of my National Service. He considered the reference given to me by my commanding officer, based on the good reports of my warrant officer and, no doubt with a nod to regimental loyalty, it secured me a junior job in the accounts department at the company. In fairness I did not let Mr Stewart down, for as well as working hard for the company I went to evening classes to improve my bookkeeping and accountancy skills. So that after five years in the job I was a real asset to the company, had long term secure employment and I enjoyed a very happy working life.

My indebtedness to Billy Johnson was part of the reason that I met up with him about once a month or so, but there was another reason too. Billy's dad was by now quite a high-powered wheeler and dealer with a number of shops and working for his father Billy was required to do some things with which, I sensed, he wasn't altogether comfortable. In many ways he was in the shadow of his father and he lacked the confidence to break away. Whilst he needed to please his father in some ways, he was not on the same wave length as his dad and he certainly did not have any friends amongst the people with whom he had to work. On the contrary, in my workplace I enjoyed working with some good colleagues and there was a lot of cheerful camaraderie. So I suppose I felt sorry for Billy as well as being indebted to him for getting me the job introduction, and it was for these reasons that I kept these monthly meetings because he seemed to enjoy and need my company and, that being so, I felt it was a payment off the debt of gratitude I owed to him.

Linda came from a family with very clear moral views. Members of St Catherine's Church, where her brother Les, was a choirboy in his childhood days, they were very much against the ideas of the black market and the spivs who had been prevalent during the war. My father-in-law, Tommy Moorfield, Linda's dad, was a ticket inspector with Southern Region railways and he had no time at all for the likes of Billy's dad who had avoided service in the war by apparently doubtful means. So whenever I said to Linda that I was going to meet Billy it was the one sore point in our otherwise very happy marriage.

"I just don't like you associating with that man," said Linda.

"But Linda," I replied, "I feel sorry for him because he's out of his depth working for his father, but he doesn't know how to break away and as well as that he is very lonely."

"It's easy," she said, "he should just go off and get an ordinary job and leave his dad to his own devices."

"Linda, I think he will one day, but he needs friends like me to be able to talk to about what he should do, and let's face it he's done an awful lot for us."

"Oh yes! He got you a job which you might have done on your own."

"You know very well that his dad's introduction to Mr Stewart made all the difference and look what it's done for us. I come straight out of the Army straight into work and it meant that you and I could get married when we did, and incidentally, remember that if we hadn't planned to get married it might have ended up in a 'shotgun do' anyway with the amazing little Carole, coming along after just seven and a half months from our wedding day. And yes, we may well have about just managed, but having such a good steady job meant that we could get a mortgage from the Finchley Building Society to buy this little house. Also it means that, after you had to give up work because Carole was on the way, we have been able to manage financially ever since. I personally feel that I ought not to let Billy down because of that."

"Well there we must differ." She said.

"Yes," I said, "but, let's not fall out about it, after all it's only a couple of hours in the pub and you know I don't drink much."

"Humph!" She said, turning away.

"Alright Miss Carrie," I said turning to my little girl, "Daddy is off to work now and I will be home a little bit late tonight, but I should be here just in time for your bedtime and I will read a little story."

"Okay love. I'm off then." I said to Linda, picking up the wrap of greaseproof paper in which Linda had put up my sandwiches for lunch.

And Linda replied with a perfunctory 'Bye' and without offering the usual peck on the cheek which was our usual parting custom. Carole at least acknowledged my departure with a kiss and a brief wave.

Car ownership was becoming much more prevalent in the early 1960's but we had not yet aspired to that status. We did not really need a car. Work, as I have already explained was a ten minute bike ride away – fifteen minutes on a wet windy day peddling hard against the elements under my yellow bicycle cape. Contact with relatives was no problem. I was an only child and Dad had been killed early in the war and, until her death the previous year, Mum had lived just off Feltham High Street in Bedfont Lane, just over the railway level crossing, a twenty minute walk away. Between our house and hers one passed the end of one road where Linda's brother Les and his wife lived, and another road where her parents together with her spinster sister lived. In Feltham High Street itself you had all the shops you needed. Across from our road there was the old Hanworth Park airfield, which had welcomed the Graf Zeppelin in the 1930's and had produced small aircraft during and after the war up until the early 1950's. Then at the other end of our dead end road were fields which led to the Southern Railway marshalling yards. So exercise locally was no problem.

Then we had buses at the end of the road which could take you for a nice day out to Richmond with all its shops and the river Thames or even, with one change, to Hampton Court. Feltham Station was at our end of Feltham High Street and, as described, that was an easy walk away. From there in one direction the train took you to Staines or Windsor and the other way to Waterloo and the heart of the city. So what point a car; at that stage it was unnecessary for family life and it meant that, even with just my income, we were comfortably off.

So that morning, that fateful morning, Wednesday 6th March 1963 I left my wife and daughter and went to the garage, put my bicycle clips round my trousers and wheeled my Raleigh cycle down the drive, pushed off, swung my leg over the crossbar and began my routine journey to work.

Ask me now to recall the weather and I would be a liar to say that I did, it was probably a fairly crisp March morning and I guess I would have remembered if it had been blowing a gale or pouring with rain, so I will suppose it was not. It was, I later discovered, the first morning of that year when there was no frost in the whole country; it had been the year of the 'Big Freeze' one of the coldest winters on record. Equally, I do not remember precisely what happened when I got to work.

The usual routine was that I arrived just before eight, left my bike in one of the warehouses walked to the office back door, as reception did not start till nine, so we office staff went in the back way and up the back stairs. Being a Wednesday, it would be the day we prepared wages for the staff who worked in the warehouse and the drivers. Unlike us office staff, on monthly salaries, they all worked a week in hand, so we had to look at their timesheets for the week ending the previous Saturday and calculate their wage, making deductions for Income Tax and National Insurance and of course for any "subs", that is cash they had been advanced and would need to be taken from their wages. Then we would need to calculate how much cash we would need overall and in what denominations of notes and coins so as to advise the bank what we needed on the Friday morning when, after collecting it, we would make up the little brown envelopes to be handed out on that afternoon.

So Wednesday morning would have been busy checking timesheets, asking people about things that were unclear or illegible. It was important work to get correct because at the end of the day when the worker opened that pay packet and read the payslip inside, they would expect it to be right, and if it was not then there would be extra work for us on Friday. In short it was busy and needed concentration and interruptions were unwelcome.

At some time in the middle of the morning perhaps not long after ten o'clock I was looking at the timesheet of Freddie Coombes one of the drivers who needed keeping an eye on, as he was prone to over claim on his timesheet. On the Wednesday of last week he was showing an hour and a half's overtime and it was unclear from the notes on his card as to why he'd worked late that particular night. I walked over to our transport manager, Jim, and raised the query with him. Looking at the notes on the driver's log he had a collection from Heathrow airport late morning for delivery to Shoreham airport, near Brighton on the South Coast. It seemed unnecessary for him not to have completed that work and be back by six o'clock, yet he was recorded as not returning until almost eight o'clock in the evening.

"Where is Freddie today?" Jim asked his assistant.

"This morning, short delivery in the van to Sunbury, and then this afternoon......"

"Never mind this afternoon. Just let me know when he gets back from Sunbury."

"You're in luck. I saw him pulling into the yard only a couple of minutes ago."

Jim picked up the phone and asked Sandra on reception to 'tannoy' for Freddie to come over from the warehouse and see him. A few minutes later Freddie arrived with his usual confident, almost truculent, manner on full display.

"Why were you not back till nearly eight last Wednesday evening?" asked Jim.

"Last Wednesday? Oh yea. Well, I picked up some aircraft parts from Heathrow that had been flown in from

Germany and did not clear customs till about twelve. They were for Beagle Aircraft at Shoreham airport. So I set off down the A 24 and onto the A 27 and out at Shoreham. Got there about two, or half past, the storekeepers at the airport were busy and, as you know with them all goods inward have to be checked before they sign your receipt, so I got away about three fifteen. Should have been back by half five but I got mixed up in that bad crash at Kingsfold on the A 24. I was second vehicle on the scene and the crash closed the road and the cops told me that I had to wait for them to see if I should give a statement. As it happens I did not see the crash, as I poled up just after it had happened. So then they said there was no need for me to give a statement after all and I could go, but by then it was gone half six. I came straight back."

His story seemed to tally because both Jim and I had heard about a fatal accident between a lorry and a car on the A 24 last week.

"That is fine Freddie," said Jim, "you will get your overtime."

Freddie turned to go and then said, as one who has a piece of news to impart that nobody else has heard about yet.

"By the way Hanworth Road is closed."

We both looked up and Freddie continued.

"I just came back from Sunbury and I came up Feltham High Street and the road is closed by the church and there were police all over. I wonder if there some trouble down at the Magistrates Courts."

We nodded and off he went. Feltham Magistrates Courts were situated on Hanworth Road but around a bend in the road, so that they would not have been visible from Feltham High Street, so whether Freddie was correct in his assumption or not was unclear, but in any event it held no real interest to us; so work went on.

Not an hour later a police constable stood at the door of my office whilst Sandra, our receptionist, flapped about beside him. Looking back I am willing to wager that the more cynical of warehouse and driving staff, like Freddie, would have had a field day with the story that a copper was in the offices and that he was asking for one of those blokes in the accounts department. No doubt that would have given rise to speculation that 'one of them shirt and tie lot has been caught on the fiddle'.

Sandra was speaking and pointing in my direction, but I did not hear a word, instead my eyes were fixed on the constable. He was a local bobby and, whilst I had never spoken to him, I had seen him from time to time on his police bicycle, doing his rounds, often with a cheerful smile on his face.

On this day, however, his face said it all.

It said, 'whilst I love this job there are parts of it which are really horrible, and this is one of those parts.'

The death knock.

Immediate aftermath

"Mr Mathieson?" The policemen asked, "Mr. Ewan Mathieson?" I nodded. "Is there somewhere private we can go sir?"

"Officer, you can use my office if you like." Said Mr Stewart, the manager, who had appeared suddenly from somewhere, no doubt attracted by Sandra's twittering.

We went into his office and the policemen very deliberately closed the door and turned to me.

"You may wish to sit down sir I have some bad news." Without taking my eyes off his face I lowered myself into one of the comfortable chairs Mr Stewart liked to have for his visitors.

"Were you the husband of Linda Mathieson born in August 1935 and father to Carole Mathieson born in January 1957?"

"Yes." I replied with my mind racing. Something was not quite right with the statement he had just made and I couldn't put my finger on it, but did it have something to do with that first word he'd used. 'Were', or did I mishear him and did he say 'are', but, before I could unscramble that conundrum he went on.

"I'm sorry to tell you sir that there's been a dreadful accident."

"Oh. No! Are they hurt? And in the hospital? Should I go to them now?"

"No sir," he said his voice dropping both in volume and tone, "I'm afraid that they're not in hospital sir because, well ……………..there is no easy way of saying this but they're both dead."

He paused as I stared at him then continued.

"Shortly before nine o'clock this morning they were hit by a car in Hanworth Road and tragically they both died at the scene."

I looked at him, so there was nothing wrong with that first question he asked me, it was appropriate for him to have used the past tense and the word 'were' when he questioned me about my relationship with Linda. The silence continued as I searched his face for a sign of hope but his facial expression simply said to me 'I can't believe I have to tell you this, but what's more I cannot believe you have to hear it'.

We remained silent whilst my mind unsuccessfully tried to unravel the information he had just given me. There was no shouting, no screaming, no crying, just a profound sense of shock and inability to comprehend what this information meant. He moved uncomfortably and filled the silence.

"I'm sorry, sir, I know this is the most tremendous shock and I wonder if there is anybody you might like to be with at this time?" When I made no reply he tried again.

"Would you like me to see if I can get you a cup of tea and perhaps I can explain to your manager what has happened?"

I suppose I must have nodded because, with what I'm sure was a profound sense of relief on his part, he left the room.

"Just be a minute or two." He said with obvious relief at being able to escape.

I can remember everything in minute detail up to that particular point, as though my mind had photographed or recorded those initial exchanges and that imparting of the dreadful news. But then my brain was obviously trying to comprehend the enormity of the information he had given me. So my memory of what followed is much more vague because I know that, at the back of my mind, I was trying to deny what I'd heard, or at least trying to deny the implications of what I had heard.

Vaguely I can recall Mr Stewart coming into the office and re-assuming his wartime role as an Army Major dealing with a welfare issue relating to a subordinate, in the way that the Army is so good at, by treating soldiers as part of the 'family'. Sandra appeared wordlessly passing me a cup of tea which was probably made on instructions with some extra sugar. I never found out because I wouldn't have liked the sugar, but, in any event, I didn't even take milk, with which it was obviously liberally laced. I do know that at the end of a long conversation with Mr Stewart and the police officer, in which my address and phone number were taken but of which I have no other recollection, Mr Stewart must have given me both the day and the rest of the week off work. He also must have spoken to the police officer about where I should go in order to be with somebody who could give me some support. They decided that I should go to Queens Road to the home of my in-laws, Linda's mum and dad and Carole's gran and grandad. I do recall that he offered to send me in a taxi at the firm's expense but I declined saying that the fresh air would do me good. After some discussion it was agreed that the police officer, who was on his bicycle anyway, would accompany me on the short ride to my in-law's home.

We set off together riding in an almost companionable silence me riding next to the curb and he outside me, almost protectively in the way that, in those days, a man would usually walk on the road side of the pavement if he was out with his lady. I suspect that on that relatively busy road cycling slowly two abreast was not to the liking of some of the motorists travelling in the same direction as us. However, the presence of the uniformed police officer meant that they had to 'grin and bear it' and wait their turn to safely overtake. In my dazed state I vaguely realised that he was not taking me on what I would have considered to be the direct route to my in-law's house, but, I just followed his lead as I was far too preoccupied to argue. I saw in retrospect that what he was doing was to cleverly avoid taking me past the scene of the accident, or, as I was later to wonder, was that the scene of the murder?

We arrived at my in-law's house and I dismounted and opened the front gate in order to push my bicycle in and to lean it in its usual place against the front wall. The hinge on the gate squeaked as I opened it and I saw a quick twitch of the curtains and moments later my father-in-law, Tommy, burst out of the front door and shouted at the policeman.

"What are you doing here? Why aren't you out looking for the bastards that killed my daughter and granddaughter?"

Tommy had been born during the First World War and when he had been old enough to get a job it was the time of the economic depression years of the 1930's. But he had been most fortunate that a friend of his father's had got him an apprenticeship on the railways and by the time of the outbreak of the Second World War he was a train driver. This was a reserved occupation and he drove trains throughout the war, being based mainly at the Feltham marshalling yards and driving freight trains rather than passenger ones. Despite his strong faith and membership of the Church of England which, I had once read, had been described as being the Conservative Party at prayer, he was a staunch socialist and trade unionist. The happiest days of his life, no doubt, came in the late 1940s when the post war Atlee government brought in what Tommy regarded as those wonderful socialist Acts of Parliament which, to him, included the Education Act of 1944 the National Health Service Act of 1946 and the National Assistance Act of 1948.

In the early 1950s he suffered an industrial accident which left him with a severe shoulder injury and which precluded him from being a train driver. However, British Railways retrained him as a ticket inspector and he took to this role like a duck to water. His very clear socialist view was that British Railways was owned by the people and nobody should attempt to defraud the people by failing to purchase the proper ticket. He was zealous in pursuit of cheats but he was equally fiercely opposed to capitalists and those whom he saw as their lackeys and that, sometimes, included the police.

"If it was the daughter and granddaughter of one of your landed gentry," Tommy went on, "you'd have caught the killers by now."

It was his anger which broke the spell of shock into which I had descended from the moment I had first set eyes on the policeman. It was as though my mind had simply shut down, but Tommy's anger brought me back to reality.

"Leave it Tommy," I said catching him by the shoulder and turning him away, back towards his own front door, "this officer has been very kind to me and I appreciate what he's done and I'm sure it's not his fault."

I shoved him in the door and turned and mouthed a 'thank you' to the officer who just nodded, lifted a hand in a quasi-salute, got on his bike and pedalled away. I followed Tommy in the door to find him crying uncontrollably being consoled by Daisy his wife and my sister-in-law Winnie, who had obviously been summoned from her office job in London. Daisy was hugging her husband and was looking over his shoulder towards me. Straightaway in the eyes of her mother I could see Linda's eyes looking at me and that was it. Tears came, not noisily just gently and for a time nobody spoke.

"I'll put the kettle on." said Daisy setting off for the kitchen, and Tommy looked at me and, beginning to recover a bit, asked.

"What did that copper say to you then?"

"He was very nice and very kindly and just told me that there had been an accident and I half expected him to tell me that they were in hospital. But, then he told me they were dead and I couldn't believe it."

"Did he tell yer how it happened?"

"Not really, he just said that they had been knocked down by a car in Hanworth Road."

"There you see," said Tommy," they didn't even tell you the truth then did they, because Mavis Hardy, who lives six doors down, was there and saw it and she's gonna be a witness for the police. Some big black car comes screeching round by St Catherine's Church and there's a bus at the bus stop on his side of the road and he's swerved out again to avoid the bus. He mounts the pavement and crashes into................"

Again he broke down into more tears.

Slowly the realisation that this was not perhaps just a simple road traffic accident began to come into my mind.

"Did….. didn't the car stop then?"

"Not according to what Mavis told us," said Winnie over her father's sobs.

"So it was a hit-and-run?" I asked.

"Seems so." She replied.

For the first time my comprehension of Tommy's anger was now more understandable. Life is full of accidents; some of them may be as simple as just dropping a cup or glass onto the floor and seeing it smash. It could be of very little consequence or, if it was a particularly expensive or prized object then it might be a bit more disappointing. But it's rare that such an event, such an accident, would have any lasting consequences. Had somebody lost control of the vehicle because of a mechanical failure or even just a misjudgement then that too would have been an accident, but obviously one with much more severe consequences. But so often with accidents of the type I have just described, and one where there is, for want of a better term, a guilty party, matters are made somewhat better if the person causing that accident admits their part in it and allows people to understand why they thought it had happened.

This was different, it sounds as though the driver of the vehicle was being completely reckless in the way that they drove, but even that could have been ameliorated somewhat by them stopping to offer assistance to the persons they had most obviously injured. But in this case he, or she, had callously driven on. So now I could begin to understand a little bit more clearly why Tommy was feeling so angry. I read, somewhere later, that anger can be part of the grieving process, and if this is true then that must be exacerbated in any situation where someone may be perceived as being patently and deliberately responsible for the death.

Winnie and Daisy made some tea and sandwiches and then we all sat in their front room sharing our grief with periods of recollections of Linda and Carole, interspersed with long silences and not a few tears. By late afternoon I felt the need for some solitude and told them that I thought I would go home. They were very much against it, suggesting that it would not be good for me to go home to an empty house and that there was a spare bed on which I could stay the night. I know they were only being kind and I could see the logic of their argument about not being on my own, but somewhat ironically I knew I wanted the solace of solitude.

It's interesting that their perceptions were about the need of family support in times of crisis. There were three children in their family and being together was no doubt something that any of their children, including my late lovely wife, would have wanted. But as an only one, brought up from the age of six by a widowed mother, I was used to solitude and that's exactly what I felt I needed. A compromise was reached in that Daisy was insistent that I must have something to eat and so about five we all shared some soup and then after a tearful farewell I got on my bike and pedalled home, arriving as dusk was beginning to fall. I opened the front gates, unlocked the garage, put my bike away, locked up again and opened the back door into the kitchen. Linda was always so organised and the breakfast things had all been washed up and left on the draining board, saucers and bowls leant on cups to allow them to dry. I went to the draining board and picked up Carole's little china bowl with pictures of bears, I ran my fingers around the rim and felt the chips caused in her younger days when she had bashed it with a spoon. I hugged the bowl to my chest and thought again of that lovely tiny little blue-eyed girl whom I had kissed less than twelve hours ago, and who now was lost to me until I could join her in that other life.

Then Linda, why, oh why, did it have to be this day when we parted, not in anger, but certainly not with the usual love and affection that had graced our relationship and our marriage from the very beginning. I wanted so much to go back and make that last parting one where we were in equilibrium and at one with each other. I knew even then that this was a regret that would never desert me. And so it has proved.

Eventually, as I stood in the kitchen, darkness fully descended and I turned on the light and worked to put away the saucers, plates and bowls, as I knew Linda would have wished me to do. The telephone rang and I made my way down the hallway and lifted the receiver off its hook.

"Feltham 2716" I said.

"Hello. Is that Ewan Mathieson?" Said the caller and when I replied in the affirmative the voice went on, "my name is Detective Constable Simon, I'd like to offer you my sincere condolences; but I have to ask you if you can assist us with our enquiries."

"Of course." I said.

"Well sir," he said hesitantly, "unless you would like me to ask her father, I would like to ask you to identify the bodies of your wife and daughter."

I agreed and he continued.

"Right. So I will send a car to your house at about nine thirty tomorrow morning to bring you to the mortuary and I will meet you there, sir."

"That's fine." I said and put the phone down.

As I hung the black cylindrical earpiece onto the hooks beside the upright telephone receiver, I glanced at the doormat and saw a number of letters, several of them were without postage stamps so that they had obviously been hand delivered. I picked them up and the top one was from Florrie, one of Linda's friends who was a neighbour from three doors down. She just wrote she was so sorry to hear the news and offered that if there was anything she could do I had only to ask. There were two or three more similar notes from neighbours. Then, there was an electricity bill and finally a fairly big envelope postmarked Inverness. I opened it to find it was from some Solicitors and the heading stated 'In the matter of Roderick Mathieson (deceased)'.

Cannot one have enough of death in one day I wondered? I dropped all the letters onto the table which held the telephone and went to sit in the front room.

Uncle Roddy? It could only be the semi mythical uncle Roddy who must have died. I say this because, so far as I knew, I had never laid eyes on him either in the flesh or even in a photograph. He was my father, Andrew Mathieson's, younger brother. All I knew about my father's family was what limited information my mum had given me, since I was only six years old when his ship was torpedoed, and he was drowned. Mum said that there was a family disagreement about what should happen to the croft which my grandparents worked and on which Dad had spent his childhood. Seemingly dad's brother Roddy was something of a favourite with their parents and when it was mooted that the tenancy was to be shared rather than go just to him, my father took umbrage and there was a big row which ended in his leaving home to join the merchant navy. Subsequently he met my mum, Hilda, who was then nursing in a London hospital. They married and they bought a cottage in Bedfont Lane, Feltham near to her own parent's home. He returned to his seagoing life living at home only during periods of shore leave. Dad was apparently quite stubborn and the rift was never healed with his parents and brother and, so far as mum knew, dad had never contacted his family again.

The phone rang again, I answered it to a man who turned out to be from the Daily Mail who told me that they were keen to follow up an article which had appeared in the London Evening Standard that evening about the accident. He had got my telephone number from the telephone book. I told him that I was too upset to be able to talk to strangers about things and put the phone down. Not long afterwards the telephone rang again and went on to ring several more times, but I decided to ignore it. I went back into the front room and drew the curtains put on the BBC light programme for some music and then at about seven o'clock there was a tapping on the back door and there was Billy.

"Oh Billy! I'm so sorry I forgot we were meeting............."

"Don't be so bloody silly." He said. "I've read the paper and I know why you didn't come to the Red Lion tonight and, what's more, if you don't want company I'll quite understand and leave you in peace. But when I heard, I thought I'd pop round to see you and on the way I called in at the Airman pub's off-licence across the road and bought these couple of bottles of Watney's pale ale."

"Come in." I said.

Even loners like me need a few friends whom they can really trust. Of course Linda was my best friend but I realised that Billy was my next best. We had shared understandings from our early schooldays which were then reinforced by our time in the Army and thereafter. Whilst we only met a dozen or so times a year, we easily took up whenever we met. We talked for an hour or so and he helped me remember Linda and Carole in a positive way he didn't avoid the fact they had died he just talked to me about all the good times.

After he left I realised I was tired and for the first time I went upstairs. I had a wash and cleaned my teeth and on my way back to our bedroom, which was at the front of the house, I passed Carole's door. I went in and I looked at her neatly made bed with her teddy bear Edward, who was made out of the kapok lining of an airman's wartime jacket and who'd been lovingly crafted by an elderly relative. I flopped onto her little bed and grabbed hold of Edward and cried myself to sleep.

The next few days were a relative blur of activity. There was the awful visit to the mortuary and identification of the two bodies. My little girl looked as though she was just asleep as apparently her head was virtually unscathed but her little tiny body was crushed, although I did not see anything other than her face. Linda on the other hand was presented with a sheet drawn tightly up to her face as apparently the back of her head suffered severe trauma. Then there was to be the Inquest which I was informed would simply be opened and adjourned. Detective Constable Simon had accompanied me to the identification and afterwards spent a lot of time talking to me, gleaning information about Linda. Most of the questions I thought were understandable but one or two struck me as a little odd.

For example he wanted to know whether Linda always took the same route to school. Did she walk on the same side of the road? Where did she normally cross? Things like that. Then, with me he wanted to know about my work and whether or not I dealt with customers, which was very rare because most of my work related to drawing up invoices and doing wages. He asked if I was ever required to chase up any bad debts on behalf of the company, but I told him that it had nothing to do with me, I simply reported to Mr Stewart who dealt with that side of things. He wanted to know about my finances and was particularly interested to know whether I owed any money to anybody. I told him that Linda and I had always been careful with our money and we never bought things until we had the cash in the bank.

On Monday 11th March I returned to work, Mr. Stewart had offered me more time off but after five days of having to fill my time I decided that being at work was much preferable to being off. The Inquest was set for Thursday, 21 March and was to take place in the Feltham Magistrates Court building on Hanworth Road less than 200 yards from the scene of the incident. We were all there me, Tommy and Daisy, Linda's parents, Winnie and

Leslie her sister and brother. Although he kept in the background, I noticed that Billy was there too.

The proceedings started with evidence of the identification of the deceased which was a statement that I had given and was read out by Detective Constable Simon. Then a Detective Sergeant Smithson gave evidence in outline of the events which went along the following lines. A robbery had occurred at a jeweller's shop in Hounslow. The jeweller had arrived at the rear of his premises at about eight twenty in the morning and unlocked his door and entered but, before he could turn to close it, two men, wearing balaclava helmets and armed with knives, pushed their way inside. They forced him to open the safe and got away with a significant amount of cash and jewellery. However, the jeweller had a direct alarm link to the police station and as soon as the robbers had fled he was able to notify the police and he gave them the make and description of the getaway car, an Austin Westminster, together with the registration number.

The details of this vehicle were radioed out to police patrols. A police car on the Staines Road spotted the vehicle and turned round to give chase. In an attempt to avoid pursuit the car had turned into Hounslow Road heading towards Feltham. It was driving at a very fast speed and the police car was not gaining on it. It went through the traffic lights at the junction with Harlington Road narrowly avoiding a collision and at that point the police car lost a bit of ground but they saw it going over the top of the Feltham railway bridge next to the station and, because this is quite a steep bridge, it was lost to view as it disappeared over the brow. When the police vehicle crested the bridge the car was not in sight and the officers assumed that it had carried on into Feltham High Street whereas, using the fact that the police car could no longer see them, the driver of the getaway car had turned immediately left into Hanworth Road. By this time it was shortly before nine o'clock and the incident was near a school where there were many children and their parents around.

The sergeant then told the court that a separate eyewitness describes the car as screeching round the corner into Hanworth Road. The driver momentarily lost control managed to re-gain it but then was confronted by a bus parked on the left-hand side of the road and immediately had to turn out to the right. At this point control was lost again and the car mounted the pavement and was in collision with the two pedestrians. According to the witness there was no slowing down of the vehicle it simply sped on and was shortly lost to view as the road bent round to the right. No witness could confirm anything about the occupants of the vehicle, which had subsequently been found abandoned in Twickenham, beyond the fact that it appeared to be two males and this fitted with the evidence of the jeweller who had reported two males wearing balaclavas had been involved in the robbery.

After this basic evidence had been provided to the court the Coroner announced that the bodies could be released for funerals to be arranged but the Inquest would be adjourned for further enquiries and we all left the court. Tommy was in better control than on the day of the incident when I had I called at his home with the police officer, but he was still fairly angry. The police sergeant came to us after the inquest and Tommy was straight on his case.

"So I hope you know who's done it then."

"No sir," replied the sergeant, "we have not yet established who was responsible, there are a number of suspects, people who commit these sorts of offences of robberies of jewellers and we are doing our best to find out who it was."

"Haven't you got any fingerprints from the car or anything?" Tommy asked.

"No sir. We've searched the car very carefully and I can tell you that it was stolen in Isleworth and the only fingerprints we've been able to lift belong to the car's owner and his family members. The car was found abandoned in Twickenham, but nobody seems to have seen it arrive and so we have no descriptions."

"But you must have some idea of who it could have been?" said Tommy.

"We do have ideas, but ideas are ideas," said the sergeant, "we want to catch these men, because there were two of them in the car from what witnesses have told us, but to catch them and get them convicted needs evidence and I have to be honest with you sir and say that at the moment there is no evidence that could lead us to charge somebody in this matter. However, I assure you that we will do all in our power to bring these people to book."

After this I was approached by a very polite young man who told me he was from the Middlesex Chronicle, a local newspaper which was widely read locally in those days. He told me that he had been at the Inquest and that he believed that if he wrote a fulsome article about the situation, it was just possible that another witness might come forward who may have seen the car between Feltham and Twickenham. Or even somebody who may have seen the people stealing the car in Isleworth or later abandoning it. He asked if I would therefore make any comment that he could use in his article. His approach was so thoughtful and polite that I agreed to say a few words to him which went along the lines of: 'this terrible crime has ruined my life and that of Linda's parents and I would be most grateful if people could rack their brains to see if they remember that on 6th March they had seen this black Austin Westminster at any time between the early morning, when it was stolen, and the late morning when it was abandoned'. The reporter was true to his word and a very sympathetic article appeared a few days later reporting the evidence from the inquest and my appeal for witnesses.

So there it seemed to be. We now had an outline of how this had happened but it looked as though there was going to be nobody brought to book for it. Fate, it seemed, had dealt me a serious blow. The love of my life had gone and my beautiful little girl would never ever grow up. Despite various offers I just wanted to retreat again. So I said my goodbyes and walked home.

Little did I realise that fate was about to intervene in my life for a second time that month.

Distant Light

With a few exceptions, as I have already indicated, I generally preferred my own company. But I did not like it if I did not have anything to do. Over the past few days I had done a number of small jobs and kept the house clean and tidy, as I knew Linda would have wished. One of the jobs I had neglected was the post and so I began to go through it. I put aside letters from neighbours and others expressing their condolences and organised them into a pile so that I could reply to each, with the top of the pile having the most significant ones and needing an early reply. I disposed of a couple of bills including the electricity bill that had arrived and then I took up the envelope with the Inverness postmark which, from the heading I had read, was presumably telling me Uncle Roddy had died and letting me know about the funeral. Well Roddy would have had to go to his grave without me because just then I had more important things on my plate.

Still, best know all about it I thought.

It was a letter from a firm of solicitors whose offices were in Church Street, Inverness, dated 5 March 1963. I have it still.

Dear Mr Ewan Mathieson,

<u>*In the matter of Roderick Mathieson (deceased)*</u>

We are acting as Executors in the matter of the Last Will and Testament of Mr Roderick Mathieson of Shore Croft, Clackmore, Sutherland. You may not be aware that Mr Mathieson died of heart failure on 2nd March 1963 and is to be buried in Stoer Cemetery on 11th March.

Should you wish to attend or obtain further information in this regard then please contact Mr McKay of this office as soon as possible.

I am given to understand that you may not be aware of Mr Mathieson's circumstances in recent times and it may assist you to know that he was generally well until just a few weeks before his death and then he was attended by Doctor Hardy, a locum General Practitioner. After some tests, the doctor tried to persuade Mr Mathieson to go into hospital but he refused on the grounds that he had young animals to care for. Because his condition was known to the doctor a death certificate was issued and his funeral expedited, as this is a rural area with few facilities.

Irrespective of your interest in attendance at the funeral there is a more pressing matter to which you must direct your attention.

You are named as the sole beneficiary by Mr Mathieson in his aforementioned Will. You may be aware that he never married and his only close relative was his deceased brother Andrew, whom, Mr Mathieson gave us to believe, was your late father. In the fullness of time a proper account of Mr. Mathieson's estate will be made to you, but by my estimation and after deduction of testamentary expenses and burial costs there will be little by way of financial inheritance.

However, as a legally established Crofter he had the power to appoint a relative to run the croft and he named yourself. There is however a legal requirement under section 10, Crofters (Scotland) Act 1955 that you must notify the Crofting Commission within two months of the date of the original crofters death of your intention to take up the tenancy or else the tenancy will be reassigned.

Mr Mathieson died on 2 March and therefore you would need to take action by 2 May 1963.

In view of the foregoing I would ask that you contact this office at your earliest convenience to advise us of your intentions in this matter.

For completeness I can inform you that the animals on the croft are currently being cared for by the neighbouring crofters Alistair and Morag McLeod.

Yours sincerely

J A McKay

Having read the letter once, I paused; then I read it again.

This letter opened an avenue of thought that had never occurred to me in the days since the incident, for I no longer referred to it as the accident. All the counselling and perceived wisdom that I had received from Linda's family, neighbours and work colleagues went along the established line of, 'you have had a tremendous shock, you are in no state to make any major decisions for some time'. Looking at things dispassionately it was quite clear that most of the building blocks of a settled life were here still. My job was secure, likewise my home; family (well, in-laws anyway) were supportive and so were neighbours and colleagues. But I had not made any decision, I had, in the absence of any alternative, acquiesced in the notion that I would carry on. And here, now was a potential alternative course.

For a while I stared at the letter whilst my mind raced.

Who was I without Linda and Carole? They had been my anchor and they had been my future. They were the reason I went to work each day, they filled my evenings and weekends, and I had already learned that without them I had little to occupy me. Oh yes! My Army training had equipped me to wash and iron and keep things tidy and so I was able to keep Linda's legacy of a clean and tidy house alive. But even these tasks went nowhere close to occupying me away from my working hours, so that more and more of those away from work periods were spent thinking about my lovely wife and daughter and dwelling on what might have been. It also occurred to me that once we had arranged the funerals and dealt with the other practical issues surrounding the incident then my life would become even more filled with unoccupied time. In turn that held the danger of my becoming sorry for myself, or angry at the fates or people who had taken my happiness. Either or both of these states of mind could lead to a state of embitteredness. Being stuck in some sort of sorrow or self-pity might actually be very debilitating, from which it may be hard to escape.

Thus, on the face of it, a change might have greater long term benefits to me than staying put. Solitude and industry was what I craved and this letter offered that opportunity.

However, was I equipped to deal with this particular change? It sounded as though it might be quite an isolated and lonely life but clearly that was not a problem for me given my personality. I had loved the Army life where every moment of every day was filled, so probably the fact that farming meant working hard from dawn till dusk was another thing with which I could cope. Fending for myself would be easy too. On the other hand there were some big unknowns and of these the biggest was my complete ignorance of the skills of farming and animal husbandry, which clearly would be the principal element to being a crofter.

Then there were the practicalities; firstly of arranging my affairs in order to move to virtually the other end of the country and secondly the ridiculously short timescale in which it would have to be accomplished. But the more I thought about the opportunity the more convinced I became that, despite the enormity of the challenge, this was something that would fit with me and if I failed to take the chance I might regret it for the rest of my life.

By about three in the afternoon I had convinced myself that this was something I should do, provided some basic building blocks were in place. I knew that a house like ours would fetch about £4000 and that we'd put up a reasonable deposit and had been paying the mortgage for five years. This left me thinking that there would be equity of over £1000 and if I sold all the furniture and other items in the house that could raise another few hundred or enough to cover funeral costs. Then with our savings, which added up to about £200 at the time, I thought that would go some way towards the purchase of a vehicle and taking into account that cost I might end up with something in the region of £900 in the bank. It seemed to me that this was sufficient of a cushion to get me through a year or so of limited income. Labourers in the warehouse at Air Transport & Freight I was well aware took home a net pay of just short of £50 per week and kept themselves and their families on that. So financially I could make the move with enough money to see a single man through for the best part of the year.

We had been a very close self-sufficient nuclear family and my primary, nay, my only responsibility for these past few years had been Linda and Carole. Now that responsibility was no longer there the only responsibility left was to myself. I could ignore or reject this unexpected opportunity but if I did would another come along? Would I always regret missing the chance? What had I to lose? Well, the only things at stake were a house and money, and if I lost both then I would have to come back, tail between legs, and start again.

Picking up the phone I got through to the operator and gave the long distance number of the Inverness solicitors. In due course I was put through to Mr McKay, and when he came on the line his tone was business-like but not particularly friendly.

"Oh! Mr Mathieson I assume you're going to tell me that you don't want to take up the option on the croft since it's taken you over two weeks to acknowledge my letter?"

I told him about the untimely arrival of his letter and at the end of my story, as well as expressing what sounded like sincere condolences, his tone became much more sympathetic.

"I am seriously considering taking over the croft," I told him, "but in order to do so I wondered what steps would be required to meet any legal requirements and whether they would cause problems in meeting the deadline, given that I had not responded promptly."

He replied by assuring me that the legal requirements only meant that I would have to notify the Crofting Commission and, that he would, if I wished, undertake that task for me. Then, I needed to visit his office in Inverness some time before the date of the deadline, there I would simply sign some papers and the whole procedure, he estimated, would take less than half an hour, including time to drink a cup of tea.

"But forgive me, are you really sure? From what I understand you never met your uncle or visited the property so I assume you have no background in crofting and Clackmore is far out on the west coast, almost, one might say, at the limits of human habitation. I would be failing in my duty if I didn't say to you that it sounds somewhat like a rash decision made at a time of great personal and emotional pressure."

Acknowledging that what he said was true, I told him that I had weighed that against what I knew about myself and what I felt was right for me, in making a future that would not be dogged by a descent into morbid loneliness. By reference to my National Service and personality, I told him that I felt that I had the potential to cope with the requirements of the life and I expressed a willingness to learn the new skills, which I realised that I would need. I went on to say that I had not finally decided, and I would take advice from Linda's family and my friends but at the point of our conversation I was ninety percent certain that this was the course I was going to follow. I told him that unless I notified him to the contrary within seven days he should assume this to be the case and to send a letter to the Crofting Commission on my behalf. He requested that I confirm our conversation in writing and I agreed to do so.

My provisional plan, I told him, was to try to arrange to get up to the croft by late June as I had to sort out lots of things including the sale of my home and other things; at this there was a slight pause before he replied.

"Well," he said, "I must tell you that this is an isolated croft in a small valley in an otherwise rocky area and there is only one other nearby croft. Mr & Mrs McLeod are not entirely young people and when they offered to take care of the animals upon the death of your uncle they made it clear that they had in mind a deadline of the beginning of May, as shortly thereafter they would have to be gathering hay and otherwise getting into one of the busier times of their year. Additionally I should point out that you too will have to gather your own hay otherwise you may face very high costs of buying winter feed. In short you really need to be there by the beginning of May."

So, we discussed the practicalities and by consulting the calendar we realised that 2nd May was a Thursday exactly six weeks hence and I committed to it, despite realising that it was a pretty tight timescale. We made a provisional appointment for me to attend his office in Inverness at four o'clock in the afternoon of Wednesday 1st May 1963, for me to sign some papers and collect others, and then the following day I could drive to Clackmore and take up residence. He told me that he would inform Mr and Mrs McLeod on the neighbouring croft and advise them of my provisional intention and my likely arrival in the afternoon of 2nd May.

That was the easy bit. Now came the difficult bits. I decided that to raise this issue immediately, on the day of the Inquest, was certainly not a good idea and in any event I needed time to think about it more myself. So the following day, on the Friday, I went to work as normal and did the normal Friday things. As usual I went to Barclays Bank, which was situated half way down the Feltham High Street, to collect the cash for the wages. Mr Stewart always arranged for me to be driven there in one of the firm's vans so that we could park outside the door and the driver could act as a sort of 'minder' for me with the all that money. By chance that day it was the truculent Freddie who was deputed to drive me.

"C'mon Mr Hewie," he said making a play of words on my name as I walked towards the waiting van, "I haven't had time for me smoke break yet."

"Alright Freddie," I said, "it's only a short trip so you will be back by half ten."

"Ah. But I bet there is a lot of money involved. How much would I pocket if I knocked you on the head on the way back?"

I think it belatedly struck him that, perhaps, given that Linda and Carole were killed by men escaping from a robbery, that his little jest might not have been the most tactful in the circumstances.

"I'm sorry.... ." He started, but I cut him off and changed the subject.

"Have you always been a driver?" I asked him.

"Yeah, pretty much. I joined the army at eighteen in 1940 and somehow managed to get into transport and spent all of the war driving vehicles. So when I left in forty six I got driving work straight off and I've done that for the whole time ever since. This job is a good one by and large because it's mostly day work and I can go home to the wife and kids most nights. Before this I was on long distance and I could be away a week or more sometimes and that was no good after the kids come along."

"Did you ever go really long distances then?"

"All over," he replied, "all round London, up the A 5 to Holyhead and over to Ireland, up the A 6 to Glasgow, yeah all over."

"What about the north of Scotland?" I asked.

"Oh yes, loads of times I've been up the A1 to Edinburgh then, once or twice, on to Inverness. That A 9 is amazing with all the mountains."

I asked him if that was the route he would take to Inverness, via the A 1 and he said he favoured that route as it was more straightforward than the A 6 Glasgow route. The only issue being that the ferry across the river Forth at Queensferry was a bottleneck and would remain so till next year when they should have the Forth Road Bridge open.

By this time we had got to the bank and I went in and collected and signed for the money. I returned to the van.

"Why so interested in Scotland?" Freddie asked. "Are you thinking of a holiday?" I nodded and he went on.

"Do you good mate after all you have been through. Are you drivin' then, cos I've never seen you in a car?"

"Firstly," I said, telling a small untruth, "I have not yet decided to go, but it is something I am considering. Secondly, you have not seen me driving because I don't have a car. But, like you, the Army taught me to drive and I'm sure that I would soon get the hang of it again."

"Yes," he said, "you'll have no problems, but don't start going up to town and doing Piccadilly Circus,

Parliament Square or worst of all Hyde Park Corner, which and it aint no corner it's just a big area of tarmac and it looks and behaves like an enormous fairground dodgems."

We both laughed.

"Here," he said, "if you're serious and you don't have no car, you just let me know, as I have a number of mates who are mechanics and we could probably pick you up a nice second hand motor and me mates would make sure it's a good 'un."

"Well, that's a really good offer and I might just take you up on it if I decide to go, but, Freddie, I would be grateful if you didn't mention it till I have made up my mind."

"Your secret's safe with me," he replied, and then adopting a mock Churchillian voice, "'Loose talk costs lives' and 'Mums the word.'" This last comment delivered whilst tapping his index finger against the side of his nose.

After work that day and, with some trepidation, I cycled round to Queens Road.

Just Daisy and Winnie were there, Tommy had gone to a union meeting. I explained my thinking to them both and their shock was evident. Daisy began to cry.

"You have become one of the family," she said, "whatever will we do if you leave us?"

But fortunately Winnie was more of a realist and also more my age and told her mum that she could understand my wish to take this unsolicited opportunity. Both, however, acknowledged that Tommy might be quite surprised to hear my proposal. And so it proved.

I stayed on at Queens Road chatting with Daisy and Winnie till the door opened and Tommy returned home.

"Sometimes I wonder if my fellow working man is bothered to give any thought to what the bosses are proposing and how it is going to affect the way we……….. what?"

He had looked round and seen our faces and whilst we were all paying him attention he sensed that there was a more important topic on everyone's minds. I opened my mouth to speak, but Daisy beat me to it.

"Ewan is thinking of moving away" she said.

"It's not quite like that," I said before Tommy could react, "but I suppose it could look that way. I have heard what everybody says about not rushing into things and trying to adjust to this changed life, and I was expecting to do that, but this chance has come up and it is time limited, there is no luxury of leaving the decision; it has to be made. You see I had an uncle, whom I had never met, who inherited the family croft in the far north of Scotland and he has died and is leaving it to me."

"So you're going to be a landowner then?" said Tommy, socialist indignation to the fore.

"No," I said, "from what I understand it is a tenancy, but one where there is a right to pass it to a family member provided that it is done within a short time scale and if it is not then the Landowner has the right to re-let to a new tenant. I will never have the right to the land itself, as things currently stand. As I said I did not expect to make a change like this now or ever, but faced with the opportunity and thinking about the sort of person I am I feel that I could cope with the relative solitude and the hard physical work that will be entailed. I need to have my time fully occupied so that I can begin to try and bear this terrible loss which is manifest to me every time I get home and open the door to the empty house. I can see that people might think I am just running away and in one sense I will be, but I am trying to think about it as though instead of it being running away, rather that it is running towards something. Linda and Carole will be with me forever until my dying breath, but will I honour their memories' best by staying here with their ghosts and becoming a lonely embittered person, with nothing to do at weekends and evenings? Or will they be better pleased with someone who has seized an unexpected opportunity and honoured their everlasting memory by making a positive decision to move forward in my life. I do not know if it is the right decision as only time will tell, but I feel it is something I ought to at least try."

I stopped and waited for Tommy's response. He stood there, still, looking at me intensely and there was a long pause until he spoke.

"Well, that's a turn up. I love all my children, but as the youngest I had a very soft spot for Linda and I will tell you now, as I did on your wedding day, that I was never quite sure that you were the right man for her, I thought she could do better. And you will remember that I said that to you at the time. But you showed me how wrong I was and you made her happy and you cared for her and for Carole. Because of this I have learned to respect you and that being so I must also respect your decision. I can see what you are saying, and you have got a lot of life yet to lead and I for one would never stand in your way. Just know this, that I know how much you loved our precious Linda and how much she loved you. You cared for her and made these last few years' happy ones. You go and take this opportunity and if per chance it does not work out you will always be welcome here."

The phrase 'you could knock me down with a feather' jumped instantly to my mind. And indeed at that moment the impact of a feather might just have succeeded in making me lose my balance. Here was the person whom I most feared being upset by my decision, actually supporting me.

After a period of silence, during which Tommy and I both stared at one another, he stepped towards me and, each of us smiling.

Warmly we shook hands.

Making Arrangements

Thinking about the funerals was a major preoccupation in my thoughts and in my contact with Tommy and Daisy, tentative ideas were exchanged but no real plans were made. But outside that issue there was much to do for what would follow now that the decision to move north had been made. It started with telling Mr Stewart on the following day of my decision and the fact that I was giving formal notice of one month as required. That meant that I was due to finish work on 19th April. Mr Stewart was very understanding but he persuaded me that I should finish on 25th April due to the fact that he needed to find a replacement for me and it was the Easter weekend 13th/14th April and holiday on the Monday. I wanted to be fair to him so I agreed on the basis that I could perhaps have some time off work unpaid to make visits to such as solicitors to arrange the selling of the house and the rest. He did agree but suggested that I might let the house instead of selling, as he thought that if I did not like what I had let myself into I would have a place to which I could return.

  This gave me pause for thought. As well as having a safety net, should I realise that the crofting life was not for me, I would have a small income from renting the house to supplement any income (or lack thereof) from the croft. It was tempting. In the end I decided against it for three reasons. First was the fact that I needed capital immediately in order to buy a vehicle and anything else that might be needed for the croft and for subsistence in the first few weeks and any rental income would take a time to accrue. Secondly, whilst one might expect that there would be a gross income generated from the rental, there would also be maintenance and repairs to deal with which might considerably limit the net income. But the main reason I rejected it was because, by its very nature, spending time and effort creating and maintaining a safety net would limit my commitment to making the change.

So I immediately arranged for the house to be put upon the market and made contact with local estate agents and solicitors whom I instructed, on the proviso that they be willing to deal with matters in the event that the house did not sell until after my emigration north of Hadrian's Wall. I then turned to consideration of the house contents. We had been married for six years and, whilst we were certainly not spendthrifts, it was nevertheless Linda's pleasure to make the home nice. So we had a twin-tub washing machine and a refrigerator and even an electric whisk in the kitchen. We did have a lovely Bush radiogram for both radio programmes and playing our collection of records, as well as a transistor radio in the kitchen. No television, but it had been on the list of things for which we were saving. Then there were cupboards, chests of drawers and bedroom furniture. There was a gas cooker and that would be sold with the house.

Clearly much of this equipment could not go with me to the croft and I wondered what would be most useful to take. As a result I put in another call to Mr MacKay in Inverness. He told me that he had visited some years ago and from memory the building was small, there was a relatively newly built kitchen to one side of the front hallway, a sitting room to the other, and two small bedrooms up some fairly steep stairs. When I explained the reason for my call being to do with what I needed to take he added.

"Well, how can I put this? Your uncle was a good crofter in terms of the management of the croft and his animals, and it would clearly have taken up much of his time, so he did not use his free time on home maintenance, if you get my drift. Indeed, I would doubt that apart from the extension, which expanded the kitchen to incorporate a bathroom, very little will have been done or bought since he inherited the croft from his father, your grandfather."

So it seemed that the place was poorly maintained and furnished. Perhaps I should consider hiring a firm of removers. A quick enquiry with a local firm to take a small removal lorry 650 miles and back would have exhausted my £250 savings on its own, without consideration of buying a vehicle for my own use. This led to the making of two further decisions. First that I needed to make a list of those things I felt would be essential to take and second, in considering what type of vehicle I needed to buy, I decided that a second hand van may be rather more useful than a car. In any event I thought that a van may be more useful on the croft for carrying things like animal feed.

These initial decisions and actions concerning the sale of the house were taken by the beginning of April and then it was time to sort out the furniture and other possessions. Without Billy's help I would never have managed, he came every weekend and we worked solidly every day. On that very first weekend we made an inventory of what was in every room and in relation to furniture I made a decision on what I would take and what I would dispense with. I gave my in-laws first refusal on any items that I earmarked for disposal. Linda's brother Les wanted the twin tub washer and gave me £20 for it. Then Billy arranged to make cards advertising the availability of the dining table and chairs, the three piece suite, wardrobes and a double and single bed, the latter was the one from the spare room. We had just put Carole into a brand new single bed so I decided that I would take that north with me. Billy advertised those items for sale in the newsagents in Feltham and also in some shops of his dad's. Within three weeks every item was sold and as things were collected so living became a little more Spartan, ending with my just having Carole's former, and now my present, bed and a couple of odd bedroom chairs to sit on downstairs with meals taken on my knee.

To transport north was the single bed and mattress, the Bush radiogram which had detachable legs, as did the bed, and one five drawer tallboy cabinet which had been my mother's. Then Billy got me some tea chests which were delivered by one of his dad's vans and into these I packed a selection of bowls, plates, cutlery, glasses and pots and pans. I did not take all and I put the remainder into another tea chest for sending to a second hand dealer who had agreed to give me a few bob for them. Bedding went into another tea chest and I probably took too much but I thought it was not likely to deteriorate and might save in the long run. Finally there was the clothing. Mine was easy; I took everything packed into a small suitcase and a tea chest. I spoke to Winnie about Linda's clothes; she thought that Daisy would probably like to go through them and save some, as well as a few of Carole's. They came one day and sorted through and took some away in a small suitcase, the rest they packed into a tea chest which went to the WRVS to distribute to the needy. In and amongst all this I acquired my means of personal transport in the shape of a two and a half year old Bedford van.

After I had given my notice my situation became common knowledge amongst my fellow employees at work. When he got to know, Freddie the driver approached me and reminded me of his offer to help me find a vehicle. I agreed and within ten days he told me that a mate of his, a panel beater, knew of a van which had been in a bump and had a bad scrape along the side. The owner was looking to sell it cheap because he did not want to have to pay for it being re-instated as the price for the panel work was, in his view, too high. So I picked up the van, which had cost £600 two years previously, for thirty percent of that and Freddie's mate put it to rights in his spare time for another £75. Yes, there were some dents which had not been completely knocked out but there was only 23,000 miles on the clock and I thought it a bargain. Insurance cost me £49 as I had no history for 'no claims' and then the Road Fund licence was another £16-10s-00p for the year

By Easter Monday April 15th I had my van, packing was done, save for the clothes I needed for the next few days, the house was on the market and there were a few people interested but as yet no offers. I had notified various utilities and others of my new address. Actually with Mr Stewart's permission he had agreed that his secretary could type the letters for me. It is really surprising how much you can get organised if you set your mind to it. Indeed I was almost ready to go and the next ten days might otherwise have been a period of limbo, were it not for the small matter of the funerals, which were set for Monday 22nd April.

Undertakers excepted, most people will have limited practice in arranging funerals; some people in large families might have more than the average but for most of us experience is limited. When my mother had died I, as an only child, had full responsibility for the arrangements. I was grateful for the help of the local undertaker and of course I was supported and helped at that time by Linda and, to a lesser extent, her family. Despite her proximity to St Catherine's my mum was a regular attender at St. Dunstan's in Lower Feltham, just across from the cemetery. After mum's funeral service and short trip to the cemetery we held a small gathering in the Three Horseshoes across the road. I thought that it would be nice to do similar for Linda and Carole but the circumstances were now very different. For my mum's funeral I, as only son and in the absence of a father, had been in sole charge as decision-maker. Things were now different as, despite being the husband and father respectively of the deceased, it seemed to me that the views of Linda's parents' ought to be given full consideration. In the occasional references to the funerals, as part of general conversation over my last few meetings with Tommy and Daisy, nothing had been decided in any detail and I realised that it was a conversation that we needed to have together.

One day after work I called round knowing that Tommy had been on early shift and would be at home as well as Daisy, but that Winnie would still be at work. I began hesitantly by asking them their views about the funeral and what form it might take and where it might be. Tommy was very clear that he would like to see Linda and Carole buried in the graveyard at Lower Feltham, where they could visit from time to time.

Interestingly that had not been my starting point; I had rather assumed that a cremation might be the best. Of course, given our relative youth, I had never discussed with Linda what should happen if one of us died. It's not really a topic to exercise healthy people under 40 with young children who hold an unspoken assumption of living to retirement and beyond. Even when my mum had died she had expressly stated she wished to be buried and so alternatives were not considered. So I was completely unaware of Linda's views. I have to say that I tended towards cremation and my initial thoughts for Linda and Carole were to take that course. Rather than have a fixed spot in the world where they could be 'laid to rest', I rather liked the idea of their dust and spirit drifting about freely, or, as Bob Dylan put it in a song which became very popular later that year 'Blowin' in the wind'.

To me Linda and Carole were still with me in spirit, they lived on in me because they had been such an important and intrinsic part of my life. In that sense it helped me to feel that they were still around, at least in an ethereal sense. Not to have a fixed spot in the ground where I knew their remains were laid would have been positive for me. The more so now that I was contemplating living the best part of 20 hours non-stop drive away and not easily able to visit their 'resting place'. But I put myself in Tommy and Daisy's shoes and thought about how I would feel if in years to come, had Carole reached maturity and married then died and her husband wanted one course and I another, it could have caused a big rift. So I felt that it was right to accede to their wishes; they could visit their daughter and granddaughter's grave and I could still take their memory, nay, even their continued spiritual presence, with me.

Tommy went on to say that whilst they worshipped at St Catherine's he had no objection to a service being held at St Dunstan's, if that was what I would wish. He said that it would be very convenient to the graveyard, but more importantly, he felt that to have the service elsewhere would mean that every Sunday when he and Daisy went to St Catherine's church to worship they would not be faced by memories of the funeral service. It was decided therefore that the funeral would follow the overall pattern of my mother's and would also include a small gathering in the Three Horseshoes afterwards.

The general content of the service was easily agreed but there was some difficulty in deciding who might deliver the eulogy. My position was clear, there was no way that emotionally I would be able to say anything and my preference was to talk to the vicar in advance, perhaps together with Tommy, and let the vicar deal with that. I had expected Tommy to say that he wanted to take a part but he told me that he recognised, as a very emotional man, he was unlikely to get through an individual part and he did not think it fair to start breaking down in the middle of even just reading a lesson and he was afraid that was likely to happen to him.

My estimation of the man, already high, went up another notch because, whilst I could see he wanted to say some things, he recognised that sometimes you should accept your limitations, especially in situations of potential high emotion. Over subsequent years I have felt sorry for a number of close family members who believed it was their right or duty to speak at a relative's funeral only to break down in public.

We went to see the vicar together and we talked to him about our memories of Linda and of Carole and the importance of them both in our lives. I am glad we did that, because, on the day, he said all the things that we would have wished to say and he managed to do it in a calm and measured way without the undoubted emotion that would have affected Tommy or I. Sometimes it's better to recognise that, when struggling with emotion, speaking publicly is doubly damned. On the one hand you are emotional about doing it at all and secondly your emotions are stretched to breaking point by the sadness of the situation. The old show business saying that 'it'll be all right on the night' does not, it seems to me, apply in these sorts of situations. If your emotion overtakes you then people listening either turn off and do not hear the message, or alternatively they become full of sympathy or empathy for you to the detriment of listening to what is being said about the deceased or hearing the message about them that you are trying to deliver.

The day of the funeral was dry but windy. There is that old proverb which goes 'March comes in like a lion but goes out like a lamb' but on this occasion, well into

April, the lion was clearly very loathe to give way. Tommy, Daisy and Winnie all walked down to Boundaries Road arriving at about a quarter past ten. It had been decided that it was only right that Linda and Carole's last journey should start from their home. It was a little difficult since there were only the two chairs left in the house and, together with the emotion of the day, it was a little awkward for us all. Just before half past ten the hearses and the one car that we had ordered arrived. The four of us were ushered into the car and the undertaker put on a bowler hat and walked in front of the vehicles. As we set off we passed many of the neighbours houses whose curtains were drawn as a mark of respect and, as well as that, a couple of them stood, heads uncovered and bowed, on the pavement. At the junction with the main road the funeral director got into the car and we went out and across to the Hanworth Road and proceeded up until we had just passed the Magistrates Courts. The cars then stopped and again the funeral director got out replaced his bowler hat and proceeded to walk in front of the vehicles for the next three hundred yards round the left hand bend and passing Tommy and Daisy's road on the right. We stopped momentarily a few yards beyond the point where the incident had occurred and then the funeral director resumed his seat in the hearse and off we went down Feltham High Street and on to St Dunstan's.

After the coffins were carried in, the four of us, now joined by Linda's brother Les who had taken his wife to the church, followed the coffins to walk down the aisle. I was staggered by the number of people there. I noticed many former staff members from the firm where Linda used to work in the canteen and also many of my own former colleagues amongst whom were Mr Stewart and Freddie the driver. I later learnt that many of Tommy's workmates and friends from church and his trades union were also there. The service went quickly for me, we had three fairly uplifting hymns and I always think that to sing together with other people brings a lot of comfort, this was even more the case because the hymns we chose were ones regularly sung in the churches in those days and also featured in the simple services we had at school as children. Over the ensuing years I was not able to go to church on any sort of regular basis, but when I did, or if I heard one of these hymns on the radio, I was taken back to that security of my childhood experience in singing these well known and loved words to equally well-known tunes. The vicar did a wonderful job in incorporating into his eulogy all the points which Tommy and I had made to him in our meeting.

It was then onto a blustery graveside where a slightly deeper than usual grave had been dug and I watched rather numbly as first my lovely wife, followed by my beautiful daughter, were laid to rest together.

Obviously, from what I have written I do recall some of the day, but there is so much that now escapes me as I think I must have been in somewhat of a daze. I can remember little of the reception in the pub, other than the fact that I stuck to tea rather than going for beer, and also I recall eating several sausage rolls since the alternative, pieces of cheese and a piece of pineapple on a cocktail stick, has never appealed to me. I do remember walking back to Tommy and Daisy's and spending an afternoon in desultory conversation and I really remember enjoying a casserole that Daisy had made for us. Finally I walked home to my near empty house and sat for some time listening to some records before going to bed.

The rituals concerning rites of passage are pretty important in moving us through the stages of life. I suppose all my preparations for the change had given me the reason to avoid thinking too much about the enormity of my loss. So the funeral brought me up short and momentarily, again, I went into a phase of being shocked. So it was very useful that the following day I was able to return to work, to have my time occupied and for the security of well-worn routine to take over. However, by the Wednesday I realised that I was making the wages calculation for the Friday and that I wouldn't be there to collect the money from the bank and put it into the pay packets. Fortunately, Mr Stewart had appointed someone to take my place, this time an older woman who was returning to work, as her children were now aged over 10 years. I was happy to show her the ropes and to introduce her round to all the people that she needed to have contact with in the firm. It had been Mr Stewart's practice to check my calculations for my own salary and to sign off on that every month. He told me that he had checked the calculations and had made a special arrangement for my money to be paid in to my account already, so that it would be cleared in the banking system by the time I set off north. I told him I was very grateful for that. When I checked the amount paid in I saw that he'd added £50 as a sort of honorarium for which I was most grateful and indeed, later, I sent a letter of appreciation.

So on the Thursday night I took my leave of my fellow employees and just before I set off home Freddie arrived, with a few more of the drivers and warehouse staff, and they all shook me by the hand and wished me well and finally Freddie made a little speech.

"Me and the lads want to wish you all the best for the future and we've had a little whip round and hope that the enclosed will be useful to you."

He handed me one of the brown envelopes which we used to pay them their wages and on it he had written *'All the best £7.06s.4d. No tax or National Insurance deducted. (PS I put in the four pence!)',* and it was signed 'Freddie'.

On Saturday I took Tommy, Daisy, Winnie, Les and his wife for lunch at the Red Lion. When I say I took them well ……….I did buy a round of drinks but Tommy insisted that he would pay for the food. Yes, it was a sombre meeting, but I think that five days after the funeral we, who had been mourning on the day and gradually been struggling up from the depths ever since, were coming closer to the surface, without yet having arrived there. It was a lovely family occasion and I knew as we parted that I was leaving behind some good decent people with whom it had been my privilege to share part of their family life. It also occurred to me that if I was able to settle into this potential new life that I might have very limited contact with them henceforth. At Daisy's insistence I agreed to write and let them know how I was going on. Tommy and Les between them agreed to keep an eye on the house by visiting fairly frequently, until the time that it was sold.

On the Sunday I was back at the Red Lion eating yet again, this time with Billy and again it was I who received the hospitality of my good friend. After lunch we went home and began to engage in the process of loading the van, as I proposed to set off on the Monday morning. The van had been used by someone whose business involved the use of ladders and was equipped with a welded on roof frame which we thought ideal for the rigid half of the single bed. So we took off the mattress for me to sleep on that night and covering the bed base with some plastic and a part tarpaulin, which Freddie had 'acquired' for me, we roped it to the roof frame. Next we took out part of the front seat. The Bedford van had a single seat for the driver and then a double seat next to the driver to accommodate two other front seat passengers. It was this passenger seat that we removed so as to allow the mattress to be slid in on the following morning. Next he helped me install some of the heavier items, so the tea chests with crockery and cutlery inside and the one with my clothes, and these were placed in the middle of the van near the front to keep the weight forward and then beside it we installed the radiogram minus its legs. We left the van part loaded, since I would otherwise not have enough room to install the mattress and my cycle the following morning.

"Well," said Billy after we had shared a couple of bottles of beer at the end of our exertions, "I guess this is it then. You're off to your new life you lucky sod. Of course, you would rather have had your old one with Linda and Carole but, given that that was not to be, at least you've got something to get your teeth into."

"Are you really that unhappy Billy?"

For a little while just looked at me.

"No. Shall we say it's worse than that?"

"Why?" I asked.

"Well, it's the old man; I think he's lost his way. Yes, he was always a spiv and that's not to everybody's taste, your Linda's family for a start, but I feel he's just getting worse. If you get my drift he is in with the wrong crowd and some of the company he keeps frankly scares the pants off me. There are some real gangsters operating in London these days and he thinks that because he's in at a low-level, that he's safe from any problems. I only hope he is right."

"What you gonna do about it?" I asked

"There's not a lot I can do," he replied, "I suppose the only thing that can be done is for me to get away from it. You're alright, I'm not asking for a room in your new house but I really will have to give some thought to what I'm gonna do with myself. I know that I'm unhappy, but I don't know how to get away."

I said to him that I would keep my eye open for anything, but I didn't think there would be much where I was going.

"Bless you," he said, "but I don't think six or seven hundred miles would do the trick with this lot. I think that if you wanted to leave the firm on a voluntary basis without their permission you would have to go a really a long way to avoid the trouble that they could give you."

"Are you under threat?" I asked.

"No not now, not this minute, but the more me dad gets into the more he gets me into what I don't want to be in, but I have to stay in it for him. What's more whilst ever I am in it I'm safe, fine and dandy, but if ever I said I was leaving some people might think that I knew too much and that it wouldn't be safe for me to be running round knowing what I know. It's then life would get difficult."

I didn't know what to say, he clearly didn't want to elaborate on what exactly he knew but I could understand, in a broad sort of way, that he had become part of something that was anathema to him but which he felt unable to leave.

"Well enough of this," he said, "I'm off and I'm going to wish you all the very best for the future." He gripped my hand and looked me full in the eyes and said.

"I'm grateful to you for being an honest and sincere friend and I know that your late lovely missus was not all that enamoured of me, nevertheless you stuck by me and I'll never forget that."

With that he turned grabbed his coat and in the act of walking out of my back door he also walked out of my life; or nearly.

By this time it was also almost nine o'clock and I had had a long day and tomorrow I was starting an adventure that would hopefully turn into my new life. I knew from a recent early morning visit to the toilet that it would be getting light about five thirty in the morning, so I set my alarm for six and thought that that would mean I could get away by about ten or so. I had a somewhat restless night, initially brooding on the unhappiness of my friend Billy, but then in the early hours I woke to the thoughts that this was my last night in the home that I had shared with Linda and Carole. I tossed and turned and was quite glad when the alarm clock rang and I could wake up.

    To a new morning.
    To a new day.
    To a new life.

The Journey

By eight o'clock in the morning I was washed, shaved, dressed and breakfasted and ready for the final packing of the van. The hardest task was to get the mattress out of the back door into the van. Billy had helped me the previous night to get it down the stairs, so that I didn't have to negotiate them but it was still quite an unwieldy piece of furniture to manage on my own. It just about fitted in, but it went right through, almost to the front dashboard, and looking to the left from the driver's seat visibility would be limited. Then I packed the last of my clothes, washed and dried the last of the crockery from my breakfast and added them and a small amount of bread and the remaining cornflakes to another box. Then I cleaned the sink, upstairs wash basin and the toilet, so that all looked smart for any person viewing the house. Finally, I emptied the waste into the metal dustbin and put the lid on.

Several neighbours, who knew of my plans for departure that day, either hailed me as they went off to work and one or two even knocked on the door if I was not visible packing something into the van. Florrie, one of Linda's best friends, arrived with some sandwiches in greaseproof paper and a slice of cake to go with them. These various brief contacts were very nice, but tended to slow down my progress a bit, particularly as I felt I ought to be reasonably sociable with some, especially Florrie. It was therefore not long before nine o'clock before I could lock the door of the van and set off on my bike to Feltham High Street.

My first call was to the estate agents who held one set of keys to the house and there I had some hopeful news, because they thought that one of the parties who'd recently viewed the house was likely to make an offer. We discussed that and I instructed them as to how much I would be willing to negotiate on price, but I told them that it may be difficult for me to be in touch with them, as I wasn't sure about communication opportunities where I was going to live. Therefore, I told them that I had fully discussed the matter with my father-in-law Tommy and that I relied upon him and his judgement and he was to act as my agent in this matter. Then to the solicitors, broadly speaking to reiterate what I said to the agents and finally, a little later than I'd hoped, but about twenty past ten I got to the bank. There I confirmed my provisional arrangements to transfer my account to the branch in Inverness and my bank provided mobile banking services once a month to service the Clackmore district.

My balance on the day was £212. 12s. 8p so I withdrew £50 leaving me just over £160 to be transferred. I do not think I had ever held £50 in cash in my pocket before and it was a little concerning as well as a little bulky as I had got it in small denominations of £1 and £5, fortunately the large old white fivers had been replaced by the smaller fiver, featuring an image of Britannia a couple of years earlier, otherwise they would have substantially increased my load. I felt I needed to have cash in hand to cover travel expenses including petrol, meals and two overnight bed-and-breakfast stops and also to have something left for a bit of shopping when I arrived.

On return home I loaded the bike onto the van, closed and locked the backdoors and went into the house. I guess I wobbled a bit at that point. It's not that I didn't want to go, that I didn't want this new life, it was just that I really didn't want to have lost my old life.

Slowly I went round the whole house, I guess on the pretext of making sure that I hadn't left anything, but really absorbing the memories. Remembering how I had felt the first time we walked in when the house looked much as it was now, empty but ready and willing to be a home, our home. I lingered in our bedroom realising how much I missed the comfort of sleeping with Linda, memories of sad times when one or other of us had been temporarily sick with a cold or flu and remembering happy times when we cuddled up to make one another warm on a cold winter's night. Eventually having toured every room I reached the kitchen and realised that this was the last place on earth that I had seen my lovely wife and kissed my little girl for the final time. Eventually I snapped out of my reverie and after one final glance around I opened the back door went outside, locked it walked round the back of the house and put the key under a stone from which my brother-in-law, Les, would retrieve it later in the day and then I went to the van.

I pulled back the sliding driver's door, started the engine reversed out and parked in front of the house. I turned off the engine went and double checked that the front and back house doors and the garage were locked, and, on my way to the van I closed the gates for the final time. I got into the van put my hands on the ignition key and before turning it I looked at the house and quite involuntarily I said out loud.

"Okay my lovely girls we are off on a new adventure and I am taking you with me." With that I brushed the tears from my eyes and turned the ignition key, started the engine, closed the van's sliding door, shifted the gear lever on the steering column to first gear and so began my new life.

Freddie had scratched his head when I had asked for his professional driver's opinion on the best route to take.

"Well then, 'You'll take the high road and I'll take the low road and I'll be in Scotland afore ye.'" he laughingly replied.

"You have options; A 6 and up the west coast but although the new motorway M 1 is open to north of Northampton you then have to cut across through the Coventry / Birmingham area. You could go to the end of the M 1 and then cut across to the A 1 but that's a bit tricky. Given you're not a regular driver, I would go round the North Circular and pick up the A1 and just follow it. But just going back to the high and low road bit, and as you are goin' in a van not a wagon, I would take the high route over Carter Bar on the A68 because it's a nice drive and you miss out all that queuing through Gateshead and Newcastle and its miles shorter than going right round the coast."

So armed with a slightly out of date AA map I set off. At the end of the road I turned to my left leaving Feltham behind me and then left again onto the Chertsey Road heading towards Twickenham, eventually passing the international rugby football ground on my left. After crossing the River Thames and skirting the centre of Richmond away to my right I turned left again and proceeded on, leaving Kew Gardens my left. Crossing Kew Green I suddenly realised that I had been going flat out since early on and it was now getting on for noon. Fortunately, I saw a place to park and pulled in to enjoy some of Florrie's sandwiches and some tea from the flask I had prepared. Then, refreshed I set off across Kew Bridge and a little way further on I joined the great outer ring road for London, the North Circular Road. This was a very busy road, parts of which were two lanes each way, with a lot of traffic, especially a lot of commercial traffic.

Picking up the A1 just south of Barnet, I turned north. Fortunately in the 1930s both Barnet and Hatfield had been bypassed and the main road skirted Welwyn Garden City but it was busy through many of the other towns like Stevenage, but progress was improved as Biggleswade had been bypassed a couple of years before. I journeyed on to St. Neots where I got some petrol and found a café for a cup of tea, since that in my flask was a bit stewed. It was getting on for three o'clock before I was on the road again, but I was refreshed by my break and the fact that there was much more by way of countryside and towns were less frequent and less busy.

One other piece of advice Freddie had given me was about a transport café on the newly opened Doncaster by-pass, which he said would be a good stopping spot and over two hours after leaving St. Neots, I was relieved to arrive at this establishment and parked amongst a large number of commercial vehicles. Apparently this cafe was open 24 hours a day and a favoured stopping spot for many long distance drivers. After more than six hours on the road, and being out of recent practice at driving, I was extremely tired. However, after a large meat pie with chips and beans and a slightly chipped, but huge, mug of tea I was re-invigorated and ready to go. When looking at the map I had thought that the halfway point up England to Scotland ran on an approximate line between Hull and Liverpool. I noticed that these two cities were linked by the A62 and my intention was to get beyond that line on day one if possible.

My objective was achieved just at about a quarter to eight and by now I realised that tiredness was beginning to affect my driving. I had checked that sunset was due about eight twenty five and so when I reached Wetherby at eight fifteen I realised that I quickly needed to find a place to stay. Over the river Wharfe and up a main street I noticed a number of hotels and inns in what must have been a former coaching stop in yesteryear. On emerging from the main street, there was a petrol station and I decided to refuel and seek some local information. Now, I was concerned about staying in towns because the van might be susceptible to being broken into, so I asked the man who served me my fuel about farmhouse bed and breakfasts. He advised me that there were two going north. I was to go on for a couple of miles and pass the Bridge Hotel at Walshford and then there were two farmhouses offering accommodation on the open road a couple of miles further on. I asked what my options were if they were unable to help me and he said that then I would just have to go on to Boroughbridge which I should make before it was completely dark.

In the event the first farm advertising 'Bed and Breakfast' was able to take me and after some discussion the farmer's wife was happy to give me a fairly early breakfast. Apparently she helped with the milking and finished about seven in the morning and made breakfast for her husband for half past seven and I could join them. From what she told me their main business through the year was with drivers and the occasional travelling salesman and very often they were looking for an early start. When she had real holidaymakers this was only during the summer and then she did the family breakfast after milking but then made a separate breakfast for the guests.

After sleeping like a log and devouring a large fried breakfast, I was on the road before eight o'clock in the morning, indeed by that hour I was passing through the pleasant little market town of Boroughbridge. After negotiating the town I was out again into very pleasant rolling countryside and I reflected on my journey so far.

For much of my life I had lived in an urban setting and was quite comfortable with built up areas and busy roads, with hardly ever a view of fields. That had been the case by and large until I got north of Stevenage and then I began to see more and more fields and even though the road was busy it was nowhere as busy as I was used to in

Feltham. I had passed by the edge of the Nottinghamshire coalfields and then after more fields and agricultural land I had passed the Yorkshire coalfields around the area near to Castleford and Pontefract. These industrial areas were the only ones that I had seen since leaving Greater London and ever since I passed across the A 62 there had only been the occasional small town to interrupt a basically agricultural landscape. It was quite surprising for one whose life was mainly spent in the urban sprawl of Greater London to realise just how big our country was, and save for major towns, how much land there was.

At Scotch Corner, right by an impressive hotel bearing that name, I could have turned off onto the A66 and gone via Penrith up the West Coast route. Instead, on Freddie's advice, I continued for about another 10 miles and then took the A 68 through West Auckland, Tow Law and Corbridge before, according to the map, heading out into the less populated hinterland of Northumberland. Just after eleven o'clock I had climbed up to the Scottish border at Carter Bar, where I found a small layby with a view over the surrounding countryside. It was a pleasant late spring day, albeit a bit windy, and after stretching my legs I returned to the van to make a lunch of the remaining sandwiches Florrie had prepared supplemented by some sips from a large bottle of R. White's lemonade which I thought would be more tasty than the stewed tea from the flask provided by the farmer's wife at breakfast earlier in the day.

It had been a long morning and I felt quite tired, indeed I closed my eyes and must've drifted off for about half an hour, only to be woken by the crunching of gravel and the loud noise of a big lorry pulling in beside me. I set off again this time going downhill and was soon in the pretty little town of Jedburgh. Although the town was busy I managed to find a place to park and I decided that, despite my snooze, I needed a substantial break from all the driving. After a walk around town I found the museum dedicated to Mary, Queen of Scots, where I spent a good bit of time. By the time I had refuelled and got back on the road it was gone three o'clock but I felt much refreshed from the exercise.

By five o'clock I was stuck in traffic in the centre of Edinburgh and it was after six when I arrived at South Queensferry and found a small cafe looking out across the Firth of Forth with a good view of the world-famous train bridge which crosses that stretch of water. Then it was on to the ferry point where I had to wait for about forty five minutes before I picked up a ferry for the twenty minute crossing to North Queensferry. We had a wonderful view of the new Forth Road Bridge and clearly it would not be long before it was completed, for sections of the roadway were already in place sticking out from each of the two main supporting towers. I remarked how well the project was going to one of the sailors on the ferry, but, as he reminded me, it wasn't good for him because once the bridge opened then there would be no more work for him on the ferry boats, as everybody would take their cars and lorries over the bridge.

Motoring on into the evening I found a small farm offering bed and breakfast a few miles south of Kinross. The journey had been quite tiring, coming on the back of the emotional departure from home, as it still existed in my mind, and then with the long day of driving that followed, I had taken quite a bit out of myself. Then again, today had started much earlier but I'd had a long morning in the driving seat and quite a long afternoon having spent an awful lot of time in traffic jams in Edinburgh. Once again I slept well but the breakfast was not to be available until after eight o'clock, so it was gone 9 o'clock when I set off heading towards Perth where I was to pick up the

A9 which would take me all the way to Inverness and my appointment with the solicitor.

Leaving Perth I was back out into agricultural country, just as I had been on the way up from Kinross, but then a section between Dunkeld and Pitlochry was wooded with not many views. This continued until Blair Atholl and I had not enjoyed the past hour or so of the journey since it had come on to rain very heavily. I passed the gateway to Blair Castle in a deluge of rain and, after going under the railway bridge, I followed the wall of the estate for what seemed like many miles along a fairly straight narrow road with huge puddles every few yards. It was clearly a busy road, for I passed a number of large lorries most of which splashed muddy water all over the van. I only hoped that the tarpaulin on the roof was protecting the bed base well enough. But then soon after I left the trees and rose up towards the pass of Drumochter the rain and its attendant clouds began to clear and opened up some magnificent views. After lunch in Newtonmore I was passing through Aviemore at about two o'clock I pressed on and just before three in the afternoon, I was running into Inverness.

Near the city centre and whilst waiting at traffic lights I asked directions to Church Street and a helpful local suggested that I go to Bank Street, which was beside the river, and I could park there and walk up to Church Street. This I did and presented myself at the solicitor's office about a quarter past three.

James McKay was a sprightly but rotund gentleman of some sixty years with a ruddy face and a very affable manner who came out of his office to greet me as soon as the secretary, to whom I had reported, had informed him by telephone of my attendance. He waddled across to meet me and greeted me like a long lost nephew, which of course I was to the late Roddy but not to him. He ordered me the promised cup of tea and wanted to hear in great detail all about my journey. After ten minutes of conversation about my journey he turned to the business that had brought me there.

"Can I say that your uncle would have been delighted to hear that you were coming to make your home in the croft. Of course he would have been greatly saddened by the circumstances which brought you to that decision. When I last spoke to him a few months ago he was aware of your circumstances in terms of your marriage, your child, and your settled occupation, and so at that point he was resigned to the fact that your decision would quite logically be to decline the offer of taking up the croft. Shortly before his death he wrote to me, reminding me of the requirements of the will, and stressing that I at least formally approach you regarding the tenancy of the croft, and he also enclosed two letters. The first was addressed to you in the expectation that you would probably decline the offer, and the other is addressed to 'whom it may concern' and I have no doubt that its contents will relate to the way he has organised the crops and the livestock in recent years so that anybody coming in would be aware of how he had managed the thing. I'm sure he would be delighted to know that both letters are being passed to you."

At this point he handed me two envelopes the first addressed, in a scrawling hand, to me and the second, to 'whom it may concern'. He then asked me to sign a couple of documents to do with the notifications of the transfer of the croft and finally he produced a set of accounts and a bill for the services of his firm.

Uncle Roddy's bank account was in credit to the tune of just under £90 on top of that there was a post office savings account of just over £450, in other words his life savings. Deducting the funeral expenses meant there was little cash in hand even together with the payment of a death grant which Mr McKay had obtained. Most had been nearly wiped out by the settlement of various outstanding bills including to a local vet and in payment of his electricity account. The account showed on the bottom line that there was a surplus of £27.10s.8p my heart sank as I thought about the solicitors bill.

"I have spoken to the managing partner of the firm," said Mr McKay, "and in the circumstances and given that your uncle had already paid us for all the other services provided to him, it was agreed that the following bill was appropriate, given your recent tragic circumstances."

I picked up the bill which simply said 'Professional services in the matter of winding up the estate of Roderick Mathieson. Total £27.10s.8p.' Realising that he had excused me from a substantial sum I offered him my fulsome thanks.

"As a matter of interest what should the bill have been?"

"Well, I couldn't possibly say since we've not actually calculated the work done. But let's put it this way It would certainly have exceeded £27.10s.8p." And with that he smiled broadly.

"So what's the plan now?" He asked.

"Well I'm planning not to go too far as I have had a long couple of days and I am not used to driving, so I plan to pick up bed and breakfast before turning off towards Ullapool."

He suggested that it was a nicer journey if you keep to the better roads this side of the country and suggested that I go up via Bonnar Bridge before turning across to the west.

"And if you do that be sure to take the 'B' road off to your left between Evanston and Alness because then you will be able to stop off at the lovely viewpoint at the top of Struie Hill."

We parted at the outer door of the offices, to which he had accompanied me, and I set off back to the van, clutching tightly my two letters from my late uncle Roddy.

On the way from the parking spot to the solicitor's office, I had noticed by the river a sign post indicating the road to Wick and so I retraced my steps and turned onto that road and followed along the south side of the Beauly Firth. Not long after five o'clock I arrived in Beauly and right beside the road was the Lovat Arms Hotel, with parking just in front, so I pulled in. Enquiries revealed that I could get a meal there but they did not start serving until six o'clock but the bar was open. I booked for a meal then returned to the van and got the letters and over a glass of beer I opened the one addressed to me and began to read.

The letter was dated 22nd February 1963 but it was obviously written over several sessions judging by changes of writing size and shape and at one point a change of ink colour and the whole was written in an untidy hand, which I am sure it is not uncommon in people who are unwell.

Dear Ewan,

The doctor wants me to go into hospital for some tests as he believes there is something seriously wrong with my heart. I am not going, even though I am quite sure that he is right. For several years now I have had periods of feeling faint and dizzy and breathless but I have put it down to just getting older. More recently the shortness of breath has become more frequent and in the last few weeks my ankles have been puffing up and I have lost a lot of weight. But I have spent virtually the whole of my life living here and I have absolutely no intention of ending my days in some hospital or nursing home in Inverness. Added to this there is no one really able to look after my animals. So in case the end is nearer than I hope, it is time for me to put my affairs in order.

If you are reading this it will be because I've gone to that better place to be reunited with my mother and father and my long-lost brother Andrew. I do not know what version of events he gave you about the family rift which led to him leaving the Croft never to return. However, I would like to take this opportunity to tell you the story from my point of view.

The day my brother left half of me went with him. I never wanted him to go and I wrote to him several times begging him to return, but your father was a stubborn man, one who, once a decision had been made, never allowed it to be revisited. To that extent he was like my father, your grandfather, a fiercely independent man who found it impossible to excuse anybody who had done him wrong. Your grandfather, my dad, was a harsh, what they would now call, Victorian father, but that was only to be expected by virtue of his own life experiences and the harshness of eking out a living on a small croft.

I was born just 13 months after your dad and we grew up almost like twins. I looked up to him and he looked after me and we did everything together. If we were not at school we were almost certainly working on the croft and what little free time we had was spent on the beach unless, on rare occasions, we went to neighbours' houses for a ceilidh. I should say that that term is now associated with a formal gathering of people, often involving music and dancing, but our understanding of the term was that it was Gaelic for any social gathering even just one family with another, just spending time together, and having what we call a blether.

If you want a description of the ideal childhood then I can tell you that we had it. Five days a week in term time walking two miles each way, hail rain or shine, to school. Before we even set off there were chores around the croft especially with the animals and when we returned home there were more chores. The school leaving age in those days was 14 and all our schooling was delivered locally. In our isolated community we heard very little about what we now call news from outside the area.

When your dad was fourteen the First World War was on and we had been well aware of this and the likelihood that Andrew would be conscripted. We had to face up to the likelihood that it would happen and whilst he and we were worried about this there was also a degree of excited anticipation on his part about going out into the big wide world. Added to this were the financial pressures on my parents to support us all from crofting and the odd jobs that dad got from time to time.

By the time your dad was eighteen the war had ended and we were both working on the croft, as our father had begun to get problems with arthritis. I suppose the thoughts that he would be conscripted and through that route would leave home had been very much in your father's mind and so when that avenue was closed to him because of the end of the war he was, on the one hand relieved that he would not have to fight, but on the other hand he was disappointed in that there would not be an acceptable way for him to see what the outside world was like. So he talked to our father about leaving home for a while, getting a job perhaps in Glasgow, sending some money home, but at the same time seeing something of the outside world. I'm afraid that did not suit our father who was a very rigid man and who said if your father left he would be leaving the family and he need not bother to return.

I could see your father's point of view entirely and given his own strong personality I wasn't surprised when, one day in early 1920, he packed his bags and left. Whilst he sealed his own fate in terms of the views of my father, he ironically sealed my fate too. For father's arthritis got worse and worse until there came a point where he could no longer do anything on the croft and it was all left to me. Our father died in 1929 by which time I was running the croft and had been for years. After father's death I made enquiries through cousins of ours, who lived in Lairg, as to what they'd heard about my brother and apparently he had occasionally written to them over the years. It seemed as though he had gone to sea starting as a cabin boy and working his way up to become an able seaman. He had mainly served with Gow, Harrison & Co who ran out of Glasgow and gradually worked his way into the good books of the company and ended up as a boatswain with them.

I wrote to him when our dad died and assured him that although the croft had been left to me I was more than willing to share it with him, but if he did not wish to return here, which I could understand, then at least I hoped we could remain friends and keep in touch. I received no reply to that, nor to a similar letter sent in 1935 after our mother passed away. The only communication was from your own mother in 1941 to tell me that his ship had been torpedoed in the Atlantic and that he was missing, presumed drowned. So, I could not even say goodbye to him at a funeral.

However, because he was lost into the Atlantic, the same ocean which washes onto the beach just a few yards from the croft, I have felt that just looking at the sea reminds me of him, and how much I loved him and how I wish things might have been different. If only he could have been able to forgive then maybe you would have known me personally, instead of through this letter. So I hope that this explanation will help you to better understand this part of your family background.

It is time for me to close now, but I must finish by addressing the reason why I have named you as the person to take over the croft. This croft has been in the family for many years now and this act of mine in naming you is to prove to you and him that despite his bloody-mindedness my love for my older brother has never faltered and had he lived I would undoubtedly have bequeathed it to him. This act of love however is a selfish one and I can die knowing that I passed the croft on to family.

But what happens after I am gone must be a decision for you. I know from various sources that you are happily married, with a little girl and that you have a settled job and you live in London. It would be wholly unrealistic for you to give up that life for a very different, hand to mouth existence on a croft. So please do not think I expect you to take up the offer, in fact you would probably be mad to do so since your life experiences are so far removed from what you would get as a crofter. So as well as this personal letter to you I have also written a letter to whoever takes over, just to tell them a few things about how I have managed the croft over the years and what I have done recently and what needs doing. Mr. McKay the solicitor will pass that letter on to the new crofter.

I do ask you one thing, and it will be a big ask I know. Please, please make it in your way to visit the croft. Not necessarily straight away, but some time. If possible bring your wife and daughter for your little girl to see where her granddad lived his early life. Make sure you walk on the beach and when you do I know you will feel the presence of me and your father, my brother, walking with you.

Good luck with your life and God Bless,
Roddy Mathieson.

It was fortunate that there were only a few folk in the bar and that I was in a dark corner, for after being rapt with interest in the story to start with, the final two paragraphs hit me like a thunderbolt. Oh! How I would have loved to be able to have taken Linda and Carole on a holiday to see the croft and walk on that beach. Just thinking about it was enough to make me feel distraught. To reflect on the fact that my little girl had only ever been on one seaside holiday, to a boarding house in Birchington, in Kent, hurt me as I felt that I had failed her in the lack of experiences I had given her in her short life. It returned me to those 'if only I had known what was round the corner' thoughts.

Once I had steadied myself I turned my focus to this man, this obviously kind and thoughtful man, who had wanted, in his own mind at least, to prove his love for his brother by leaving the croft to him, at least in a token way, via his son; me. Yet he also acknowledged that as things had stood at the point of his penning the letter the likelihood of my wanting, or indeed being able, to take up the tenancy was most unlikely, and yet he thoughtfully absolved me from any guilt in not doing so. What a shame I had never met him; he must have been a nice bloke.

My mind was beset with all the thoughts which the letter provoked and I cannot now recall what I ate, or even where I stayed the night. It was another farm beside the main road, somewhere between Dingwall and Evanton and it was used to catering for drivers and commercial travellers. I availed myself of the offer of an early breakfast and I was off before eight the following morning. As suggested I took the 'B' class road before

Alness and after winding up a long hill and traversing an undulating plateau, at about half past eight I reached Struie viewpoint, about which the farmer's wife had also told me. I pulled in and was greeted with the most marvellous view across the Dornoch Firth. There was mist still on the water but the high land beyond was clear as a bell as the sun tried to burn off the mist below. A train on its way from Inverness to Wick, I assumed, passed toy-like below my viewpoint.

I dropped down to Ardgay and over the metal bridge to Bonar Bridge and at a junction, where the road north to Wick went to the right, I turned left and headed towards Lairg but long before getting there my route to the west coast required me to bear off to the left. Not long after that turning I reached my first single track road with passing places. This was a new driving experience for me; stretches of road not wide enough to allow two vehicles to pass, with occasional passing places marked with a white diamond shape on a post and some with an exhortation to not park in these refuges. To start with, as I ventured west, there were some stretches, in little hamlets, of wider bits of road and I passed through good arable land which increasingly gave way to forestry. I gradually climbed up and after passing Oykell Bridge, and it's very smart looking little hotel, I was out onto moorland.

This made the driving easier, as forward visibility was improved, and just as well because I encountered a lot of fish lorries loaded with the day's catch from Lochinver, roaring down to market. These professional drivers, with a long way to go, were disinclined to stop in a passing place if they were not forced so to do and came ploughing on at breakneck speed. I soon learned that it was as well to pull in and let them by rather than risking the next layby, which meant stopping them. So progress was slow. I guess it is about forty miles from leaving the Lairg road to

Ledmore Junction, where the road up from Ullapool is joined, but what with getting used to the single track road driving technique and the numerous fish and farm vehicles, it must have taken me the best part of an hour and a half, an average speed of less than 30mph by my calculation.

By ten thirty I had passed the Inchnadamph Hotel and reached the turn to Lochinver, which the signpost advertised, was eleven miles further on. Now by looking at the map I knew that I did not need to go into the village in order to reach my destination, but, I was aware that I needed provisions and to top up fuel for the van, as it was not clear whether I would get any of these things nearer to the croft. If indeed there was nothing closer, then it would mean a return journey of over twenty miles to get to Lochinver and back again. So I decided to not take the risk and therefore I went down the hill towards the sea, past my turnoff to the right signed for Drumbeg, and took a sharp left over a single track river bridge and on into the village.

The map shows a place which is the biggest substantial centre within a huge area, so I was prepared for quite a town; that is not what I found. It is situated on a wide inlet from the sea, quite a natural harbour. In a very broad schematic sort of way it resembles a square that has had one side removed which constitutes the seaward side and into each of the remaining two corners runs a river. The first, the Inver river, over which I had entered the village leads to a ribbon development along the landward side of the road for about three quarters of a mile till you get to the other corner where another, smaller river enters the bay. Along this road were to be found a mixture of houses and shops including a baker, grocer, garage and petrol pump together with a doctor's house, police house and bank. The only building on the seaward side of the road was a church built onto a very small promontory. Once past the second river, the road turned seaward and after a couple of hundred yards ended at a fish quay and sheds on the seaward side and on the landward side an imposing castle-like building which advertised itself as the Culag Hotel. Set back from the hotel, where the road ended, was a bar, a ships chandlers and a Seamen's Mission to serve the obviously very busy fishing industry.

I turned around at the hotel, since I could go no further, and headed back to the shops which were situated at the corner of the village where I had first entered. I got fuel for the van, noticing the significantly inflated price per gallon which I realised was due to the added costs of getting the stuff delivered. Then to the grocers for some staples like tins of corned beef, sardines, beans, soup, cornflakes, butter, milk and the like; once again the prices were more than I was used to paying. Finally to the bakers for a couple of loaves and some floured rolls and he offered a range of sandwiches and pies and so I took two of each.

It was almost midday and I was tempted to stay in the pleasant village and eat a sandwich looking out at the sea, but the desire to get to my destination was overwhelming so on I went back over the narrow Inver river bridge and up about two hundred yards to my turnoff, signposted to Drumbeg. Now if my travails on the single track road earlier in the day had been a test for my driving, they were as nothing to what awaited me on the last dozen miles to my turn off to the road to the croft. A ribbon of tarmac tackled steep inclines and declines and there was no verge, all you had beside you was a steep drop which would have taken you down into one of the innumerable small bodies of water which I passed; these small lakes I later came to know as lochans. After one particularly long rise I was confronted with a right handed, right-angled, bend round a towering rock face to my right whilst being confronted with a two hundred foot drop on the other side. Fortunately there was nobody coming the other way.

Eventually after counting the turnoffs, all of which were to my left, I came over a rise and looked out across a valley about half a mile wide. The road swung right going down and inland a little to cross a bridge and then turning right in the distance as it rose up the other side of the valley. However my turning was just before the bridge and I swung onto an even narrower strip of tarmac, with grass growing in the middle. After a short while I passed a croft and sitting on a bench by the door a man lifted a laconic finger of greeting and I waved in reply but carried on. The road dropped easily away and gradually opened out to a view of a small bay and in the distance I could see the croft house, as Mr McKay had described to me. What a lovely view on that fine spring day with a grey blue sea sporting a few white caps in the distance and a beach with what looked like a picture postcard cottage down by the sea.

At last the road dropped down to the valley floor and turned right so that it ran along above the shore, and indeed in places it was semi covered by windblown sand, then on to a little stone bridge. Just beyond the bridge I turned right onto a gravel track and rose up to a parking place directly outside my new home.

Oh my!
What had I done?
They say never buy a pig in a poke.
Always look carefully before you buy.
Caveat emptor.

An arrival

Well I was not actually buying, I was a tenant, but I had already got the impression that the landlord allowed you to hold the land but anything upon it was an issue for the tenant and that included the maintenance of the property.

Sitting in the van and devouring one of the baker's delicious sandwiches, I considered the aspect. The picture postcard croft house from half a mile away was much less appealing up close. Architecturally it was typical of what I came to think of as a local Scottish style. A front door was flanked on each side by a window, whilst above were two peaked windows coming forward out of the low roof. From where I was parked I could see some ramshackle outbuildings at the rear and also what looked like a scrapyard of old agricultural equipment. The paintwork on the house windows and door looked well overdue for attention as did the peeling whitewash on the outside walls.

Fortified by my sandwich I decided that it was time for action, although it would not be dark till late I realised that, if the outside was anything to go by, there would be a lot of work to do inside before bedtime. I thought that my priority was to look and see what those conditions were like inside and how I would be fixed for the night.

The key was under the plant pot to the right of the front door, as I had been advised and I retrieved it and put it in the lock, but try as I might it failed to turn. I circumnavigated the property but found no other door, so I returned to the front and cursing I waggled the door handle and the door opened. It had not been locked at all, mainly because it had swelled and the lock arm and the receiver were no longer aligned. I entered a hallway.

Immediately opposite, one pace away, was a set of stairs and to my right two paces along was a sitting room with a fireplace. It held an ancient three piece suite which had been moved towards the rear of the room and towards the front, nearer the door, was a single metal bed frame minus mattress.

Along the hallway back past the front door, a total of five paces, was what I can only describe as a relatively modern kitchen/dining room. Originally it had been a room similar in size to the sitting room, but an extension had been created at the back of the house which provided, as I was to discover, a bathroom with bath, basin and toilet – this latter I later found was serviced by a septic tank. Within the old room, as I first looked upon it, was a large table with a variety of hardback chairs around it, then towards the back of the room and the entrance door to the bathroom, was a kitchen area which comprised a traditional white stone sink (no doubt original), a relatively modern electric cooker, small fridge and even a top loading washing machine. I later discovered that there was a small portable spin dryer that could be used with the washing machine and which I was to find very helpful.

Trying the electric light switch failed to cause the bulbs to activate so I went in search of a mains box and switch, this was easily located in the kitchen area. Once switched on the light I had tried came on and so I investigated further and was able to put on the power to the fridge and to locate an immersion heater switch too. For all the rest of the place was very dated, Roddy's kitchen, bathroom and electrics in general were more modern than in my old Feltham home.

Back to the hallway and the steps upstairs were very steep, just two steps up before it began a ninety degree turn to the right, another dozen or so narrow steps and then it turned sharply to the left, and two more steps until you reached the landing. Immediately to the right was one bedroom and then you passed along the narrow landing to another; neither of these rooms looked to have been in use recently, the furthest one being empty, apart from a variety of boxes and had clearly been used for storage and what had once probably been the main bedroom had a double bed frame with no mattress on it. Despite not being used for some time and apart from being dusty there was no evidence of dampness in either room and they could clearly be used as bedrooms.

I went down the stairs noting that, again apart from being dusty, the carpet was fairly threadbare and this was true of the big rugs that were on the wooden floors in each of the downstairs rooms. Looking at how things were, I assumed that as his heart condition developed Roddy had decided not to use the upstairs and had obviously laid out some money to create a new kitchen and toilet area so that he didn't have to go up and down the stairs. He had then lived in the two rooms downstairs, probably due to his condition and the fact that where he did expend energy it was out on the croft, managing the land and the animals and not in keeping house. At this point I suppose my domestic centred, town living, army and Linda like experiences kicked in and instead of prioritising, as a farmer would have done, looking at the land and the animals, I resolved to clean and tidy the house.

After the deluge of rain around Blair Atholl the previous day, I had been lucky enough to experience only dry weather and in fact on this, my last day of northward journey, it was one of those beautiful spring days with puffy white clouds and a gentle breeze. It was ideal weather for cleaning. I had been loath to leave Linda's cleaning materials behind and I quickly found the tea chest in which they had been packed. A good old hand held scrubbing brush, some Dettol, a sweeping brush and a dustpan and brush were soon by the door. The kitchen dining area seemed the logical place to start and the first thing to come out was the rather greasy ancient rug which covered much of the floor. I rolled it and carried it outside and then took all the small items like chairs and put them out as well. Starting at the very back I cleaned the bath, the toilet, the basin and then working forward I gave a good clean to the whole kitchen, including moving the washing machine and cooker out to clean behind them. Then on hands and knees I scrubbed the whole of the floor from back to front and having done so I opened the front window to let the whole area begin to dry out. I then turned my attention to the sitting room and out went the bed frame but I could not move the armchairs or the two seater settee, so having first removed the front room rug I then scrubbed that out from back to front, only this time I found the window was jammed and would not open and that would need later attention. I had decided that the sitting room rug, whilst dirty, was not greasy like other had been so I took it to a nearby fence and whacked it with a broom handle on a number of occasions and left it there to air in the breeze. By this time it was late afternoon and I was quite tired with the physical exertion.

To make a break for myself and to allow the scrubbed floors to dry I tried to take stock of my new home. It was on a slight rise above the little road which had brought me to it and I noticed that the road went on and curved away up my side of the valley and disappeared over the crest. I made a mental note to explore this further at some stage. The other side of the road from the croft was a grassy area where a number of rabbits were happily nibbling in the spring sunshine. Then the land dropped away and all I could see was the sea itself, but I later discovered that over the ridge was a beach, part sand, but mainly rocks and large smooth stones, many of a reddish hue.

Round the side of the house I discovered what I later learnt to have been the original croft building or at least the old black house that had preceded it. Originally it would have been a thatched building, but after the new croft house was built then somebody had made it into a barn where a few animals could be kept. On the ground floor, in the old part of what would have been the black house and then above it there was storage space for hay and the like. The structure was built with substantial timbers and the sides and roof were clad with corrugated iron sheets bolted onto them. It was not pretty, but it was clearly serviceable and on the far side was a sort of Heath Robinson carport arrangement, crudely built with various bits of wood and which provided shelter for at least two cars, again covered and backed with corrugated iron. One of the bays was empty but the other housed quite a smart, but small, David Brown tractor.

Behind the house the land rose gently upwards and was mainly grassy with a few outcrops of rocks. Looking to my left there was the road that I described before as, going to 'know not where', and then the ridge ran out to form a headland jutting out into the sea. To the right, the height of the land at the top of the ridge fell a little as it went inland. It was clear that the area between the small river and the ridge offered good grazing for animals. Down towards the river itself there were fields of what looked to me like long grass interspersed with a few rocky outcrops.

My eye was taken by a movement across the other side of the river and I could see a minibus coming down the road. I watched it for a moment and then began to retrace my steps around the front of the house, expecting that the vehicle would pass the end of my road and continue on over the hill. Instead of that it turned into the entrance of the croft drove up and parked near to my van.

The driver's door opened and out stepped a young woman and before I could take in what she looked like she was followed immediately by a Collie type dog which ran like the wind and came to a sudden stop just before the croft house's open door. Whilst I had been watching the dog the woman had come closer and, as I turned, she greeted me with a quietly confident "Hello". The last syllable was an emphasised 'oooh' rather than an 'oh'.

Now I have always been shy around women. As an only child with no sisters to allow me to understand that gender and the fact that my mother kept me on a fairly short leash, I had been amazed by the stories of how my fellow army mates perceived, and dealt with, the fair sex. Of course I had had no need to worry about finding ways to meet girls because Linda had found me at school and I was content with that. Linda was about five foot six inches and I was two inches taller. We were city children of rationing, about average for our generation. The woman before me was an Amazonian creature of six foot or more, but whilst she was obviously big boned and had a long face and hair she was without an ounce of excess flesh. Two brown eyes stared at me out of a weathered face which bore a long scar on one cheek.

"I am guessing you're Ewan," she said, and when I nodded she went on, "well, I'm Catriona McLeod, most folk call me Cat. My dad is Alistair and we've been keeping an eye on your croft since Roddy died. My dad told me that he'd seen you passing by about midday. We live at the croft on the other side of the river so that's our land over there," she said pointing across to the other side of the valley, "and you have this side of the river and we are the only two crofts in this wee valley."

"I see", I said, "so where does this road go to I said pointing over the rise?"

She replied that it went up and over the hill and dropped steeply down to a rocky inlet which was also sheltered by an island. At the end of the road there was a jetty with a ruined boat shed beside it. But halfway between the top of the hill and the jetty was another house and that belonged to Douglas Cameron, a bit of a recluse, who fishes for crabs and lobsters and the like in the inlet and in the narrow passage around the island.

"His house, yours here and ours are the only three places that are currently lived in along this road at all." She told me.

"Anyway," she said, changing tack, "I see you've been busy cleaning out and I'm sorry we did'na have time to do anything about that. We knew it was a bit of a mess, but spring is a busy time on a croft, well actually I mean all the year is busy, but spring time especially so, and there has been no time to do any cleaning. But my mother has made a stew and is insisting that you come for your tea as an apology for no doing any cleaning."

"Well," I hesitatingly replied, thinking that after all my exercise having a prepared meal would be wonderful, "I ought to get on and finish off here by returning some of the stuff from out here, if the floors are dry and then unpacking the van."

"You ought to know, that in this part of the world, it is extremely rude to refuse an invitation like my mother's, and I am guessing that as a new white settler amongst us natives you might not want to cause upset right at the start. So you'll come?" And I nodded.

"That's agreed then. And just in time because you see that over there," pointing to the seaward end of her side of the valley, "that's the south west, and that cloud coming up means that rain will be with us in the not too distant future, so why don't I give you a quick hand getting that stuff back in before it all gets soaked?"

She made a move towards the door and the dog immediately rose up "Lie down" she said quite curtly to it and the dog immediately did as she bid.

"Oh! By the way, meet Roy, your dog; his predecessor called Rob belonged to your uncle Roddy and when Rob died he bought this one and named him Roy; after Rob Roy the highwayman whose fame was improved by Sir Walter Scott in his novel. No doubt Roddy's sense of humour."

So this was why the dog was sitting staring at the door, this had been his home and maybe he thought Roddy might be there.

"I've never had a dog."

"Well now you have one; because we have two of our own and we have just been mindin' him for you. Come on let's get you organised and then we can go for our tea."

And with that she strode off into the croft house. As she walked I noticed that she had a slight limp, favouring her left side which made her look somewhat ungainly, guessing that I was watching her she turned.

"Oh! Saving you asking, I limp because I had polio when I was younger and suffered a lot of muscle wastage on one leg. Given the much greater suffering many other folk had from that terrible disease, I'm lucky just to be left with a wee limp and nothing worse."

With this she picked up a dining chair and stepped into the front door immediately turning to the left, so clearly she knew the house.

"My. My. Somebody's been busy. Freshly scrubbed with Dettol and nearly dry too. You get the carpet from the fence," she ordered, picking up another chair and I did as I was told. Within no time at all we had replaced the furniture, with the exception of the bed frame, which I did not need, and the greasy carpet from the kitchen dining area with which I had decided to dispense. She then asked if she could help me with anything from the van and I hesitated.

"What would be helpful is if we can get the base of the bed from the roof rack of the van and the mattress out, as they are both a bit awkward. But do you think you'd be all right with that."

She looked at me and smiled.

"I may have a limp, I may be a girl, but I clip sheep, and they take some catching, turning over and holding, and I tote hundredweight sacks of animal feed around and I do plenty other heavy lifting as well. So just show me what we're shifting before this rain arrives."

We lifted the base of the bed off of the roof and found the tarpaulin had done a good job as it was a touch damp in one corner but overall not too bad at all, given all the weather it had been through. We manoeuvred it through the front door and along the passage into the living room. I decided that until the upstairs was cleaned I would be like uncle Roddy and use the living room as a bedroom. I screwed on the legs and finally we got the mattress out and took that in and dropped it on the top of the base. She remarked on the fact that I had a bicycle and she said that it would be very useful in getting around to the local shop, about three miles away, but as petrol was expensive it was often better to use a bike than a vehicle. She said that she did cycle but, as her childhood muscle wastage caused some difficulty for her, she also had a pony which she could ride when she didn't feel like cycling or walking.

"Come on put your bike and the dog in the minibus and we will away up for our tea." She said.

"Ok, but let me lock up."

At this she burst out laughing. Then, as that subsided, she looked at me.

"Firstly, folk round here do not normally steal so nobody locks doors and secondly there are no folks round here at all anyway."

At that moment, as if to prove her wrong, a battered Morris Minor estate car came over the top of the rise behind us and motored slowly past. The driver, an unkempt looking older man stared at us before raising a laconic finger in greeting, my second such greeting of the day, and a gesture to which I was to become accustomed as a form of greeting, and one which I have gone on to adopt.

"That is your other near neighbour Dougie Cameron." she told me. Going on to explain that Dougie was a particular friend of her father and mother and that he was like an uncle to her.

Despite her amusement I insisted on locking the Bedford van, pointing out to her that all my worldly possessions including documents and most crucially pictures of Linda and Carole were there. She turned from amusement to seriousness and said that she fully understood.

"By the way," she added, "we were all so terribly sorry to hear of your tragic loss." Explaining that the solicitor had indicated the reason I had decided to take on the croft and start anew.

I stored the bike in the minibus and we drove the half a mile to the McLeod home where I was greeted by Morag, Cat's mother. As with so many of the folk I was destined to meet over the next few months and years, she was very welcoming and showed an immediate interest in me and was clearly pleased to have conversation. At the same time it was clear to me that she was not a well lady, her eyes were somewhat shrunken into her head and her pallor was a whitish grey. Nevertheless she fussed around making me welcome before going off to the kitchen leaving Cat to introduce me to her dad.

Alistair was a weather-beaten man with skin like leather, marking the fact that his life as a crofter had been supplemented by occasional work on building sites and on summer road maintenance. He greeted me warmly and wanted to know all about my trip up. We were soon chatting equably and I took to him quickly. He offered me a "dram" which gave me a problem. I am not a tee totaller by any means, I have drunk beer, in moderation, all my adult life, but the taste of whisky, gin or rum is not at all to my liking. Bearing in mind Cat's reference to refusing hospitality gave me a dilemma. But better I thought to be honest and so I explained my position.

Drawing in breath in that unique highland, west coast and islands way he said.

"There are two good reasons you have told me that. The first is I like a man who is honest, and secondly I hate the idea of wasting good whisky on somebody who does'na like it, especially when it's ma own whisky."

My mother brought me up on adages, one of which was 'honesty is the best policy' and so I thought that I ought to be grateful to my mother, reinforced by Linda and her 'straight as a die' family for allowing me to learn to put into practice qualities such as that. I often wonder, in retrospect, how it would have turned out had I simply acquiesced and accepted the offer of the whisky and then gone on to either show my dislike of it, or more likely, to have left it hardly touched. Had I done that I'm sure that Alistair might well have been a bit more suspicious of me. As it was, in his quiet and understated Highland way, over a very pleasant meal, he drew me out in terms of why I had decided to come and take over the place from uncle Roddy. There was an acknowledgement, as with Cat, of my loss but I was not pressed into saying more than I wanted to; which on the day was not a lot.

Morag too showed a great deal of interest in me and, as I was to learn, in an area where communications were almost exclusively personal, people had a deep and abiding interest in any fellow human being they met. By and large it was not a nosy sort of approach, it was straightforward interest. The other side of the coin, however, was that if the person was staying around the locality, folk were interested to know what they might bring to the community, because, as it was an interdependent community, they did not want people who were unprepared to join in and contribute. Over many years I became accustomed to the somewhat pejorative term 'white settlers', which was used to describe people who had come up from the south, often England, and who could afford to buy a property that perhaps local people would otherwise have utilised, and who very much wanted to do their own thing. I guess the term came from the old days of the American Wild West where Native Americans were invaded by Caucasian people, from the settlements that had originated on the east coast and who wanted to bring their own way of life, and to replace the lifestyle which the indigenous locals had enjoyed over many, if not hundreds, of years previously.

On the other hand Cat was silent for much of the meal, adding a few bits here and there just to show that she was involved in the conversation, but at the same time I felt that she was listening and watching intently and she was being slightly less open than her parents. Also I felt that she was regarding me with a degree of wariness, which, in some senses, was contrary to the apparent openness of our first exchanges at the house.

Both a shower of rain and an hour and a half had passed since my arrival, and pleasant though the meal and company had been I was beginning to feel the effects of my long drive and the unaccustomed hard work of cleaning out the house. It would be something after eight o'clock when I began to make my move, citing the above reasons and the fact that I probably needed to make up the bed and do other things before the light faded. I was assured that the light would not be a problem since it would still be possible to see at ten o'clock at night at this time of the year but nevertheless they understood my need to go.

As we moved towards the door, Roy, who had hitched a lift up in the minibus, appeared as if by magic from somewhere, Alistair asked me about what I had planned in terms of managing the croft.

Hesitatingly I told him about the notes that uncle Roddy had left me and which I had not had time to look at, but would try do so tomorrow.

"Ahhhh," he said, and with a certain hesitation added, "we are really needing to get the hay in and you should know that your uncle Roddy's tractor has in the past been used both by him and us and a number of other crofters around to pull the machine for cutting the hay and later on for bailing it. When we knew that you were due this week we agreed that we would put off the cutting until next week and see if you were all right about that."

"What if I am not all right with it?" I asked. "Or, if I'd not been coming till a little later in the year?"

He looked me in the eye, formed his mouth into a thin straight line, which eventually ended up turning into a bit of an embarrassed smile, drawing out the first word as, at the same time he drew in breath.

"Weell, I'm thinking we may just have borrowed it anyway."

We both laughed.

"Well then," I said, "I suppose you can still borrow it anyway."

Again the smile.

"But we need to borrow you with it."

I too laughed and agreed but said that I hadn't the first idea how to drive a tractor and I probably couldn't even start it. He told me that Dougie Cameron my other neighbour, over the hill, behind my house, had been an engineer before he moved to his current home and became a fisherman. He said that Dougie was incredible with engines and in the past he had helped Roddy by ensuring that the tractor was in good working order. So it was agreed that Alistair would have a word with Dougie and either tomorrow or on Saturday we would all inspect the tractor, do some maintenance on it and also seeing that the cutter and the bailer were serviced and ready to be used.

With that I bid them good night, got on my bike and with my new family member lolloping along beside me, I pedalled a few times to get going and then coasted down the valley and I only needed to pedal again on the short slightly uphill rise from the far side of the bridge to my front door.

"Well, Mr Roy."

I said, addressing the dog, who considered me with a look which seemed to suggest that he was doubtful if I had ever possessed any marbles but, that if I had, I had recently mislaid a substantial number of them.

"What do I do next?"

And what I did was very little, because tiredness and fresh air, together with a hearty meal, had pretty well exhausted me. I got the foodstuffs from the van just dumping the tins and things into cupboards and putting the fresh things, which I had bought in Lochinver, into the fridge. Then, finally, I retrieved some of the bedding from the van, made up the bed and in fairly short order I got into it.

"Well uncle Roddy", I thought lying there just before the very necessary blackness of sleep engulfed me, "I'm here. I don't know whether you would be pleased or not to see what sort of a helpless crofting soul I am. But at this stage I'm sort of encouraged by my contact with the McLeod family and, I feel that in Alistair, I have a potentially very helpful teacher. I will do my very best for you and try to make a go of this new life and I will do it for you, the stranger who has given me this chance and for Linda and Carole who, I know, will always be here beside me."

I was at the end of a few days of phrenetic activity of a sort most unusual to me.

Tiredness and a relative contentment equalled immediate, deep sleep.

Part 2 Renaissance

New Beginnings

There was a scratching at the door, Roy obviously required a comfort break so I rose and opened the door on a beautiful morning with the sun just about to light the house, as it had lit the hillside above us. It was barely five o'clock yet I'd virtually enjoyed seven hours of a quasi-death experience, by which I mean I had been fast asleep and not moved at all, from what I could tell, the whole night through. I felt refreshed and ready to engage in my new life. New experiences are exciting, there is something captivating in being in an out of routine existence. I had led a very settled life and with the exception of the army experience, I'd always lived in the same area but I had still had a few experiences which marked themselves down as different from the humdrum or the ordinariness of daily life. The first time I'd been to London and seen Buckingham Palace, my first trip on the Thames, the first time I'd been on a trip down to Brighton and seen the sea, these things were stimulating because they were out of the ordinary.

    Standing by my door looking out inland, but hearing the sea, I felt a tingling of excitement of what may lie ahead. After all, I told myself, starting again was what I wanted to do in order to try to let go of some of the horrors of the recent past. It was a chance I knew I needed to take, but, at the same time I wondered however I would manage to move away from the sedentary, set in his ways person that I had become. But Alistair's comments last night suggested that possibly, if I joined in with him and other members of the local community, I would not only have the opportunity to learn from others I could also become part of a supportive network.

I went and unlocked the van (old habits die hard) and began to unload the rest of the things into the house. Clothing I put in the cupboard that Roddy had used in the corner of the living room which was my temporary bedroom. Various small items of furniture together with boxes of various odds and ends, including cutlery, I again dumped into my bedroom to be sorted later. I returned the front seat of the van to its rightful place, as I had taken it out in order to accommodate the mattress on the way up. Then I set to in the kitchen and made myself some breakfast and, following this, I put as much as I could away in cupboards. This I had I just about finished when I heard the minibus coming downhill at about a quarter past seven. I assumed it was coming to my house but it went straight past and on and over the rise. Not long after afterwards it returned and this time it did come into the parking area outside the front door. The engine was not turned off and I heard men's voices and I heard Alistair shouting 'bye, bye just now' as the minibus turned and left, obviously Cat was off to her work. It had come out over last night's meal that she worked part time delivering some local children to school in the morning and then worked on the croft with her father till it was time to return the children at night.

"Morning," said Alistair, "Cat said that you may have left these items off your shopping list." He handed me some milk and four eggs.

"But here is the most important item from the dog's point of view."

And he handed me a bowl.

"Boil up of tatties and oatmeal and I am sure you will be feeding him bits of your grub too."

In my ignorance of caring for animals I had ignored the fact that the poor dog needed sustenance.

"Oh!" I said. "He has not had a drink."

"Dinna worry he'll ha been down the stream already. Now," he said turning, "this is Dougie."

And I looked at a man of my own modest height, with unkempt hair, probably mid to late fifties. He did not look at me but grunted what I took to be a greeting and looked off into the distance. Obviously Dougie did not do much by way of social chit chat. It turned out that Dougie had been a mechanic, but he became victim of a breakdown, not the sort that could be fixed at the roadside by the Automobile Association or the RAC, but the sort that required psychiatric hospital and medication. For many years he lived with his mother in Ayr and between admissions to hospital he fixed cars on a cash in hand basis.

When his mother died, about twenty years before, he had come to live with his dad in the croft over the hill from me. Apparently his father had left his mother when Dougie was still a baby. The isolated life was good for him and he helped on the croft as required, but he also used his engineering skills and repaired vehicles and boats. Through this latter work he came across a boat that was pretty old and the engine was beyond repair. He was virtually given the boat and had it towed to a mooring near the crumbling jetty below his dad's croft. Then over time he acquired an old tractor engine and adapted it to drive the boat's propeller. After that he set about fishing for crabs and lobsters which he sold to local hotels or to the fishermen in Lochinver to add to their own catches.

His father worked the croft but after his death, ten or so years ago, Dougie was not up to managing it very well and he came to an arrangement with uncle Roddy whereby Roddy would manage the animals on his land and Dougie maintained the machinery which was owned by Roddy but used for the benefit of a loose crofters co-operative in the local area. Other crofters who benefitted from the tractor's use in ploughing, hay cutting and bailing helped Roddy and Dougie by arranging to get bulls to the cows, rams to sheep and animals to market for sale. The tractor was a boon for many, but in some fields hay still had to be gathered by hand as the ground was too studded with outcrops of rock to allow the benefit of mechanisation.

So, Dougie entered my life. An inauspicious uncommunicative start for what was to become a relationship of great mutual respect and indeed would lead us to be business partners of a sort – but there, I am getting ahead of myself.

On that day the three of us went to look at the farm machinery to assess its readiness for work. It quickly became apparent the tractor had been used after Roddy's death and the truth was 'leaked' into the conversation in a gradual way with these confessors careful to watch my reaction. When it became clear that I was not going to raise any objections Alistair finally said.

"Dougie took an ullage of the diesel in the tank before we started to use it and we have made up the contents to the same ullage level."

"That's all very well," I said, "but what about the wear and tear."

They looked at one another, obviously taken aback that they may have misjudged my earlier comments, which seemed to suggest that I was OK with their use of the tractor. Then with an intake of breath Alistair said.

"Well we could come to some……….."

And then he saw the smile on my face and we all laughed together.

That summer was such a wonderful time for me. My learning about this new life was exponential; managing cattle and sheep, cutting, bailing and stacking hay, driving the tractor and the implements it pulled and working with new neighbours. Morag ensured that I had some hens, and so they were to deal with night and morning, but the eggs were very welcome. As well as that I had to manage, that is attempt to manage, my own household. Just cooking, washing up dishes and washing clothes took every bit of spare time and as a result the upstairs still had not been cleaned and my bed remained downstairs.

I was up and breakfasted by six o'clock in the morning and many is the day that work would start immediately and I rarely finished before seven o'clock in the evening and after cooking, eating and clearing away it was straight to bed for ten at the very latest. It was wonderful medicine for my bereavement 'sickness', for though I was still mortally wounded from the loss of my lovely girls, my life was so filled with work which required my full attention that I had little time for reflection.

Occasionally something would be said that would sting me into tears and cause great distress to the speaker, but gradually neighbours and I got to realise that there was nothing negative about these reactions, in fact they were positively cathartic. I have already said that the locals were at ease talking to you and I came to welcome their frankness and they in turn were able to approach the subject of Linda and Carole and allow me to express feelings, and this was the most helpful of all.

On Monday June the 10th I finished early and loading my dog into the van I made my first trip to Lochinver since arriving. When I arrived there I bought some supplies and some sandwiches and a bottle of beer. Up to that point Cat had been kind enough to post a couple of letters for me to Tommy and Daisy.

I then went to the phone box and made a call to Feltham and got through to Daisy, Tommy and Win being at work. We had a little cry together when I explained that my call was in remembrance of Linda's birthday, but we could not speak too long as I did not have a lot of coins to feed into the box. Daisy thanked me for my letters. She told me that there was nothing new from the police about their investigation or any suggested date for the adjourned Inquest.

After that I filled up with fuel and then on the way back I took the turn that led down to the dunes at Achmelvich, which Cat and Alistair had told me about. After following a narrow road down a steep sided valley for a few miles I found the tarmac petered out into a series of tracks in the back of the dunes, I parked and let the dog out of the van. We had become apparent friends, we were always in each other's company and I had started talking to him especially on days when I had been without much human conversation. When addressing him I had continued to call him 'Mr Roy' and the name had stuck.

We walked down to, and across, the beautiful beach of fine white sand and then after our walk I went to the van and got some refreshment for us both and took up a place in the dunes, where I sat and stared at the gently breaking waves and thought of Linda on what would have been her twenty eighth birthday. I sat, and ate, sharing some with Mr Roy, and drank my beer till late in the evening. The dog sensed my mood and instead of his usual frenetic running round was, for once, happy to sit with me and watch the tears fall from time to time.

The fact that I had not been to the village in six or so weeks was due to the fact that I got most of my stores from the travelling shop, which came once a week. If there were special items not available there, either Cat or another neighbour would offer to get them for me. That said I tried to be frugal as I knew my finances were not that good.

Dougie became a regular visitor over that summer. Three or four days a week he would arrive in his Morris

Minor estate, whose green coachwork was very jaded. The doors when opened revealed space for carrying a crate or two of crustaceans, when he had them to sell, and further forward towards the driver's seat the rear seats had been removed and were a storage space for mechanical tools and spares. I suspect that Dougie had continued to frequent my croft (notice that – it was most certainly my croft now) after Roddy's death and before my arrival, to make use of the shed which housed the tractor. There were some obviously home-made shelves whose foundation was an old cupboard with the front doors removed. Within and upon this were a variety of tools, spares and parts all fairly neatly stored. Above the cupboard were some lengths of offcut wood nailed between the wooden stanchions and into this various long nails had been hammered and upon these were hung a variety of larger tools and parts.

Dougie's little croft had no outbuildings and it soon became obvious that this was his workshop. Whenever I found him there he would grunt 'hello' and continue with his task in hand. Gradually we got onto speaking terms. The terms were that I spoke and he grunted. But as the weeks went by he began to communicate through the medium of talking about whatever task he was on with. He would explain in detail what he was doing and I, with no understanding of engineering, became interested in his work. He was a law unto himself, some days he was there and some days not and there was no obvious pattern to it.

As I got to know him it became clear that whilst mechanical work was his first love, he also enjoyed his lobster and crab fishing and when he was not in my tractor shed he was out tending his pots. The catch was used to barter for other things from neighbours but mainly to sell to hotels and the Lochinver fishermen who would give him ten percent less than the going rate, but they would pass his off as part of their catch.

Occasionally I would offer Dougie a sandwich and a beer at the end of the day, when he was still at work, and on those occasions, from say midsummer on, we would talk and gradually he came to open up to me about his illness in the past and his contentment now.

Overall, Dougie and I were on comfortable terms by the end of August and one way or another we saw one another on four or five days on average in any one week, as every day was a working day. It was on one day in early September that he asked.

"Have you noticed a black Commer van passing by recently?"

I recalled hearing a vehicle a day or two before and said so, and he went on to tell me that it had passed his croft and come down to the rather crumbling jetty when he was just arriving after mooring his boat to its buoy. The occupants had spoken to him and asked him where he lived and whether there was any problem in using the slipway; to which he replied not. This seemed to please them and they asked about mooring a fishing vessel in the inlet and Dougie said that there was nothing to stop them doing so. At this they told him that from time to time a friend of theirs may do so and that soon they would arrange to lay a mooring well away from his and that they would leave a dinghy on the beach by the jetty.

When I asked him how he felt about it he shrugged. Replying that it was a free country, that he had no power to stop them and he hoped it was not a permanent thing. I looked at him and there was something else he was not saying, so I asked why he was being guarded.

"Not ma type. Too full of their selves, and I had a feeling that they might have been a wee bit less friendly if I had raised any objections. And they spoke awful, like I was unable to understand them. Just like you. Bloody 'white settlers.'"

And for possibly the first time since I had known, him he nearly smiled.

Nearly.

The summer had progressed with adaptation to my new life continuing apace, my contacts were expanding, albeit restricted to neighbours and crofters whose land I visited with the tractor. It became clear that not all could repay me in kind, so a little cash changed hands especially to cover fuel costs. There was some income also from towing the occasional vehicle out of ditches, a not uncommon occurrence with the narrow single track roads. However, the requests normally came via local contacts since I could not afford a telephone.

But with these contacts and Dougie's skills I talked to him about doing car and tractor repairs for local folk and paying me a small percentage, for the use of my shed and equipment. Ultimately this led to a good little business but again I am running ahead of myself. For my part I did the paperwork and invoicing and dealt with tax issues. Later that would lead to my becoming known as a cheap accounts and tax person and in time would lead to a steady, if quite insubstantial, income stream.

Apart from neighbours and local crofters my only other contacts were with the mobile shop and library, the scavenger lorry men (I would have called them dustmen in my former life) and the local postie. The latter came in a van from Lochinver, often arriving early in the afternoon he would throw the mail into the front door as there was no letterbox. Usually I would be out but when I saw him he was always up for a chat. From him I was able to get some local information but as I was, to him, still a newcomer he did not say as much as he did to old trusted friends like Cat's mother Morag. So, I got all the real scandal from her!

Do not think I was out of touch. I liked the radio and following my mother's love of classical music, I listened to concerts in the evening, not so much that first summer but in the winter. I tuned in to the BBC news sometimes and as an old Tottenham Hotspur fan was delighted when the week after my arrival I learned that the 'Spurs' had won the European Cup Winners Cup in Holland beating Atletico Madrid 5-1. Later significant events of that summer were the Profumo affair and later still the Great Train Robbery. So I was up with the news via the radio and it was nice to have my music and to be aware of big events, but really I had little time for leisure and I was more bothered about what was happening, or needed to be done, on the croft than anything else.

I have said before that I did try to keep in touch with my former in-laws and Daisy wrote and I replied. Generally they were chatty letters about what was happening at their end and mine. There were few other letters except formal ones and so the postman was a very infrequent caller. In late July I got a letter from Billy. I had written once to confirm my arrival and exact address and I had outlined my situation. He had acknowledged and gone on to wish me well. The life on the croft overtook me and I rather forgot him I am afraid to say. The letter that arrived from him was short and unsettling. It gave no sending address, although the post stamp was Hounslow, where he used to live.

Dear Youee, (this was his nickname for me)

Things are not too good for me down here. The lot my old man got in with seem to get more bent and troublesome than ever. It seems that drugs are the new thing for the lot he works with and I have a nasty feeling that there is going to be trouble. I have decided that I do not want to be around when things go pear shaped and so I am working on a plan to emigrate to see if I can get away from it all.

Whilst I am still at my old address I would ask you not to write to me there as I do not want anybody to have any idea where you are as your house might have to be a bolthole for me if things get bad down here. I do not expect it to come to that. But it might. In a few weeks or months I will drop you another line with contact details.

Cheers, Billy

Of course, this was an unsettling letter and I found myself wishing that I could help this old friend in some way but in the circumstances I had to be guided by what he asked of me and rather than doing anything I resolved to leave it to him. He was obviously working on things and he was looking to me for help only if and when the time came. So meanwhile it was business as usual.

Looking back, this letter, coming as it did at the time of my joy of immersion into this all enveloping new life, appeared then as an insignificant item.

In reality the letter was akin to cirrus clouds.

Those harbingers of a storm that is not even yet upon the horizon.

Incidental consequences

Astronomically speaking autumn runs from the September equinox to the December solstice and occurs roughly in the third week of each of those months. For me the fact that we passed the equinox was demonstrated by the fact that, as we entered October, it was no longer possible to work much beyond six thirty in the evening, as the light was beginning to fail. I realised that in about three weeks, when the clocks went back an hour from British Summer Time to Greenwich Mean Time, I would be working in the dark at five pm or thereabouts. Work on the croft for me and for my group of associates, with their own crofts, had been hectic with sheep shearing, another hay cut and a myriad of other jobs like fence mending which had ensured a non-stop summer. I was fitter than ever and brown as a berry, the latter not just being from a fair amount of sun but also the wind burn, for still days were few.

My ongoing relationship with Dougie I have already outlined; but there were others. Alistair was a regular fount of knowledge for crofting advice and he often walked down on good days. If I was passing with the tractor, or very occasionally on some errand on my bike, it was *de rigueur* to call for a cuppa and a chat. Morag was always delighted to see me and to impart all the local news. Indeed one day in September she assured me that the local opinion was that I was OK. I gathered from this that, so far, people were of the opinion that I might be considered as more of a boon to the community than a drag on it. However it was also clear that these were very early days and there was still opportunity for my rating to fall from the significantly high level of 'OK'. I never left her house empty handed of some foodstuff or other. In addition I was invited to an evening meal about once every two or three weeks.

My ad hoc visits were usually to Alistair and Morag alone as, when not doing school transport, Cat was sometimes contracted to take kids on a field trip of some sort or otherwise to offer transport for medical purposes. I also learned that she occasionally was required to do some cover work when local district nurses or midwives were unavailable. It transpired that she had trained as a nurse in Glasgow and worked there for a few years before her return to the croft. She did a lot of the heavy work on the croft helping out her father.

She was generally there on the days I went for an evening meal and she was polite and cheerful, but I sensed a sort of reticence. This did not preclude cheerful social interaction and in many ways she was quite a joker, it reminded me of the jokiness of some of the men from my army days and perhaps it reflects the necessary light-heartedness required by folk who work in difficult jobs like the forces or nursing. Sometimes the tasks to be faced are very stressful and therefore, those facing such tasks need to be able to joke and let off steam when they are with colleagues but away from the tasks themselves.

On the non-human side my relationship with Mr Roy had also improved. He seemed to welcome the fact that I had been told it was necessary for me to feed him, and when I proved able to meet this requirement on a regular basis he warmed to me. As with the time it had been Linda's birthday he began to recognise my moods and to respond to them. It was clear that I was a focal point in his life and to be fair he was a constant companion for me and quite often I talked to him about all sorts of things and he never once interrupted. He was a working dog and there was no need for me to take him 'walkies', because he had more than enough exercise with me. If I was in the fields with animals he busied himself walking with me. If I went on the bike to see Dougie or Morag he would lollop along with me and if I went in the tractor he would ride in the very small space behind the driver's seat or, if available, in an attached trailer and if I went in the van he travelled with me. In short we had become inseparable.

As much as I liked him I realised that I was allergic to his hair, fortunately this allergy was mild, unlike my quite serious allergy to cats about which I had known since childhood. So I decided to do some home improvements so as to arrange for him to be able to sleep in a porch that I would build. With advice from Alistair, and help from Dougie and the availability of some old breeze blocks that had 'arrived' at the croft during the war, no doubt having 'escaped' from the government building of coastal lookouts and guard posts that had been erected in the area, work commenced. A shallow trench was dug for footings and then the breeze blocks were laid to form a porch about six feet by six. They were loosely tied to the house with building ties but over the years this had to be replaced by a more professional builder. Where there were later windows, the first edition of the porch had wooden sides. It was a Heath Robinson structure – so named for the cartoonist of First World War renown who drew many improbable contraptions. Whilst ugly and of doubtful long term viability, it did provide a wonderful cofferdam against the fierce winds and so the house would be warmer because the draft had to get by two doors. It also made room for a dog kennel where Mr Roy could reside in the nights.

After a while I did have to get a cat to control the mice in the outbuildings. But this was fortunately an independent soul who kept its distance from me in return for a little food and water placed in the outbuilding. It was unnamed and terrified both the local mice population and Mr Roy in equal measure. And talking of cats, there was the Amazon, Cat, my neighbour. She was always friendly but reserved, especially when I had my meals in her parent's home, and our contacts were limited to these occasions or sometimes working together. In farming breaks there were often others with us, either Alistair or maybe another crofter neighbour. So, in the main, conversations were superficial and about the work in hand, albeit our interaction was always cheerful and, sometimes even, jokey.

One evening in late September I was sitting on an old chair outside the croft trying to prolong some inconsequential bit of mending for the two reasons of enjoying the evening sun and having some relaxation after yet another full day. Mr Roy, who also had endured a busy day of running round after me, was matching my mood and laying in the sun, suddenly he sat up, ears raised. I assumed some of those pesky rabbits had ventured too close and momentarily he would race away after the coneys and chase them till they disappeared from view, below ground. Up he rose and off like a shot but not toward rabbit land but down to the road. What his ears had picked up was the sound of a horse. He would have heard it before me on a still day but there was quite a breeze which, to the human ear, made the sound of the hooves inaudible. Mr Roy greeted Cat on her horse by loud barking and running around the beast in manic welcome and he was joined by Cat's dog Willy, who became equally agitated until she said something at which point Willy lay down, but Mr Roy kept up his antics.

Cat trotted up the gravel track from the road and dismounted close to me and I rose to meet her. She was in everyday clothes and no rider's helmet. Whilst she was tethering the horse to my fence I was between her and the setting sun and, for the first time, I was really able to study her. Big boned as she was there was not a spare ounce of flesh on her and she was bronzed by the same elements as had given me the leathery looking aspect that stared back from my shaving mirror in a morning. Despite her slight limp, she seemed to glide effortlessly over the ground and for the first time it occurred to me that she was a good looking woman. As soon as that thought passed through my mind my guilt was ignited and would keep me from sleep a good bit later that night. How could I possibly harbour such a thought when my dearest Linda was not yet more than six months dead?

"You need to teach that dog some manners," she said as she came towards me, no doubt unaware that I had been studying her.

As observed in a Gilbert and Sullivan song in Trial by Jury I was 'in the dusk with the light behind me', so she would have been unable to notice my confusion and embarrassment at the thought which had just occurred to me.

"Can you whistle?" She asked.

Pursing my lips I gave a poor rendition of 'I love a lassie' the old Harry Lauder favourite.

"Well I won't ask which of the lassies round here you may love," she said, and my face must have gone pink again and my guilt rose exponentially, "but, one thing's for sure."

"What's that?" I hesitatingly asked.

"You can't bloody whistle."

She then began to explain to me how you can teach a dog, like Mr Roy to obey certain commands and she demonstrated this with her own dog Willy. Using fingers in her mouth she sent him off on a long run away from the croft and then using a combination of whistles and guttural commands like 'lie down', she rounded up a few unsuspecting sheep. The demonstration was impressive and I could see the benefit of having a dog to help you to herd sheep and cattle. She explained the general principles of the training required and we also established that I could not master the art of the loud whistle, using fingers in the mouth. Within a few days she would have sourced for me a dog whistle and my training of Mr Roy could begin.

Lying awake in bed that night I wrestled with the unwanted emotions of the day. I had to acknowledge that for the first time, since Linda's death, I had seen a woman and recognised her as such. Of course there had, in the ensuing months, been contact with a few women and some might have been attractive young hotel or shop girls, but my dealings had been with a human being, gender quite inconsequential, but now I had seen somebody whose gender seemed significant. I supposed that it was not just a gender related thing, because there was also the frequency of contact, the fact that we had shared in pieces of work and I had got to know that she was a reliable workmate and the occasional meals at her home meant that we had seen a bit of one another in a social setting too.

But that guilt was there. My lovely Linda; we had been together since our schooldays, happy in courtship and happy in marriage and happy in parenthood too. She was gone, ripped from life by some awful person and what would she have done if the tables had been turned? She would have got on with life in Feltham, been supported by her family and she would have been loyal to me in grief and she would not, for a substantial time, have entertained any feelings for anyone else and certainly not within such a short time of my death. I rationalised that, in my recent work, the reproduction aspects of livestock management had been a frequent consideration and that perhaps that had subtly awakened my innate sex drive, indeed there had been a couple of erotic dreams recently which had caused guilt feelings of their own. So, only when I had resolved to try very hard to ensure that there were no indications on my part that I had any feelings for Cat, which I argued to myself that I did not, was I able to drift off into a fitful sleep.

Roddy had trained Mr Roy so the commands like, 'come by' to get him to move clockwise, and 'awa to me', to get him to go anti-clockwise were known to him and he just needed to get used to hearing them from me and not the way Roddy would have spoken. By far the greater amount of learning was required from me in terms of remembering the commands and using them correctly. But gradually we got there.

Because of my resolve to ensure that Cat did not get the wrong idea I suppose the dog training sessions were a little less companionable than they might otherwise have been. If she sensed any change in my behaviour she never questioned me about it. And in any case our contact had been on a fairly work colleague level up to that point. However that changed when I had a little accident.

Working as a single-handed crofter, as uncle Roddy had done, has the benefit of allowing one to decide on the undertaking of specific tasks, subject to season and weather, and allows you to choose what to do and when you can do it. Some drawbacks may be seen in the fact that, if you have no one to cook your meals, you can tend to skip them or to have a fairly restricted diet. A crofter with a wife or partner will have to work round the demands of that other person, but equally they will receive some support in terms of meals being prepared, clothes washed, and the like. But perhaps one of the biggest threats to a single-handed crofter is the fact that nobody has a clue about what they are doing or where they are doing it and what time they are likely to return. Therefore, one of the greatest dangers is of succumbing to an illness or an injury whilst away from the croft house and being unable to return to it. If there's nobody expecting to raise the alarm at your failure to come home then you can be in serious trouble.

It occurred to me after my accident that they have made films out of what might have happened. Me having an accident out on the croft, out of sight of the road or hailing distance of any help. Mr Roy licking my wounds and then rushing off to a neighbour's where he barked and barked, until somebody followed him and rescued me. But of course, that only happens in the cinema and usually to that wonderful dog "Lassie". Fortunately for me, my accident took place at Alistair's croft house, where Dougie and I were helping him transport some fence posts on the trailer. We had unloaded the fence posts and the trailer was one that Alistair used to keep at his place so we were unhitching it from the tractor. Alistair released the mechanism and swung the tail around towards me and as he did so his hand slipped and the unsupported trailer dipped down the two or three feet from its level position. Unfortunately, the metal coupling, on its way to the ground, scraped down the side of my leg and the pain was instant.

In no time it was obviously bleeding quite badly so we went to Alistair's house and on lifting my trousers I could see that there was a long deep cut on my right calf.

"Doctor." said Dougie.

I replied that that seemed unnecessary and I was sure it would heal but he was quite adamant

"That's too deep it needs stitches."

Morag entered and she agreed and so the three of us men set off in Alistair's car to drive to Lochinver, with an old towel wrapped around my leg and getting slightly redder by the minute.

It must be an interesting job being a doctor in an isolated place; you have to be able to deal with all sorts of things that doctors in an urban community would probably refer to a hospital. Our nearest hospital for real accident and emergency was probably two hours' drive away and if one had to summon an ambulance that's two hours each way for the ambulance. So doctors like ours were quite used to the sorts of injuries sustained by crofters, road workers and fishermen and were able to set broken bones and apply stitches. Doctors who work in such settings must have a high degree of self-confidence as well as a high degree of professional skill and ability in dealing with emergency situations.

The doctor pronounced Dougie's diagnosis to be the correct one; stitches it was, eighteen of them in all, followed by a dressing. The main concern was that, as my trousers had been ripped as the metal cut through to my leg, the doctor felt I needed a tetanus jab, which he gave me, and that it needed to have a close eye kept upon it, with the dressing changed regularly to ensure that infection had not come through the dirt on my trousers, or indeed any dirt or rust that had come off the metal coupling. Thus it was agreed that I should see a district nurse regularly over the next few days, to ensure the wound healed properly without infection setting in.

"Very fortunate," said the doctor, "since you have this week's district nurse living just up the road. One of our two regular sisters is on holiday but Cat can easily pop down and keep an eye on you."

Overnight and the following day I have to confess that my leg felt very sore but despite this the actual inconvenience it caused to me was fairly limited. I was certainly able to go about my crofting duties without any great difficulty. I could however see the sense in having the wound inspected on a regular basis to ensure that I developed no unwanted infection. So on the second day, having passed messages via Alistair, I attended at his house in the mid-morning, as arranged, to see nurse Cat. She had just returned from her school run and was dressed quite normally as she would have been for taking the children to school. She explained that she was going to change into her nurse's uniform and set off on her other duties after she had had a look at my leg.

She changed the dressing and pronounced the wound to be apparently free of infection and to be healing nicely and she thought it would not be long before she would be able to remove the stitches. A couple of days later a similar visit and inspection with a similar positive outcome led to her suggesting that we leave it for a few more days and then she would arrange to remove the stitches. For one reason or another it suited her to make me the last on the list of her visits planned for the coming Saturday and so I agreed to be sure to be at home from four o'clock onwards and she would call in at my croft once her other duties had been completed and then it would be an easy trip home for her.

I made arrangements to do jobs around my house on the Saturday afternoon but by about six o'clock with the light fading I repaired indoors. With all the demands of summer work on the croft I had still done nothing about shifting my bed upstairs as I had originally planned. However, I thought that as winter drew on and the days got shorter I would be able to use the longer evenings to properly clean out the upstairs rooms and scrub them ready for moving my bed and returning my current bedroom to its original role as a sitting room.

At about half past six Mr Roy alerted me to the approach of a vehicle and the little car that Cat was given to use when working as locum district nurse pulled up outside. Mr Roy gave Cat his accustomed welcome and she came in with an apology for lateness and explaining that one of her cases had taken a lot longer than she had anticipated. It was in some ways quite startling for me to see Cat wearing her uniform as district nurse, this put a whole different complexion on my understanding of who this woman really was. Before this point she had been a fellow crofter, with a little job bussing children to and from school. But here before me was a professional woman who must have undergone a lot of training and who had a very great deal of experience in dealing with the injured and sick.

"I think it'll be best if you take your trousers off," she said, and obviously she saw my face and the surprise registered there, so she explained, "it may get in my way removing the stitches and to be quite honest there is nothing in the male anatomy book to cause me any surprise. In any event, I assume that you have underwear on?"

Of course I did, but perhaps I was a little embarrassed by my concern as to how long I had been wearing the current pair of shorts and I was also aware the that the washing machine, which I used infrequently, had a tendency to turn that which had originally been white into an interesting shade of light grey. However, I obeyed her command and at her request lay face down on the bed and she began her work.

To deflect my discomfort from the pull of the stitches being removed, I enquired how it was she had gained her nursing skills. In that unusual situation, of me face down on the bed looking to the side and she, concentrating on her work on my leg, began a tale which I suppose I might not have come to hear had we been in the situation of being face-to-face.

She told me that she had an extremely happy childhood and coped alright when, aged eleven, in common with all local children, she had to go away to Dornoch on the other side of the country, to attend secondary school; boarding in a girls hostel in that town. Then in 1950, at the age of fourteen she had developed polio she had to go away to hospital for several months. Fortunately, her condition was less serious than many others who suffered from that dreadful disease but, as she had originally told me, some muscle damage in one leg had left her with this slight mobility issue. But being away did two things. Firstly, she saw the work of the nurses and it impressed her and she thought it was something that she might be able to do herself. Secondly such reading materials as were available in terms of books and magazines, and particularly the latter, showed her a life outside of what she was experiencing in the relatively isolated community in which she lived. Not unusually for someone at that impressionable age she was drawn to the idea of working in a big city and of course becoming a nurse would enable her to achieve this objective in what might be felt, by her parents, as a constructive move. A bit similar to the position Uncle Roddy had described my father as being in when the prospect of going into the Army in the First World War had first been an option.

She said that she had worked hard at school, as a result of this successfully applied to become a trainee nurse in Glasgow with an offer of accommodation in a nurse's hostel. Every minute, she said, was a learning experience for her and she was eager to develop her knowledge and skills and effectively over the next five years she did so, becoming qualified as a state registered nurse.

By now the stitches were out and she told me that she had applied a much smaller dressing and that within a couple of days I could simply remove it myself. As I was getting dressed, and she was repacking her medical bag I asked her what had brought her back to Clackmore.

"Various things," she replied, "one of which was the fact that I knew that managing the croft on their own was just beginning to be a bit more difficult for mum and dad."

"And of course," I said, "you had this locum work that would keep your hand in as a nurse."

She hesitated.

"Well no not really. I came back in an unplanned sort of way and there were no opportunities for me to do any medical work, and actually I was quite lucky to get the school transport job. When I returned there were the two district nurses but the workload was limited so that they each covered the other for holidays. Then, and it was only last year, when it was felt that one person could not do all the work that was necessary in the week, was funding agreed to cover what has become my locum post."

"Anyway," she said, "that's me finished from my week, but…… ," and she was obviously on the edge of saying something else but stopped herself; and somewhat perfunctorily left.

Along with others, we had cut peat in the high summer and now it was time to collect it. An autumn working party rode out on the tractor with me to collect what we had cut and to load it onto the trailer for delivery to various croft houses. We all met at Alistair and Morag's croft house and when we arrived there were about eight other local crofters all assembled, as Dougie and I arrived in the tractor, with Mr Roy prowling on the trailer. After loading the crew onto the trailer we set off on to the end of our road to where it joined the main road and then went left for two hundred yards or so. Then just after the bridge which spanned the stream, which in turn eventually led down to its mouth in the bay by my croft house, we turned right. The first hundred yards or so was tarmac and then the tarmac branched to the left and led to an old shooting lodge, our track became stony and turned to the right, to rise up to the moor where the peat was cut.

The lodge had been for sale for a while and I think most of our travelling army were surprised to see down towards the lodge that there was a large furniture lorry, a horse box and also a black Commer van, and signs of activity as though the lorry was being unloaded. As I was driving I was unaware that some of the trailer riders had waved but that the men by the van had not returned the greeting. The general opinion was, as we loaded the peat onto the trailer, that they must have been miserable white settlers like me. Within days the jungle telegraph had established that it was indeed some rich white settler, from London, who had taken the lodge. It was of little consequence to me.

Then.

For a couple of weeks the new occupants of the lodge were a long way from my thoughts until one day, I was just returning home from the direction of Dougie's croft when I heard a horse coming along the road and I looked up expecting to see Cat. Of course, a moment of thought would have made me realise that she would be at work at this time of the day and not out riding. I was somewhat shocked to see that the rider was a woman, but dressed in nothing like the apparel in which Cat would have ridden. This was the real full outfit, the like of which I had once seen when Linda and I took Carole to see the Richmond Royal Horse Show. Riding hat, immaculate short black riding habit, blouse with cravat and pristine cream jodhpurs.

Drawing abreast of me she reined in.

"Is this the way to the jetty?" She enquired.

I assured her that it was and then asked if she had come far, she hesitated, as though unsure as to whether or not she should speak to me. After all in my workaday clothes I would have looked a real yokel. Reluctantly she deigned to inform me that she and her husband and little boy had moved into the lodge.

"Welcome to Clackmore, no doubt I will be seeing you around."

She looked at me properly for the first time.

"You're not from round here."

"No. I moved here from England earlier in the year."

Instantly she looked at me intently and quickly said she must be getting along. It was only after she had ridden off towards Dougie's and the jetty that I realised that despite her immaculate appearance, she did not speak in upper crust English, the sort of accent heard from many of those who came to this area of Scotland for the 'huntin' and fishin' but her accent and speech suggested that she was from west or southwest London.

The same as me.

Day off

Tattie week, I was advised by my local cultural tutors, namely Alistair and Dougie, occurred in mid-October. Apparently this week had been devised in the 1930s as a way of crofters and farmers keeping their children off school for a week, to help with the potato harvest. I don't think that was observed much in our neck of the woods, but probably that was mainly because of the limited availability of land with enough soil to grow potatoes meant that you didn't need that many hands to harvest the crop. I gather it was much more the norm in more fertile areas of Scotland and indeed the school holidays were apparently adjusted to account for it.

As I dug up my potatoes I said a murmured 'thank you' to uncle Roddy whose note about croft management had advised about when to plough and plant, and how to store, crops. This harvesting and storing turned out to be another week or so of hard work, but as it drew to an end I began to realise that the demands on me, made by my sheep and beef cattle, were now fairly limited and I was looking for other tasks to do in the daylight hours. A perennial job was fence maintenance but beyond that I was, for the first time since my arrival, allowed to look up, as it were, from what had been the constant demands of the croft through the summer months.

Dougie had begun to talk to me about expanding his mechanical work. He had realised that, unlike my deceased uncle, I was open to the idea of his using some of the barn in order for him to use as a garage in which he could repair the odd local vehicle under cover. He explained that Roddy had not been too happy about it, but he hoped that I might be a bit more open to the idea, because he felt that there was a bit of money to be made in vehicle and farm implement repair and maintenance. A few weeks before I had received a letter telling me that just over £800 had been paid into my account, this being the proceeds of the sale of the house after deductions of mortgage repayment, estate agents and legal fees. I had approached Alistair, Morag and Cat about paying for the work they had done in maintaining the croft between Roddy's death and my arrival. But they wouldn't hear of it, eventually, however, we settled on the fact that Morag needed a new washing machine and I provided the money to pay for that.

From Dougie's perspective his ability to repair vehicles supplemented his very modest income from his fishing. Indeed there was no way he could have lived off what he got for selling crabs and lobsters. I think he had begun to realise that he needed work and this for him was an important opportunity. Dougie's croft house was smaller than mine and in need of repairs; furthermore he had no outside storage or working facilities. He tended to live day-to-day and in some senses it was almost surprising that he realised that he needed another income stream, but I suppose he had gone on so long in great poverty, using up things as best he could, but now he began to realise that he needed to do something if his croft house wasn't to crumble about his ears. I pointed out to him that, whilst I had been happy to let him use the barn on an ad hoc basis for repairing the odd vehicle under cover, if he was to make a go of things certain developments would be necessary.

To start with he had an extremely limited set of tools, then especially in the winter we would need to run some electric out to the barn and I was unhappy about the idea of him working underneath vehicles using a couple of bricks to keep them off the ground. This would mean we needed to construct an inspection pit. Whilst looking at me and nodding I could also see Dougie's heart was sinking because there was no way he could pay for the improvements that would be needed. But then his face changed when I told him that I was prepared to put up some money to buy some more tools and to have the electricity moved and to help him dig an inspection pit. And so it was agreed that we would go into partnership together, I would put up some money towards the improvements that we'd identified on the understanding that he gave up this cash in hand work and I would do the billing and accounts and the profits would be shared between us.

It was a risk, I could just have seen what turned out to be over £300 of capital outlay disappearing down the 'Swanee', but I had grown quite fond of this monosyllabic man. He would have been happy just to spend his life on his beloved fishing boat catching his crabs and lobsters but was also prepared to use his other skills in engineering and motor mechanics, and I wanted him to be able to succeed. At the same time there was potentially something in it for me in terms of a minor income stream to support the limited earnings from crofting. Not long after this, and armed with some money I provided for him, Dougie went off to Inverness for the day and came back with all the tools he required and, typical of the man, he brought me the change left over from his purchases.

Incidentally, over time, this very small scale venture did actually achieve two things. It brought in a small income to the repay the capital outlay and supplement my crofting and Dougie's fishing and, as time went by, and given Dougie spreading the word about my bookkeeping skills, I also attracted a few local bookkeeping accounts which also over time added to my income. So increasingly, by the end of tattie week, Dougie and I had become relatively close. I say relatively because Dougie was unlikely ever to be close to anyone, however his closeness was to be measured by the fact that most days he would be round working in the barn, unless he judged the weather to be nice, in which case he might not come for a couple of days due to his being out in his beloved boat.

Earlier in the summer during a run of very settled weather Dougie had offered to take me out in his boat on a fishing trip. I had to decline because at that time even working seven days a week and most of the daylight hours there was always a backlog of work to be done. But, about the third week in October, the pressure that had kept my nose to the grindstone was lifting and, despite the fact that I had earmarked the day to begin the cleanout of the upstairs rooms, I was tempted to take what would be my first day off since June. Accordingly, I set off on my bike cycling up and over the hill down past Dougie's little croft to meet him at the jetty.

The tide was fairly high and Dougie had been out before me to bring his little boat from its moorings and to tie it up alongside the old, somewhat crumbling, jetty. Nearby was what appeared to be a former boat shed which, though roofed, looked in a poor state of repair and was minus a door. I leaned my bike against one wall of the building and walked over to the jetty accompanied by Mr Roy, Dougie had given special permission for him to sail with us, and we climbed aboard.

The vessel was about 20 to 25 feet in length with a beam of about 8 feet; there was a small, very thin, 3 foot wide cabin area right forward. The cabin itself comprised a flat roof framework which supported in it two forward looking windows one with a small electric 'Clearview' screen – an electric driven circular panel which, when activated, threw off water by centrifugal force – thus allowing the clear view forward when out in rain or heavy spray. Each side had a window and the back was only half enclosed by a solid fixed partition and the other had a door which gave access to the steering wheel. In the enclosed side was a small stool and some storage. The helmsman also had a stool but his back was open to the elements as the door, once opened outward, was clipped back to the fixed side. The roof extended back for about two feet from the cabin which provided a very small sheltered area for working. Also behind the helmsman's side of the cabin was what turned out to be an electric winching contraption which could be used to raise the lobster pots.

 Once aboard Dougie started the engine and went aft to release the stern mooring rope and he then briefly motored ahead so that the bow line pulled the nose of the boat towards the jetty and the stern pivoted away. Going quickly astern he let go the bow line and, after clearing the jetty, turned towards the open sea. Dougie explained that we were in what was effectively a very large bay of which you could not see the far side, because an island filled most of it; the island itself was uninhabited. The entire coastline around the bay and the island was rocky but it was well protected from the worst ravages of the weather. In short it made it quite a pleasant habitat for crabs and lobsters which was what Dougie was all about catching as an inshore fisherman.

 As we turned upon leaving the jetty we passed by a small rowing boat which Dougie explained he had moored to the buoy a little earlier. Because of the tidal range, his boat could not be moored at the jetty, but the buoy marked a place where his little fishing vessel would stay afloat at all stages of the tide and so the practice was to row his little dinghy out, attach it to the buoy, climb aboard his fishing boat, untie that from the buoy and set off leaving the rowing boat there. Then on return he would repeat the operation unless he needed to go alongside the jetty in order to discharge his catch first. He stored his catch live in wooden boxes also attached to the buoy and when he had a good enough catch and when the weather suited he would chug round to Lochinver and barter a price with the local fishermen who would include his catch in their shipments. Alternatively he would load the crustaceans into the back of his Morris Minor and drive to town.

As I looked to my right or, being at sea should I say starboard, I saw a trawler of about four times the size of Dougie's little fishing boat. Dougie caught my eye.

"Aye it's here. It's that the Commer van gang who've got their selves a small trawler. Arrived a couple of days ago and laid a mooring and the van came and picked a couple of lads up who had brought it here and so far as I know she hasn't been used since. If I had a vessel like that I'd want it out and working and paying its way, not moored up and doing nothing."

My first ever fishing experience provided me with a wonderfully relaxing day. We chugged along from lobster pot to lobster pot with Dougie hauling in, extracting the catch, re-baiting, and lowering away again. I found the crabs and lobsters terrifying, reminding me of large spiders, which have never been my favourite beast. The air temperature was cold but the wind was not strong and I was well wrapped up. As requested I had brought a sandwich and Dougie provided a large flask of tea and from time to time he used a smaller flask of something probably a bit more potent, but which having had the message from Alistair, he did not offer to me.

As we headed back towards the jetty in early afternoon Dougie drew my attention to a horse with a saddle on that was cropping the grass near the jetty. As we came closer a figure I had not noticed rose from the rocks beside the jetty picked up the reins mounted the horse and rode off up the road.

"I've seen her down here once or twice," said Dougie, "she just comes and sits and then goes away again. From what I hear she's the new lady up at Newton Lodge. She just about gives you the time of day, but, tae me she always looks sad."

This must be the smartly dressed young woman whom I'd spoken to briefly a few weeks earlier, although I had not noticed her riding past my croft at all recently. I made a mental note to ask Alistair if he knew anything. As it happens I forgot to do that, but it would not be long before further information was forthcoming.

A few days later Callum the postie arrived early in the afternoon. I had been in the barn with Dougie when the scrunch on the gravel of Callum prior to applying the brakes of his post van at the last minute, was sound enough to summon me. Even if Mr Roy had not, a good half minute earlier, started his usual war dance, of greeting which was no doubt possibly threating to interlopers, depending upon his recognition of them or otherwise.

"Bloody nuisance you are," Callum said addressing the dog, "and," as he caught sight of Dougie emerging from the barn behind me, "you, Dougie, are bloody worse."

These comments were made with a huge smile on Callum's face and it was a customary greeting for the two of us, because if we had mail to be delivered, which fortunately for Callum was an infrequent occurrence, he would have to drive about an extra mile or more to come down our dead-end road. This added 10 or 15 minutes to his working day, including chat time. He regularly informed us of this fact in a good-humoured way. Despite his complaints about the extra mileage and time he had to expend, he still needed to check out whether there was any information we could impart; because gossip was his stock in trade.

"What have ye got to tell me then?"

"Well," I said, "I had cornflakes for breakfast and Mr Roy told me that he is really missing a nibble of a postman's leg."

At mention of his name Mr Roy, who had been sniffing some inconsequential item looked up and stared at me and I addressed him directly.

"You like postman's legs don't you Mr Roy?"

Realising he was being addressed he barked in reply.

"Give up," said Callum, "I have enough problems wi' dogs as it is. Anyway your dog's a softy."

So saying he leant down and fondled the animal's ear. From behind me Dougie piped up

"Trawlers arrived in the bay and laid a mooring. We got some men coming to and from in a Commer van. And a lassie on a horse comes down from time to time."

This was quite a long speech for Dougie, but it imparted in very few words all the newsworthy items that he felt should be shared with Callum. He obviously took the view that if he was to expect information from Callum then he, Dougie, should whenever he could, impart new snippets of information to this postie spider at the centre of our local intelligence web.

"Well I can help you with some of that fulsome report," replied Callum, "I did'na know about the trawler, but it's all to do with Newton Lodge, which as you know has been taken over by some Sassenach."

"Careful Callum", I interjected, "I am no Pict either."

"No," he responded, "I understand that, but aside from your funny ways and bloody silly accent you are a friendly enough guy who has worked with the locals. This bloke up at the Lodge is as miserable as they come and he employs those couple of Sassenach eejits that drive yon Commer van. Also he's married to yon lassie with the horse. They have a wee boy aged about five who is due to start at the school soon. There is also a housekeeper and very recently they've been joined by a Scot, who says very little but he gets regular mail from Macduff."

"What does this owner man do then?" I asked.

"Would'nae we all like to know," said Callum, "but whenever you try to start up a conversation with any of them there is no response. And then just the other day some lads I know from Inverness, who are in the telephone division of the General Post Office, arrived in two vans and they are going to be connecting the Lodge to the telephone. That'll be costing them a bob or two."

"Oh Callum. Getting in the telephone, now that sounds very fishy. They must be Russian spies."

"Could be," he said, "after all they are about to start a war with America with all those missiles heading for Cuba".

Of course I had been joking, but his reply was no doubt prompted by the news on the radio which was full of the advance of Russian ships carrying what looked like missiles, and bound, it was understood, for Cuba.

Taking in his breath, and in all seriousness Callum said.

"Aye, you could be right they could be spies."

"Give me a break, I was only joking." I said.

"Whell, as they say, many a true word spoken in jest." Replied Callum making his way towards his van.

As he drove away I reflected upon what silly nonsense we sometimes talk in these jokey, bantering, light-hearted, social conversations.

Because, after all, it was so unlikely that the occupants of Newton Lodge were engaged in espionage. And most certainly the last thing we would have wanted was to have spies on our doorstep.

And of course we didn't have.

It was worse.

Social Christmas

Early in November Cat had somewhat hesitatingly mentioned to me that there was a group of musicians, based in Strathpeffer, who were due to come and play in Lochinver on the Friday night 15th November. She asked me whether I liked Scottish country music and if so whether we could go together. She went on to explain that she knew I liked music in general as I regularly used to listen to music on the radio and obviously she had seen my record collection. Whilst most of the records were of classical music and piano music especially, I also liked Gilbert and Sullivan and for a complete change I occasionally played my Errol Garner 'Concert by the sea' record which I found to be a very cheery sort of music, although to be fair, given the events of this year I had not played it much recently.

"Well," I said, "I am not sure I know what you mean; is that bagpipe music."

"No," she said laughing, "not necessarily. It could be pipes or a harp, but I think these guys just use fiddle and accordion. They do play slow music but in the main it's fairly upbeat. They are just playing in the bar, so you just have a drink and laugh and a bit of a sing maybe."

I was hesitant, this would be my first social outing since the incident and the old guilt trip about my enjoying myself was still very much in my mind. But the days were shorter now and despite the fact that I'd completed the cleaning of the upstairs and, with Dougie's help, moved my bed up into one of the bedrooms I was finding that the evenings were getting longer and playing the radio or records was a pastime of which I could only take so much. So I thought, why not and that is indeed what I said to Cat.

We drove in my Bedford van to Lochinver and I had a really lovely evening. The band were terrific, the audience warmed to them and clapped along. Some of the extremely cheerful and high tempo pieces were wildly applauded. I consumed about three pints of beer and became reasonably cheerful myself, it being the first beer for several months. Many of the local lads were drinking beer and whisky chasers and they got exceedingly, exuberantly cheerful. Cat started on beer but moved onto Babycham which, she told me, was a throwback to her Glasgow nights out.

We sat with one of the district nurses and her husband who was a fisherman and a group of his mates and they all obviously knew Cat very well and clearly they had been briefed about the reason for my coming to the area. So, despite their customary local interest in other people and whilst they were keen to know all about how I was settling into crofting life, no mention was made of my reason for being there.

On the way home Cat and I were full of the spirit of cheerful liveliness that had pervaded the evening's proceedings. No doubt this slightly euphoric mood fuelled by much more alcohol than I was used to imbibing, led me to drive a little more speedily than I normally did. On one of the bends I nearly overcooked the turn and only just rescued the van from ending up in the ditch.

"Oh dear," I said, "that was a bit silly."

To which Cat agreed but then started to giggle which made me laugh too. On we went, fortunately slightly more circumspectly, until our turn off onto the road down towards our respective crofts. Again I took the turn quite sharpish and had to clap on the brakes as I came suddenly face-to-face with the Commer van. Fortunately our tiny single-track road does have twenty or thirty yards of double track as it exits the main road, and it was in that space that I managed to bring my vehicle to a halt, but of course the other vehicle was trapped on the single-track part and couldn't move. I knew it was my job to reverse but in my semi-intoxicated state it took me a moment for my brain to engage and for me to attempt to put the vehicle into reverse and, of course, I missed my gear. The other vehicle, believing that I was just going to sit there, then started a tirade of hooting before it saw me manage to catch my gear and begin to reverse. I reversed and pulled to the left allowing him enough room to pass beside me.

I wound down the window to bid them a cheery apology, but before I could do so, and as the van drew alongside me, it stopped and I was subjected to a tirade of abuse delivered forcibly in a south London accent from a thuggish looking man who was behind the wheel. He questioned my driving ability, my parentage, and finished off with some really derogatory remarks about Scottish people. I was somewhat taken aback, but upset all the same, and would have replied had he not quickly engaged gear and driven off.

"What awful folk." Cat said.

Somewhat sobered and shocked by this unexpected verbal aggression at the end of our pleasant evening, we continued the last three hundred or so yards of our journey and pulled up outside Alistair's Croft.

"I'm really sorry those pigs spoiled the evening. Do you want to come in for a nightcap? Mum and dad will be in bed, but I'm sure it won't be a problem."

I thanked her and said that I would get off home and she nodded. She went to put her hand on the door handle but then turned back.

"Thanks for this evening I really enjoyed it."

As I started to say something in agreement to her she suddenly lent across and kissed me very fleetingly on the cheek and then she was gone.

I drove home with my mind in somewhat of a turmoil. A kiss? What did it mean? She was a neighbour, a workmate and a friend and I was content with those descriptions of our relationship, but did a kiss mean that she was also becoming more than a friend?

Mr Roy, who had suffered a lonely evening, bounded out of his kennel to greet me as I arrived back home and as a treat for his unusually being left to his own devices, I took him indoors for a while. The kiss, inconsequential as it was, had set my mind buzzing, yet again with the confusion that stemmed from my loyalty to Linda. In the end I rationalised that perhaps, after all, a brief chaste kiss at the end of an enjoyable evening was nothing to feel too guilty about. Having cleared my head of the guilt and with the alcohol induced tiredness building, I bade Mr Roy good night and sent him out to his kennel whilst I trooped reasonably contentedly up to my bed.

The night out together had subtlety changed the relationship between Cat and me. Clearly it was not 'loves young dream', but when we met thereafter I felt a greater degree of connection between us and I guess an outsider would have noticed that we smiled at one another more frequently than had previously been the case. I had received an invite for Christmas dinner with Alistair and Morag several weeks before, and Dougie had been invited too. I looked forward to this event because by now daylight hours were restricted to the times between half past eight in the morning and three thirty in the afternoon. On the other hand my farming duties were mainly limited to taking hay out to the cattle and sheep if the weather required it and looking after the hens. Otherwise I began to deal with a few maintenance issues in the house and outbuildings as well as, on occasion, being called upon to help Dougie.

Christmas Day was due to fall on the Wednesday that year and about five days earlier, on the Friday, there was an occurrence which I was only able to subsequently piece together with information from Dougie. About three o'clock in the afternoon I was finishing my chores outside the croft house when the Commer van passed by. As was usual these days the front bench seats were occupied by three men. Without Dougie's later input that would have been the sum total of any witness statement, had I been called upon to make one. Dougie, however, saw so much more. The weather had not been too good and certainly the sea conditions were not conducive to his making a trip round in his little boat to Lochinver to sell his stock of crabs and lobsters. He had therefore decided to retrieve his catch, floating in the wooden boxes beside his boat, to bring them ashore and take them in his Morris Minor to Lochinver. He was conscious that this was a good time to do it as they would just about reach the markets for Christmas.

He boxed his crustaceans and set off for Lochinver, where he made a good deal on selling his catch and after a few drinks in the bar drove home. In due course he went to bed but the presence of the amount of alcohol in his body eventually required him to get up, at about two in the morning, in order to relieve himself. His croft house had not been modernised and the toilet was still outside. On making his way there he noticed working lights on the trawler which was back on its moorings and he watched out of curiosity. He saw that a couple of trips were made in the dinghy bringing back some objects from the trawler which, once landed, he thought he could see were being unpacked and loaded into the Commer van. Eventually he could see that on about the third trip out to the trawler the lights were going out and all the men were climbing into the boat to get back to shore and so he went inside and went to bed. A little while later he heard the van passing by.

This story would not have come out had it not been for a chance remark over our Christmas meal and it led to a discussion of the new family in the district. Alistair and Morag both had tales, from various sources, about their standoffishness and how all the residents at the Lodge seemed unwilling to enter into conversation.

"When you live in a small community," Alistair opined, "whether you like it or not, any failure to engage with local people will make them resentful. If you live in a big town and you need some help there is probably some firm or another who will offer a service to meet your needs. That's not so in our part of the world, if you can't manage it yourself you probably need your neighbour's help. Therefore, if you want your neighbours to help you then you have to engage with them."

Cat suggested that maybe they had moved up here for peace and quiet and to get away from things.

"Could be," said Alistair, "but people's curiosity will only be made worse by not communicating with folk, even if their reason is private and they do not want to discuss it. Look at Ewan, you could say he fits the newcomer bill, but he's made no secret of his reason for being here, he talks to people and works with them and so he's become accepted."

"Well," said Cat, "Jeannie the schoolteacher says that maybe we'll get to learn more about them all now that the wee boy, called Henry, is to start at the school in the New Year. Apparently it caused a bit of a stir when his mother, who goes by the name of Sally, turned up at the school to ask about him attending. She was 'made up to the nines' and dressed like a glamour model and arrived in a big flash car. Apparently she said very little, except to confirm that the boy was Henry Porter and has just had his fifth birthday. About the only details she was prepared to give was the address of Newton Lodge and then the telephone number in case of emergencies. Beyond that the teacher could get very little out of her."

The conversation moved along and Cat and I offered to get to work on the dishes, in doing so we overrode Morag's protestations that it was her job. I pointed out to her that my only contribution to the meal had been to supply some bottles of McEwan's beer and two of my chickens whose necks were wrung by Dougie, as such slaughter was still far beyond me at that time 'miserable squeamish townie', as Dougie had chided me. Cat helpfully pointed out that whilst two persons could be accommodated in Morag's kitchen, three would have left no room for movement. Cat set about washing and I took up a drying cloth. She asked me whether I had enjoyed my day.

I confessed to her that I had been having a difficult time coping with the Christmas season. Every radio programme seemed to be full of carols and talk of presents. I had, therefore, tried to avoid the radio for a while choosing instead to play records on the radiogram. It was not as though Christmas had been a huge event in my previous life. I only used to buy a present for Linda and she looked after presents for other people. Since in those days I had no other immediate relatives on my side of the family, about the only Christmas card I wrote was to Billy. I had decided that this year I would not to write any except to Linda's mum and dad, her sister and her brother and his wife. I had chosen cards with the legend 'Seasons Greetings' thus avoiding the usual 'happy' adjective which was wholly inappropriate so soon after the death of Linda and Carole. It felt as if they were duty cards and after consideration I decided against sending one to Billy, his last letter had left me feeling a little uneasy about him and something made me feel it might be better not to write to him, indeed he had asked me to not do so. I had therefore, been a little put out when unexpectedly Callum the postie had delivered a card from Mr Stewart at the old firm, in which he wrote that all my colleagues down there hoped that life was going all right and sending me kind wishes. There was also a card from Mr McKay the Inverness solicitor.

Working away with the drying cloth, actually it needed more than one in the end, I told Cat about the sort of Christmas that I might have experienced had it not been for the incident and my removal north. In that old life I would have worked up until about four o'clock on Christmas Eve and with Christmas being on the Wednesday, I would have had Wednesday and Thursday off and been back at work on the Friday. Prior to Christmas there would have been some activities of the Christmas nature in which I would have participated. There would have been the purchase and erection of a Christmas tree to go in the front room, which task I would have done together with Carole. Also it was my responsibility to climb on the chairs to hang up any paper chains that my little girl had made, with parental help of course. There would also have been a visit to church for a carol service but not the Midnight Mass, because we felt that was too late for a little girl of Carole's age. In the run-up to Christmas this year I had been aware of all those things which, in other circumstances, I would have been doing and it did feel a bit emotional and my mind kept going back to Linda and to Carole and I did wonder how I would feel come Christmas Day.

By this time we had finished the dishes and returned to the front room where, having enjoyed a hefty repast several bottles of beer and innumerable whiskey chasers, we found Dougie and our hosts fast asleep. We picked up our glasses and moved a couple of the dining chairs and sat and looked out the window. Their croft was sited so as to look down the valley towards the sea and somewhere down there was my croft, but in the darkness it was invisible. There were the occasional flashes of white which would no doubt be waves crashing on the headland in what was obviously quite a strong wind which would have whipped up a lively sea.

"So how do you feel today?" asked Cat.

"Well," I said after some thought, "I suppose I felt a bit empty not having a little girl to bounce into my bedroom with a bright red stocking filled with a few presents, probably including an orange and certainly some sweets, and watching her delighted face as she pulled out each item. But I suppose I knew this was coming and I knew it would have to be faced yet in all the awfulness of the situation, of being without Linda and Carole, I realise that things could have been worse."

"In what way?" Cat asked.

"Well, in the way that if I had remained in my old job, in my old house, these reminders and memories would have hit me much harder. The day of the incident when I went to their house I could see Linda's eyes in her mother's and her sister's faces and that would have been the case if I had been having Christmas with them, which undoubtedly I would have done if I still lived down there. People say that you shouldn't make a move after a significant bereavement until you settle down a little bit. I can certainly understand why that might be right for some people but for me coming up here has made me change my life and in doing so some of the emotional ties to my old life have been taken away."

We sat in silence for a while and then Cat asked me how I thought her mother was looking. I replied that I thought she looked in reasonable health, although maybe a bit on the tired side. She went on to explain that she was getting a bit worried about her mum being so tired, but maybe it was just the hard demands of a crofting life together with her getting just a little bit older.

Dougie caught a snore in his throat and erupted into a loud fit of coughing which had the effect of waking Alistair and Morag from their slumbers as well.

"And what are you two talking about?" Asked Morag, in a sleepy voice.

"I have just been telling Cat how lucky I have been to find this assembled company here, in my time of need. I came here as a stranger and you have offered me great friendship. I was saying that if I had remained in my old home and life this Christmas would have been extraordinarily difficult, as it would have faced me starkly with my missing wife and daughter. My memories do make this time particularly emotional for me but I can still recognise that, without you folk, things here things would have been so much worse."

Morag put a hand to her mouth and searched her sleeve unsuccessfully for a handkerchief.

"We were not looking forward to some southerner, with no idea about crofting, coming to take on Roddy's place," said Alistair, "but you have far exceeded all that we could have reasonably hoped for as a new neighbour and friend. Also, nobody I have spoken to around here can believe how well you have adapted to your new life, in what is in fact only about eight months or so. And now I'll let you into a secret. We invited you here for Christmas because, as a Sassenach, we knew that's what you would have celebrated. But if you want to be somebody who is looking to put in his papers to become a true Jock then you need to realise that, whilst Christmas is okay, the real celebration comes on the 31st of December!"

"Hear, hear to that," echoed Dougie, "and now I'm away to ma bed if we are going to dig that pit in the morning."

"What pit?" Cat asked.

I explained that Dougie and I had agreed that he could do a lot more mechanical work if we dug an inspection pit on one side of the barn. This work had been planned for Boxing Day. So Dougie and I bade our farewells and gathering up Mr Roy, who had been waiting in Alistair's porch, we walked in companionable silence until our paths diverged at my croft house and he plodded on towards his.

Christmas was over.

I had survived.

And a New Year beckoned.

What might it bring?

Historical Echo

Well first of all the New Year brought quite a bit of snow. Fortunately on Alistair's advice and with the help of Cat and our two dogs we had brought our respective herds of animals much closer to our croft houses, so that it was easier to provide them with fodder. Dougie and I had completed digging the pit in the barn and the walls and floor of the pit had been lined with the remaining breeze blocks. The winter toll on mechanics and electrics in vehicles brought Dougie more than usual amounts of work. With the weather often being poor Dougie spent most days in the barn, which was now fitted with an electric supply. Sometimes he would be called out to vehicles that would not start or which had broken down. But other than that he began other work which would add to his ability to provide a better service. With his new welding tools he adapted a couple of old trailers to create one trailer upon which he could load a car that had broken down and tow it in to make it easier to be worked upon.

 I had grumbled about the ancient tractors and other farm implements that uncle Roddy had abandoned. Dougie began work on some of these rescuing parts to add to his stock. He drained oil and sold it locally, just for use in oil cans to lubricate farm machinery parts, in little salvaged tins with screw tops like those which formerly held the toilet cleaner Harpic. Any more valuable metal that he found he cut off with his new acetylene burner and eventually sold these for scrap sometime later in the year when he went down to Inverness with a trailer load. When he couldn't do any more he then cut up the remaining rusted stuff and I was glad to see the whole croft looking a little bit more tidy. Early in February I noticed him loading some rusty scrap metal into the back of his car and asked him what he was doing with it. Dumping it at sea he replied.

"Are you allowed to do that?" I asked.

"Who's going to stop me?" He replied. "Anyway I only dump it in the inshore rocky areas where trawlers won't go and snag their nets."

I have to say I felt a little concerned about this until, sometime later, when talking to a recently retired merchant navy officer who had served in tankers and he told me not to worry. According to him all ships threw all their rubbish over the 'wall', as he referred to the ship's rail, they pumped out sewage that was untreated and in tankers they used to wash the tanks and then pump the resulting sludge over the side.

"They said you weren't supposed to do it but if you are out of sight of land there was nobody to stop you," he told me.

Immersion in my new life was such that it was with a profound sense of shock that I opened a formal looking letter, postmarked Feltham, which I had not noticed the previous evening as Callum must have left it in the porch the previous day. The letter was informing me that the adjourned Inquest on Linda and Carole would be reopened on Friday, 20th March.

With my head momentarily in my new life I actually considered not going. I was not needed; I had been told by the police at the first hearing that because I had given my identification evidence and there was nothing else useful I could contribute to the actual cause of their deaths, I would not need to be called to give evidence again.

A moment's thought, however, made me realise that I owed it to Linda and Carole to attend and even more to Daisy, Tommy and the rest of the family. I immediately pedalled up to see Alistair and told him that I needed to journey south and suggested the provisional dates that I would need to be away. Upon being told of the reason for this Alistair assured me that there would be no problem in his looking after the animals, but in fact there wouldn't be much of that needing to be done. He did point out to me however that lambing normally started in April but that sometimes there were a few early lambs so maybe, if I was going to go south, it would be better to be back as soon as possible.

Off I then went to the telephone box up at the main road and spread my coins on the top of the black metal box, putting a first few into the slot I dialled Tommy and Daisy's number and waited ready to press button 'B' and regain my money if the call was not answered. However very promptly the phone was picked up and, pressing button 'A' my money dropped, and I was connected to Tommy who was off shift.

"So you've heard then?"

"Yes," I replied, "and I'm ringing to see if it would be all right to stay with you for a couple of nights."

To which he replied 'of course' and we went on to agree that I would arrive on Thursday the 19th but I would only stay the two nights, the Thursday and Friday, as I would need to set off back on the Saturday. He suggested a longer visit, but I explained that the journey down and back would take two days either way and it wasn't fair for me to leave neighbours to deal with the seven day a week chores that were associated with crofting. Although sounding disappointed he said that he completely understood. My visit was agreed, and I signed off before I had the need to insert any more money. My mind was in a bit of a turmoil as I cycled back. On the way I called in to see Alistair but as he gone up into the fields I confirmed with Morag the days I was going to be away. She said that she would be sure to tell Alistair when he came back. I then cycled the rest of the way down towards my croft.

Just as I arrived at the bridge over the stream before the turn off to my house, I saw a figure coming up from the beach leading a horse. It was the woman I'd seen before, the 'not a hair out of place equestrian', only on this occasion there was more than one hair out of place and her previously immaculate jodhpurs and coat were smeared with sand.

"Been in the wars?" I said. It was difficult to determine her expression before she replied and there was clearly wariness, but also vulnerability in her manner.

"I was just cantering on the beach and my horse tripped I guess and threw me off, now he's a bit lame and we're a long way from home."

I suggested she just walked the few yards up to the croft house and we could have a proper look at the horse. I was still learning about animals and horse lameness was not something that I was knowledgeable about, but she seemed to know what she was doing and explained he'd need some rest and probably lots of cold water on his leg to reduce any inflammation. We tethered the animal and I invited to her come in and sit down, at which she was extremely hesitant.

"Me husband, he'll be wondering where I am," she said, "I have to let him know. Can I use your phone please?"

"Well you could do, if I had one," I said, "but I don't have a phone and nor does anyone else down this road and the nearest phone box is a mile away up at the road junction."

Just then a potential saviour appeared in the form of Callum the postie. I explained to him that this was the young woman from Newton Lodge and she had had a fall from her horse and the horse was now lame. I wondered if he might be able to give her a lift back home where she could arrange for the horse to be collected. He showed me the passenger seat of his van which contained a large number of parcels, as did the back of his van which was pretty full and he also said, rather too loudly and no doubt for the benefit of my 'guest', that it was against the regulations for him to give a lift to folk. Now I knew this latter to be a lie, because on many occasions he had given people lifts, but I suspected that this was a payback by Callum for the attitude of those at Newton Lodge in terms of their rudeness and standoffishness. However, in discussion it was agreed that Callum would call in at the Lodge, for whom he had mail anyway, and inform them of what had happened and also ask them to send a horsebox down for the animal.

"Well," I said when he had driven off, "I guess you had a bit of a shock so maybe best if you do come in after all."

Again the hesitation, but this time realising the wind was quite cool she decided to take up my offer and we went into the house. I got her to sit at the kitchen table whilst I went off to put the kettle on. She sat slightly turned away from me, looking out of the window and I was able to study her as I waited for the kettle to boil. I guess she was about my age, may be a bit younger, with blonde straight hair which I assumed would normally be immaculate but which after her fall was a little less so.

"How are you settling into your new life up here?" I asked, and she almost jumped at the sound of my voice.

"Ah! Well," she said, and after a pause, "it's different; not what I'm used to."

"What were you used to?" I asked and she replied that she used to live in a town. To which I said.

"A town? I would have guessed that, with your accent maybe you are from London and, if I had to stick a pin in the map, I might plump for Richmond."

"Hammersmith, actually." She replied impulsively and then, almost as though she had committed a *faux pas*, she changed the subject.

"How long till that postman can pass the message to Newton Lodge?"

"Maybe you just heard him coming back from my friend Dougie's croft which you will have seen when you take your horse down towards the jetty over the hill. Also I know for a fact that Morag at the other croft on our road usually puts the kettle on when he passes her house coming down and he generally stops there for a quick cuppa on his way back. After that his next call would be at the Lodge, but I'm guessing you could have up to half an hour before he passes the message and they can set off and come for you, assuming somebody's able to come straight away." I added.

This was clearly a message she had not expected to hear. And she became a bit agitated and stood up.

"Perhaps I had better walk back." She said and started for the door.

On about her second step she clearly winced with pain.

"You don't look up to walking down the 50 yards to the road, never mind doing the other couple of miles to the Lodge. Anyway I said tea is ready come on sit down and take the weight off."

She still hesitated but then gave in, accepting what she had now come to realise was the inevitable.

"How badly are you injured?" I asked.

She replied it was just a fall and so I enquired which parts of her had suffered the greatest. She explained that she had come off over the shoulder of the horse, but hadn't tumbled right forward and had managed to stick a leg out to break her fall. She thought that was how she had turned her ankle, because then she collapsed onto an elbow and her shoulder. She did wonder whether she had cut her elbow, as there was a gash in her riding jacket. I said that perhaps it needed looking at and at this she was very reluctant, but eventually I persuaded her to at least take her jacket off and see if it was bleeding. As she took the jacket off there was obviously blood on the elbow of her white shirt. It didn't look bad, but again I persuaded her to roll up the fairly loose sleeve and together we looked at a very small cut which had already almost stopped bleeding. As both her jacket and shirt had been cut through, I did suggest that she might have some sand in the wound so I went off to get some TCP which had been left over from my own accident, together with a small plaster. She agreed to my applying the TCP but absolutely refused the plaster as she explained that her husband could get very jealous and he would not like to think that I had dressed the wound.

The cut being at the back of, and slightly inside, her elbow was difficult for her to see and she agreed to me using a bit of cotton wool and I dabbed away with the old TCP. In doing so I was briefly able to study her, just in her blouse and without the riding jacket. Standing up she was about five foot three or four, she was quite buxom and her face was fairly thickly coated with makeup which I thought was completely unnecessary because clearly she was a bonny young woman. I completed my ministrations and she was very quick to put her jacket back on and to do the buttons up. However my act of personal service to her had clearly broken what, for her, was some quite hard packed ice and over tea she somewhat hesitatingly began to talk.

Although she was still very guarded I learnt confirmation of the fact that, Cat had told me, her name was Sally, that she had grown up in Hammersmith, that she had worked as a hairdresser and photographic model until she met her husband and whom she described as being a little bit older than herself. I learnt about her likes in music but clearly when I mentioned some of my gramophone recordings our musical tastes were as chalk and cheese. Popular music was her forte. The Beatles, Gerry and the Pacemakers, Cliff Richard and many more top of the 'poppers' were reeled off by her, far too many for me to recall. Very gradually she began to relax until totally unexpectedly our peace was shattered by the arrival of a black Humber Sceptre, which skidded to a halt in my croft house yard.

Immediately Sally jumped up.

"Don't tell him you've looked at my arm or that we have been chatting." She whispered to me.

Quickly, but with obvious discomfort and a wince of pain from her ankle, she moved to the door to intercept the incoming missile in the form of a stockily built man, dark-haired, going bald, in his early 50s, who was storming towards the house. He was ignoring the frantic attentions of Mr Roy. Although I was still making my way towards the door I heard his unaffectionate greeting quite clearly.

"What have you done, silly bitch?"

"I had a fall off me horse on the beach and I have twisted me ankle and couldn't walk the horse home 'cos he's gone lame and this man sheltered me and sent a message to you."

The man looked at me again and muttered something that I could not make out and then, without further comment he grabbed hold of her arm, presumably to escort her to the car, at which point she yelped

"I've hurt that arm!"

"Just get in the bloody car." Was his response.

Throughout all this Mr Roy, sensing an unwanted intruder had continued barking and circling around him and at this point the man swung his foot towards the dog.

"Hey!" I said. "Bouncing in unannounced is not a serious problem for me but lay one leg on my dog and I will make sure he bites the other one of yours off."

By this time Sally was in the car and the man turned to me.

"Mind your own bleedin' business!" And with that he turned and strode back to the car and with a spinning of wheels he drove off. Sally was looking straight ahead and made no acknowledgement of me as they left.

By this time a second vehicle had arrived; our friends in the Commer van which was fitted with a towing bar attached to which was a horse trailer and I watched as the men put the horse in the trailer and then hurried to follow the car, which was long gone and out of sight up the road.

"Well Mr Roy." I said, who was still panting from his exertions in what he may have thought was guard duty, although in that respect he could clearly do with some extra training. He cocked his head to one side and looked at me as though about to engage in intelligent conversation, so I addressed him directly.

"That, my friend, was one nasty man. And if at first I couldn't understand why that girl was so standoffish you only have to have witnessed what happened to her to begin to understand."

When I later reflected on what had happened, I could not believe the arrogance of a man who would turn up unannounced and allow somebody else to witness his awful behaviour to his wife.

I mentioned the episode to Alistair, Morag and Cat one dinnertime, as I was passing their house a couple of days later. After describing the incident in some detail I went on to say how appalling it was that any man should be so awful and aggressive towards his wife.

They listened carefully and intently as I drew my story out, but, for one of the first times with these three friends, I sensed that the shutters had come down and that it was not a subject they particularly wanted to develop. As soon as I'd finished my story there were a couple of 'aha's' and the subject was swiftly changed to the crofting business of the afternoon.

Whilst I was mildly surprised, at the time, it was not an event of such great importance and certainly it soon disappeared from my consciousness. It was just a bit of scandal or gossip that I was indulging in and whilst this was normally right up their street, they obviously did not want to pursue it today.

So I put it aside as being inconsequential.

But it wasn't.

As I would later discover.

Southern sojourn

For the next few weeks I kept busy feeding animals, helping Dougie and improving the croft and its surroundings. During this time Dougie reported that the trawler had gone out for the second time one night. He commented that they must be catching gold bars because just one night's fishing would not enable them to stay in harbour for the three or four weeks in between. He had tried to engage the men in conversation but they were unresponsive he thought the trawler skipper might have talked but after a glance at his companions he also stayed silent.

February brought a bit more snow so the animals were to feed more often but I was enjoying a very full life. My fitness was incredible and I was enjoying working hard. None of my animals were kept inside in the winter as they were hardy beef cattle or even hardier sheep so there was nothing in the way of mucking out but their feed needed supplementing by regular trips out to scatter straw.

Doing this constant chore of animal feeding made me think of Roddy, as this was probably the last regular work he had to undertake before his untimely death. Just a year ago many of these animals would have welcomed Roddy's visits to their domain, just as now they welcomed mine. Looking back, my keeping myself occupied was obviously a necessity of the crofting business, but at the same time it was keeping my mind off the 20th March and I was really not looking forward to that. My humour was not improved when, on 15th March, somebody on the radio was blethering on about it being the 'Ides of March' and the fact that they were a often described as the harbingers of doom.

Thanks for that, I thought.

On Wednesday the 18th I set off on my journey with a small suitcase. Alistair took me to Lochinver to catch the post bus which, in due course, dropped me off at Lairg and I walked to the station where I had a long wait for the train from Wick which would take me to Inverness. I had hoped to get a train to Edinburgh in time for an overnight one to London. In the event there were some unspecified delays and when, eventually, we could leave Inverness it was already dark and my arrival in Edinburgh, on a train that stopped at every station was so late as to ensure that I missed the overnight London train. So I had to doss round in Edinburgh until I was able to pick up an early morning 'Elizabethan' service down to London which whisked me, capital to capital, in little over six hours. From King's Cross I travelled to Waterloo and then took the service down to Feltham, arriving mid-afternoon.

The last leg of my journey had been in an electric powered Southern Region train and I realised how much cleaner they were than the steam trains I had used for the rest of the journey. There were no remnants of steam and smuts on the door handles and in the carriages. The great metropolis of London, I realised, was far more up-to-date than the rest of the country. But to be fair I had enjoyed my whole journey, not least because it had provided me with a couple of days of rest from manual labour. Also the sound of the train travelling over the tracks had proved to be quite soothing with its clickerty-clack noise and I found it quite easy to sleep through large sections of the journey. It also provided me with thinking time and I guess the sleep was a way of trying to deny what I suspected would be quite an ordeal to come. Most of my thoughts, however, related to Clackmore and I realised how much I had grown accustomed to my new life in the ten months I had been there. The freedom, the fresh air, the development of my crofting skills including those of animal husbandry which, I reflected, were likely to be sore tested not long after my return, as lambing season would be upon me. Never having wanted a dog I was amazed at how much I missed the company of Mr Roy and also the presence, I can't exactly say company because he was a man of few words, of Dougie. I missed my friends Alistair and Morag, and then of course there was Cat.

Why did I even think about Cat at all on the way to the Inquest into the death of my beloved Linda? I suppose it was in the context of thinking about my local friends and Cat was one of the four people with whom I most frequently had contact. In addition she was someone not far off my own age and of course she was a woman. Yet Cat was different from Linda in so very many ways. Whereas Linda had been small, buxom and rounded, Cat was tall, angular and wirily thin. My interaction with Linda had mainly been family centred whereas with Cat it was all work-related and in that sense she was more like a work colleague. As I had come to know her, I had come to enjoy her openness, honesty and industry and also to have enjoyed what little social interaction I had had with her. As more women had entered the workplace after the war so the increased opportunity for meeting and socialising with members of the opposite sex had increased as a means of development of personal relationships. But Cat was just a friend; wasn't she? Eventually I changed my mental subject and returned to wondering what I would face upon my return to the old home town.

Alighting at Feltham, I walked out into the station yard and immediately my anxiety levels rose. To start with the volume of traffic was so great to a person who might only see one or two cars a day, and even on a journey to and from Lochinver I might only pass a half dozen vehicles. I crossed the High Street, avoiding traffic with some difficulty and went into the Hanworth Road. Slowly I descended the little rise beside St Catherine's church and passing Cardinal Road School on my right, I crossed Cardinal Road and realised that I was standing on the spot where my wife, my beloved wife, and my beloved little daughter had died. I stood there somewhat transfixed looking at the ground, was I, like Lady Macbeth, looking for spots of blood? If so, unlike Shakespeare's villainess, it was not guilt that brought me up short, it was, instead, abject grief.

I don't know how long I stood there in that dazed state, it probably wasn't that long. I was broken out of the trance by a voice calling my name and I looked up to see Freddie, the driver from my old firm, who had pulled up in the van he was driving and he shouted across the road to me through his open window.

"Euwee." He called and when I looked up he said.

"I fought it was you. How yer doing?"

Crossing the road and standing by his open driver's window I said that I was on the way to my mother-in-law's just round the corner in Queens Road.

"I just got off a train as I am here for the Inquest tomorrow."

"Oh. Yeah I had heard about that."

"Yes," I said, "it's the only logical way to reach this end of Queens Road from the station I could have gone back over the bridge up to the Harlington Road turned right over the back bridge and come in the other way but that's about a mile. This way it's only a couple of hundred yards."

"But," he said, "this way it's just past the spot……."

"Yes." I said.

After a short silence we began to chat about his work and the expansion of my old firm, about which I was glad to hear, and he was interested to hear how I had gone on in my new life. I asked him to give my regards to all my old friends at work and with that he shouted 'good luck' and he set off. Once again I was grateful to Freddie. He brought me out of a rather dark moment and back into the normality of life. He had acknowledged that he remembered why I would be standing at this particular spot and I could have chosen to say something more. On this occasion I chose not to do so but it was right that he gave me an opportunity and, on another day, maybe I would have talked more about the girls. It was important that I was in a bit more of a stable emotional position because as soon as I knocked on the door of my parents in-laws' home, and Daisy opened it, there were Linda's eyes staring back at me and we embraced, and we both cried.

    We sat and talked over a cup of tea that she made and I noticed that she had lost a bit of weight, but she said she was keeping okay, she also reminded me that Tommy was getting closer to retirement; he was now into his early sixties. Brother Les was doing well at work, he and his wife were still without children. Linda's sister Win remained unmarried, but she had got a good secretarial job in town, town being London. In fact when Win came home from work a bit early the three of us had tea, since Tommy was on shift until eight that night. They were all keen to know about my new life and I have to confess that I quite enjoyed telling them all about it and how happy I was. One of the dark winter evenings I had used some time sketching a little map of Clackmore. I have it still and I will put it with these papers. This was quite useful in describing the location of the croft house and my neighbour's houses and the jetty which Dougie used for his boat.

    It was Win who reminded her mother that there was a note for me which had been delivered by my old friend

Billy. Apparently he had called a couple of weeks earlier to ask what arrangements I had made for coming to the Inquest. When Daisy had told him, he produced a scrap of paper and an envelope which he had brought with him and scribbled a note and asked them if they would give it to me. I opened it and read.

"Can't meet you on Thursday. Can't do Inquest. Meet me for 20 minutes only at the Red Lion 7 PM Friday. Very, very important. Billy."

Tommy got off shift at eight o'clock that evening and had arranged a day off for the following day. He arrived home red-faced and excited, the obvious bearer of news and clearly from his demeanour it was news to his liking.

"That copper's been in touch with me with some news that will come out at the Inquest tomorrow and he thought we would like to hear about it before then. Apparently a few weeks ago there was another of those jewellery robberies this time in Richmond. The description of the robbery by a couple of men surprising a jeweller who was just opening up his shop and then the robbers making off in a getaway car that had been stolen, was similar to that Hounslow job which resulted in Linda and Carole's death. A few days later they found a body in the Thames at Putney and it was that of a known criminal and in his pocket were some of the items from the Richmond robbery together with a suicide note. The note indicated that he had been driving the car involved in the Hounslow robbery last year and had caused the death of two pedestrians and it and it had been preying on his mind. The most recent robbery had brought the events back to him and he felt he could no longer go on living."

Daisy, Win and I all looked at him somewhat open mouthed.

"The bastard's dead," said Tommy, "at least that's something."

We had a general discussion whilst Tommy ate some supper. I think the general conclusion was that we were all pleased that at least now somebody had acknowledged responsibility and it was something that the culprit had at least shown some remorse and indeed it had affected him so greatly that it led to his own demise. On that note we all went to bed to get some rest before the court hearing the following day.

It was helpful for the police officer to have given us warning of this development before we were all sat together in the Coroner's Court the following morning. The police officer giving evidence effectively told the tale that Tommy had given to us, and the only extra piece of information that came out was that the deceased person, with the suicide note was a man with a previous conviction for robbery and who'd served time in jail, his name was Harry Evans. Then we learned that he'd drowned, and that he had been found on a mud bank beside, rather than in, the Thames. It was also stated that his death was known to be by drowning, as his lungs were full of Thames water, but also that he had serious head injuries, probably as a result of a jump into the water from a height, for example a bridge.

Given all the circumstantial evidence regarding the most recent robbery, its modus operandi, the jewellery in Harry Evan's pocket and the suicide note the police were confident that this was the person who had caused the death of Linda and Carole. The Coroner however said he understood the police position but on the other hand he did not feel that it constituted sufficient evidence to say, without doubt, that Harry Evans was responsible. In the circumstances he recorded a verdict of unlawful killing and added that whilst it was probable that Harry Evans had been the driver, this was not proved.

Given the briefing that the police had given us the day before and our chance to consider it we felt this was a reasonable decision and went home to have some tea about five o'clock, all of us feeling now we might begin to put this most dreadful episode into the past. Never to be forgotten, of course, but at least we had an explanation of what happened and maybe we could get on with our lives.

In this new and slightly more positive vein of thinking I left Tommy and Daisy's house not long before seven to walk the few minutes into the High Street and on to the Red Lion. I went into the saloon bar and was about to order a drink when a man came up to me and asked if I was Ewan and, when I said I was, he said a man called Billy was outside and would like me to pop out and see him. How peculiar I thought, but anyway outside I went. The pub was the first building on the far side of the Longford River there was a bit of car park in the front and a service road ran down the side, round to a delivery area and more parking in the rear. Billy hailed me from the shadows, towards the rear of the pub and invited me to follow him round the back where he had parked a car.

"Jump in."

Billy ordered before I could formally greet him and so saying he himself got in behind the driver's wheel. I climbed into the passenger side and shut the door but before I could speak he started.

"Sorry about all this but I hope you can understand. I'm gonna tell you a load of stuff which I don't want you to repeat to anybody and I'm also leaving some things out, so that if you get questioned you can truthfully say you don't know the answers. Right! First up I'm in a rush because later tonight I am catching a train out of London and by tomorrow night or the day after I will be on a ship with a one way ticket to somewhere nobody is going to find me."

Billy's story ran like this. From the time of my departure the previous year he had begun to realise that his dad had got in with a seriously bad crowd. Gradually his dad got sucked into what was going on and in turn Billy became more involved. In addition to all the other low-level bits of wheeling and dealing which had always been going on, and which had sat uncomfortably with Billy drugs, in the form mainly of LSD and amphetamines, had now become part of the operation. These drugs were very popular at dances and where pop bands played at local pubs or bigger venues. More recently things had moved on from the so called 'pep pills' to harder drugs including heroin and cocaine.

The low-level wheelers and dealers, and spivs like Billy's dad had been recruited to undertake or facilitate the movement of these drugs. Those few who had objected to this change in trade to hard drugs had been disciplined by the man running this particular group, for there were several in the London area, but this one operated in the south-west part of the capital. The type of discipline related to people's level of responsibility in the organisation, some very low level 'foot soldiers' had received severe beatings and threats of worse, to themselves or their family, should they suggest leaving or start talking. The few of those higher up the ladder who had expressed unhappiness seemed to have just disappeared.

Billy reminded me that for some time he had wanted to get out, but the longer things had gone on the more his involvement gave him a lot of knowledge about the operation and he was aware that if he tried leave now he might be the next to 'disappear'. Consequently he had been planning a disappearance of his own. He told me that he'd been in contact with an old acquaintance from the army (he had once told me about a mate who had got himself a successful new life in Canada, but he didn't mention that location in this conversation). A few months ago Billy had finally been able to track this man down and using a post office box address wrote to this man and laid his situation out and asked if he could help him to start a new life.

He received a reply in short order saying that he could be housed and found work as soon as he got there but there was a question of long term residence, since presumably he would be coming on a British passport and that would limit his stay. They arranged to speak on the telephone and after discussion his friend was able to purchase a new identity and passport for Billy as a citizen of his new country and this had been posted to him. He was using this passport and the new name to travel later today. Once abroad Billy planned to stay for a while with his friend to build a work record and then he would probably move to another part of his new country and start again. He acknowledged that the purchase of a new identity was more dishonesty but his view was that, from now on, he was going to go straight and this final 'crime' was the lesser of two evils.

Billy told me that so far as was possible he had covered his tracks and was going to take the car up to town and dump it near Waterloo station so that anybody looking for him might think that he had travelled south and maybe even crossed the channel. He was then going to travel up to Euston and go north. He had been saving money and had the better part of £4,000 cash sewn into the lining of his suitcase to take with him, most of which would go in payment for the new identity for which his friend had laid out.

He said that he had no intention of writing to me because it might compromise me if people thought of checking with me to see if I'd heard from him or, even worse, that they could get an address through which they might be able to catch up with him. He assured me that he had never wanted to get into this drugs business and that he had not done anything beyond knowing what was going on and not telling the authorities. But technically he was sure that he could be said to have been involved with the supply of drugs which would lead to a lengthy sentence.

"Now, you may wonder why I have asked to see you to make this sort of confession and tell you this story. That is because I owe it to you to tell you what else I've learnt about in this awful world which my dad got me sucked into and which up to now I've been too weak to get out of. This gang is run by Eric Porter, who used to be known as 'Knuckles' because of his favoured use of a knuckle duster in his early days. Up until a year or two back Knuckles, who is a very nasty man, was just generally into crime, for example, crimes like robbery. According to one of his close associates, who I was talking to one night when he was drunk, said he had heard Knuckles boasting about how it was him that was the getaway driver on the Hounslow job the very one committed with Harry Evans and which led, as a consequence of his being chased, to the death of Linda and Carole. Knuckles was the getaway driver."

"But wait. At the Inquest the police said Harry Evans killed himself because of his feelings of guilt about killing them, so it can't have been this Knuckles bloke."

"Youee. This is big time gang stuff which someone like you would not understand. The coppers were still investigating the death of your two girls and it was getting a little hot for our friend Knuckles, because apparently some people were suggesting it might be him that was involved. This suggestion probably came from some person related to one of the many 'disappeared' souls, but I don't know that. What I do know is that Knuckles decided that the heat was getting too much and, having done no robberies for a while, he persuaded Harry to do the job in Richmond with him. After that it would not have been hard for him to get people to stage-manage a 'suicide' for poor old Harry and ensure that he ended up on a convenient mud bank. Then arrange for an anonymous phone call to be made from a phone box to the 'Old Bill' so that they found him whilst the planted evidence was still fresh. It was smart leaving some jewellery from the Richmond job in his pocket and the suicide note was probably typed and, no doubt, some forger was paid to scribble poor old Harry's signature at the bottom.

By doing this Knuckles took all the heat off himself and, of course, the cops had solved the case and they were happy. Now I understand you may not believe this but sad to say I am pretty sure this is true from various bits and pieces I have heard on the grapevine, although it's not enough in terms of hard evidence or I could go to the police.

Anyway I've just got to get away and I'm not sure whether I should tell you the next bit or not but I'm going to because I think you need to know. The story is that Knuckles has ploughed a lot of his ill-gotten gains into some manor near the coast. This is because he's moving from being a little local 'Major', running his own little local show to a 'General' organising the supply of these drugs to lots of other little 'Majors' all over town. As far as I understand it, the drugs come out of Holland by ordinary regular ship which takes them somewhere near where he has moved to and somehow they get the drugs in and transfer them here to London where they get dished out via the little local operations like the one my dad is in."

"I'm sorry but I got to go." He said glancing at his watch.

"I need to be ditching this motor no later than nine if I'm gonna get up to Euston for the train. It's been nice knowing you, thank you for supporting me all those years, I'm sorry I made a mess of my bloody life but hopefully I'm gonna try and put that right now. I hope I have not directly hurt too many people, after all I've only driven stuff around, but I know that's no real excuse. I've told you the truth as far as I know it and it may cause a bit of upset, given that the authorities 'ave told you another story. I advise you stay away from Knuckles at all costs. If any of his henchmen come looking for you to see if they can find me then you know nothing, but if some reason they tried to put pressure on then I've written something in this little envelope that you could threaten to go to the authorities with, in order to get them off your back.

Inside this envelope you will find another envelope which has been sealed and endorsed by a Notary Public and it contains a copy of a letter I will take with me setting out all the bad things I know about Knuckles and his organisation. Most of it is hearsay, but I have been able to put down dates and times and places in relation to some things that could be traced clearly back to him and would provide evidence enough to cause him a little personal trouble. Put that in the hands of a solicitor somewhere and then there's just a little handwritten note which, if stick comes to lift, and you are really under pressure or threat you could show to Knuckles or any of his associates and tell them that there is a three page letter detailing past deals, some of which can easily be proved. That should put the wind up him as this note will give him the idea of what type of detailed information might be in the letter. Say that if you are harmed then the solicitor holding the letter has been authorised to hand it to the police. I think that should be enough to keep you from harm."

With that he pushed an envelope at me then hurried me out of the car. I walked round to the driver's side and through the open window he asked.

"Is it all working out up there?"

"It's good."

"I am pleased," he said, "thanks for being my friend all these years and I hope one day we can see one another again, but this is my only chance and I've got to take it."

He started the engine, proffered me a hand, which I shook, and getting the clear message that he needed to be off, I wished him the very best of luck.

With a quick wave he engaged gear and drove briskly off.

I did not go straight back to Tommy's, instead I called into the Red Lion and got myself half a pint of Watney's Red barrel bitter and took it to a corner seat and pondered. So much information; so quickly imparted. An overload of it really which now I was only beginning to assimilate, on the back of which a number of questions that I would like to have asked Billy arose. This was now not going to be possible.

One conclusion I did reach and that was that there was no way I was saying anything to Tommy and Daisy about Billy's story. Like me, today they had received an answer to a huge question mark in our lives and Tommy's face alone said what a relief it was for him to be able to understand about the death of his granddaughter and daughter. It would be cruel to undermine that feeling and so there was nothing I could say.

A more pertinent question, however, was where did I stand in relation to this new information?

I decided that consideration of that question was for another day.

Altered landscape

Having bid goodbye I left behind Tommy, Daisy and family in a happier place, because of what the Inquest had resolved for them as I began my journey home. A journey home! Wow, would I ever have thought just about a year ago that I would have so quickly seen Clackmore as being home. I very much doubt it.

The journey south had held some anxieties about the return to Feltham to Linda's family and the Inquest, but I had utilised that journey as a rest from the hard physical labour of the previous ten months. Sleep had come easy to the soothing noise of train wheels passing over the rail joints. Whilst the soothing noise was just the same going north, the ability to sleep was held firmly at bay by the issues raised in Billy's story.

First there was poor Billy himself. He had always been uncomfortable with the spiv like operations of his father but, by and large, one supposes that those operations were at the margins of the law sometimes stretching marginally one way, or marginally the other. There was no doubt, however, that the involvement of drugs was well beyond the pale and I could imagine Billy's conscience, already sore tested by those offences of the margin, must at last have come to a sticking point. I was delighted for him that he had found a way forward and I was sure that his escape to life in a new country would suit him. I was glad that he had somebody on his side to see him get started and I felt sure that in the fullness of time he would make a decent new life for himself. He was not, at heart, a dishonest or anti-social man as I well knew but he was held in thrall by his father and had gradually got sucked into things which he knew morally did not suit him. I was glad therefore that he was able to make this break and no doubt the information in the letter was at least some partial salve to his conscience.

Although he conveniently avoided mentioning it, I was pretty sure that Canada would be his destination. He had referred to Euston station and I was pretty sure that trains to the north-west ran from there and so he could be making his way to Liverpool from where, I assumed, it was quite possible to get a ship to take him to Canada. That was a vast, still expanding, country and who knows, maybe he like me, might find somewhere in the backwoods where he could establish himself in a new setting on his own terms.

Then there was the much more difficult and knotty problem of Harry Evans and his suicide or, as Billy would have it, his murder. Criminals offend against the rules of society but this does not disbar them from human emotions and if you had unintentionally, in the heat of the moment, in a chase where you were trying to avoid pursuers, mowed down and killed two pedestrians, it was quite possible that subsequently you could become ill with the guilt of what you had done. In those circumstances, again like any other human being, your mind could be so overtaken by the guilt that you would ultimately become ill enough to take your own life. It is also possible that the commission of an offence similar to the one where your guilt is centred might be sufficient to cause you to come to that tipping point.

As against that, Billy's description was of the man Knuckles becoming concerned that the police were getting closer to pinning the deaths of Linda and Carole on him. It was not beyond the realms of possibility that he might be in a position to arrange the murder of poor Harry. I recalled from the evidence at the Inquest that Harry had drowned, that the water in his lungs was Thames water and therefore was consistent with a man throwing himself into the river and drowning. On the other hand his body had been found fairly quickly, as a result of an anonymous tip off, on a mud bank in Putney and he had clearly not been in the water for very long and though soggy, his suicide note was still easily decipherable. So Billy's version of events was pretty extreme, but not totally implausible. Furthermore, why had Harry bothered to keep some items from the Richmond jewellery raid in his pocket. That was a moot point.

So, I wondered, what was in the note that gave a sample of what was contained in the more lengthy letter. At this point I decided to open the envelope. Inside was a torn off half sheet of paper on which was written:-

Deliverer = PACCO gives Date and time then Channel 16/8. Receiver = GAEKP Spiro - PD355 201063 del to Boyo Richmond 231063 25,000

It was nonsense as far as I could see, and how this was supposed to be of assistance to me in the event of some gangsters approaching me when trying to find Billy I did not know. However Billy obviously believed that this information might well be sufficient to afford me some protection and I was grateful for that. Inside the first large envelope was another one which was sealed with two signatures across the opening flap and endorsed also by a Notary Public, whose full name and address was printed there. I thought I would do what Billy said and send it to Mr McKay, my solicitor, for safekeeping.

I turned the issue over and over in my mind and came to the most obvious conclusion, that is to say, that there was no obvious conclusion.

Then there was the man Knuckles and the information that he had moved the centre of his operations to some coastal area and he was operating in a place where he could take charge of drugs that were arriving on a ship that had, at some earlier point, visited a port in Holland. Probably then this would be on the east or south coasts as they were the nearest to that country. The importation could be effected through some arrangement with some dock workers in a big port, or equally it was possible that they might use a smaller port, but it would have to be a port of sufficient size to accept a vessel coming from Holland, even if that were only a coaster. There again, I thought, even a large quantity of drugs probably was easy to conceal in a small pleasure boat. From my childhood reading of the 'Swallows and Amazons' novels of Arthur Ransome, I remembered his descriptions of empty coastal areas in the region of the River Orwell and Walton-on-the-Naze in East Anglia and such areas would be hard to police against determined smugglers in small craft.

Once again I could reach no firm conclusion and whilst I was tempted to open the envelope with the formal letter of further information that Billy had given to me, I thought to myself that even if his story about this man was true, there was no way I could involve myself in trying to rain on his parade. First of all I had no idea where his parade was and secondly, if I started off down that road then I might create the sort of trouble that Billy was fleeing from and that would not be fair on him. If this man had been the driver of the car and he had gone to such great lengths to conceal himself from the law then the chances of me bringing him to justice were remote, but if I embarked on doing so I would endanger my friend who was trying to break free.

My total return journey had been much more speedy that my outward one. Having travelled up to town from

Feltham in the rush hour and crossed from Waterloo to King's Cross Station I had been able to catch the nine thirty morning 'Elizabethan' express service to Edinburgh arriving something before four in the afternoon. My service north, to Inverness, afforded me the lovely views over Drumochter Pass that I had first sampled on my drive north. But it was some twelve hours after I had started out from London when I arrived in Inverness and just too late for the onward train to Lairg. At the newsagents I purchased a small writing pad and a large envelope and I wrote a letter to Mr McKay, the solicitor, asking him if he would be kind enough to arrange for his firm to keep safe the enclosed envelope. I explained that the envelope contained some information which a friend had given me and which needed keeping safe, possibly for some years, but that I was not really at liberty to say more than the fact that it was personal information and not, so far as I was aware, anything untoward. I felt I had to say this, but in writing it I did have the fingers of my left hand crossed. I finally asked if there would be a charge for this service and if so I would gladly pay it. I then went round to the offices which were, by this time, closed and pushed the envelope through the letterbox.

Then after a meal in Inverness, I went and sat with one cup of tea in the station buffet till it closed and then I hung around until I could get the first train north in the morning. Being Sunday I was concerned that lifts might not be so easily available but only about twenty minutes after arrival at Lairg station I was lucky enough to pick up a lift with a fish lorry off to Lochinver. Then with an even more lucky lift in the form of a tourist couple off to drive the scenic route via Drumbeg to the Kylesku ferry, I was dropped at my road junction by mid-afternoon. I called at Alistair and Morag's but they, and Cat, were out so on I went to my house to be greeted by an ecstatic Mr Roy, whom I later learnt had stayed around the house all the time I was away, fed by Cat and Dougie.

That evening Cat arrived on horseback, accompanied by Willie apparently out on an evening ride for leisure purposes. I was just doing some washing up when she came in the front door and shouted hello. I grabbed a towel and shouted.

"Sorry I heard you arrive, but I wanted to just finish these last few dishes so that they could all drain."

"That's fine." She said and I offered her a cup of tea. Whilst I busied myself in the kitchen she sat down and there was some small talk between us. When I finally managed to get sat down on the chair and looked at her I could see this was something slightly more than an ordinary social visit.

"I told mum and dad that I would come down and find out how you'd gone on", she said.

So I went on to tell her the official tale relating to Harry Evans and the fact that now Linda's family were at least content to know who the perpetrator was and also the fact that the event had ultimately caused him to take his own life. I went on to say that I was pleased for them that they were content with this finding.

"But, you are not?" She said perceptively.

"Well," I replied, "there are just one or two things that sit a little bit uncomfortably but perhaps that's just me being pernickety."

I guess on another day she might have taken that bit of conversation forward, but it was clear that her mission to see me was an ostensible one, not to say that she wasn't concerned and wanting to take the news back to the family, but there was an obvious overriding issue on her mind. So I let her move on to that.

"I've come to ask a favour." She said.

"Anything."

"How do you think my mum is looking now?" She asked me.

"Well.... ," I said, drawing the word out, in order to give myself some time to think, "she seems to be prone to get very tired." I said quite neutrally.

"I am really worried about her," said Cat, "and I am afraid it's something awful like cancer."

As she said these words her eyes filled and tears began to roll. I pushed back my chair, walked round table to where she was sitting and put my hand on her shoulder, by way of some demonstration of solidarity or comfort. She immediately turned towards me and grasped me around the middle and spent fully two or three minutes sobbing uncontrollably.

"How long have you been worried about this?" I asked.

She replied, with words that came tumbling out in almost staccato fashion.

"Over these last few months she has been complaining of dropping off to sleep, even sometimes in the morning not long after getting up, she has had cramps and pains and although I have told her to see the doctor she refuses to do so - and has sworn me to secrecy. I suppose I should just speak to the doctor myself, but I do not want to drive her away from me. I'm a bloody nurse for God's sake, I should be able to make some diagnosis in general terms but I am baffled."

I muttered something about how sorry I was, but my mind was in something of a turmoil as this Amazon like, fiercely competent and independent creature, held me in a bear hug of an embrace with the side of her face pressed hard against my stomach as she was in a sitting position and I was standing beside her.

"I'm sorry," she said, pulling away and cuffing her eyes to wipe away the tears, "I shouldn't have done that, and I didn't come here to break down, but I suppose it's all been getting too much for me trying to carry on in the normal way when I know things are quite abnormal. I don't think my dad realises how quick her decline has come on and how serious it might be. Although, maybe just recently, he has noticed that she has become a bit of a caricature of her old self. The problem is that I have more knowledge of these things than my dad and also she has told me more about her symptoms than she has told him. Anyway, as I say I didn't come here to cry or to look for sympathy, rather I came to ask you to do dad and I favour?

You may not have noticed but in the last few weeks either dad or I've been working around the house so that we could frequently pop in and just keep an eye on how mum is doing. Now it just so happens that dad requires a minor operation on his eye, well actually he needs both eyes doing but if he can get one of them fixed that puts us on for a while. We have to go down to Inverness for this and it's only a day procedure. We can be away first thing in the morning and back by evening time, but there's the question of leaving mum. Now she would say just go, and she knows all about it since it's been planned for some considerable time, but we need somebody to look in on her. There are a few jobs roundabout the croft house relating to fencing that needs mending and I wonder if you'd be kind enough to consider coming and doing some of these jobs. Then from time to time maybe you could pop in to keep an eye on mum. In return dad or I would do some job or another for you at some point in the future."

I told her that I would be happy to help in any way that I could and enquired the day that I would be required. So it was agreed that on the appointed day I would arrive in the morning, not long after they'd gone and Morag would be told that I would be coming to do some fencing jobs because Alistair couldn't do them until this sight was fixed and it wouldn't be possible to do that sort of work for a week or two after the operation.

It was a 'dreich' day with a fine drizzle and I was quite soaked by the time that I had ridden my cycle to their croft. I called in to see Morag and said that I was there to do some fencing and was offered the customary brew of tea. Given the real purpose of my visit being that of untrained carer, I readily agreed to be out of the rain to begin to dry out. We chatted about this and that as we drank our tea and then she surprised me with a question.

"It's a long time since my folks died, but Alistair and I were not long married and looking back I must have coped fine given Alistair's support. But can I ask you if you have found it hard to cope with bereavement?"

Bereavement seems to have been an occasional feature in my life, as it is for everybody. First my dad, whom I can hardly remember, and then of course much later, by the time I was married, I lost mum. Finally of course there was the most recent event, the incident, which left me without a wife and child.

"Well," I said, "yes it is hard. But I am guessing it's hardest when you haven't got some person or persons or something to focus on to help you to move forward. When my dad died my mother told me what had happened, that he'd been lost at sea, where he had been serving his country and that's what happened in times of war, some people were killed. I therefore was able to see my dad as some sort of mini hero, somebody whom I could admire and be proud of and who, in some ironic sort of way, gave me kudos with friends because 'Ewan's dad was killed in the war doing his bit'. But after the obvious period of being very upset it was possible for me to move forward, not least because my mum was so supportive, and also at that age your ability to conceptualise issues like death are limited. You tend to accept things as facts and maybe only later do you appreciate your loss.

Bereavement for me as a child was instant and dreadful, but just as children fall and bang themselves and get up and carry on so, to a certain extent, most children can put awful episodes behind them, or at least that was the case for me. But my mum was there for me and being school-age there were things I had to do and get on with and, between these two vehicles of assistance, I was able to put the event behind me without too much pain. There was also an issue relating to the fact that my father was, in any case, a somewhat missing element to my life. Oh yes it was wonderful when he was home on leave, we did everything together, but then he was away so much of the time as well and it might have been harder for me had he been a normal dad, who was at home every evening and at the weekends, but that wasn't the case. So perhaps his death and my bereavement were not as difficult to cope with in those particular circumstances.

With my mum it was different; she'd been a constant throughout my childhood. We had been very close until my teenage years, at which point I think I had been reasonably challenging and made life difficult for her. I wonder why it is that parents, who have, in many cases, given so much love and care suddenly become the people whom we want to challenge or deny. It's only natural, we want to move away from their version of life and try to engage in what we think will be a better way of doing things, because we think we know that we will be better than our parents and their ways and values will be superseded by the way we think things should be done.

But even before I left the home that mum had made so secure for me, I found my soulmate in Linda and after my period of National Service in the army we got together and I'd left my mum somewhat behind. I'd not meant to neglect her in any way and of course we saw quite a bit of her, living as close as we did. Nevertheless she was left behind to manage on her own with her local friends but, looking back, she probably had a fairly lonely sort of life after I got married. So when she died I wasn't ready for the impact. What's the old saying 'you don't miss things till they're gone' and so it was with me. She had been there throughout my life and so I wonder if there is a correlation between the length of your involvement with somebody that relates to how you feel about their death.

But once again, just as mum had supported me through the issue of dad's death, I now had the support of Linda through my mum's death. And furthermore, instead of school, there was a settled job and then there was also my own child to consider and whilst mum's death pained me greatly the challenge of ongoing life and life's responsibilities enabled me to go forward. I did wonder how hard it must be for people who suffer bereavement at a time that they have no such support and even worse, if their life is also without another focus, like work or interests."

I told Morag that I could not explain to her the awfulness of losing Linda and Carole. I told her that I spoke to them sometimes, when I was on my own, as I felt their presence or thought I did; I wanted them to be with me even though rationally I knew they were not there. I said I could not begin to explain the pain that I felt and I also said that I just could not really talk any more about how I felt about them because it was still far too close. But I said that I was not sure that I would have been able to cope had the opportunity to come up to the croft not arisen. My old life would have revolved around going to work and coming back to an empty house. Whilst I enjoyed the work it was very much a routine sort of job which was rarely upset by any out of the ordinary occurrence. Cycling back-and-forth from an empty house was something I might not have been able to cope with and, in those circumstances, there would have been nobody else to whom I could turn. Of course Linda's mum and dad and her family would have been generally supportive and I have no doubt I would have had my meals cooked from time to time but that would not have been the close support which I had obtained from Linda when my mum had died.

"And do you get angry about the people who took your wife and daughter away?" Morag asked.

"I've been angry about losing them but I still do not know enough about the thinking of the person who did it and I'm angry that they did what they did but despite the Inquest I would just like to know more. Why it happened seems to be clearer but, more pertinently, why did they not stop to help? But then I've also thought that sometimes I've done things that I've run away from. I broke a window once throwing some stones, I ran away and I was not caught. On one level I thought to myself 'I've got away with it' and then, on the other hand, I did feel really guilty. If I'd have gone and owned up straightaway there might have been some harsh words said and I would have had to find some money to repair the damage but, having made the initial decision to run away, it was then even harder to return to the scene and own up to my misdeed. I have even wondered if the car driver had stopped around the corner and then thought 'I can't face it' and gone on. I have no way of knowing what their motive or their reaction to the incident was and I suppose that's part of wanting an answer that makes me more angry at this stage, than the deed in itself.

In a funny sort of way, the time the Inquest has taken and the fact that still there is no real clear answer to what happened, has prolonged the bereavement process. I feel sorry for people who feel so angry about a loss, to the extent that they must continue to find someone to blame, however remote the possibility of doing that might be. For they will forever be stuck in a process of finding it difficult to carry on with their lives. But I think what I'm trying to tell you is that this fortunate opportunity of coming here to the croft, with its heavy demands on my time and energy, has probably allowed me to avoid many of the problems which this bereavement would otherwise have caused me. So in a way, and at the moment, it may be my bereavement process is in limbo because my new life has kept me so occupied."

For a while we sat in silence.

"I needed to ask because I'm worried about Alistair and Cat and how they'll cope when I die."

I remained silent because Cat had not told me whether Morag was aware of the fact that she seemed to be quite ill.

"You don't need to feel you've got to keep any secrets," she said, "I know I'm not well and I know that Cat knows that I'm not well, but maybe Alistair is less aware of how poorly I am. I wanted to know how you saw bereavement because I want to be able to encourage my two to be as positive as they can be when, if whatever I have got means, I will no longer be here."

"Woah," I said, "you are not that ill are you?"

"There is a lot I could say but I feel that I am so exhausted, even after a long sleep and this must mean something bad. Perhaps cancer; and that may be an end for me. I have had sixty seven good years, well I guess that is sixty six good years and one that is turning out to be nay so good. For about sixty three or four of those years I hardly had a day's illness in my life and I was fit as a fiddle, helping work the croft walking here and there and then suddenly, after I got past sixty life began to become a little more difficult. It was not overnight, it was small things, this joint ached, that toenail got sore, it wasn't as easy as it used to be to get in and out of the bath or to bend down and cut my toenails or put on my socks. So there was this subtle realisation that my body machinery was beginning to get worn. Then this real overall exhaustion began to set in. Throughout my life from childhood, I've known that at some stage I was going to die, just like everybody else. But it's not the sort of thing that you dwell on, in fact most of the time it's not something you even acknowledge it's just part of life knowing that there will be an end. That said, you deny the fact that there's going to be an end, if you're lucky enough, like me, to have been a normally healthy person.

Of course I've had issues like influenza, chickenpox or measles and in a woman's case childbirth, but for most of us living in our sort of society these things are relatively inconsequential and only in exceptional circumstances are they likely to lead to death. But as the body parts get worn so you must more readily face up to the fact that your time here is limited. And so it has been for me, gradually beginning to have to face the possibility of an end. But I feel that these signs are ones that mean that I may not be going to get better from this and, in fact, it might signal my time to go.

I'm not too bothered about leaving this life behind, because I know it has to be. I do believe in God but I am worried about the experience of dying and in some senses if somebody could tell me a bit more it might be helpful. But I only know of one person who's come back from the dead and, whilst I'm willing to believe in Him, I just wish He had told us more about what it's like, that actual moment of passing from conscious living to......... whatever lies in front.

My concern is for Alistair and Cat and how they will cope. Alistair is going to take it very hard and maybe it's something to do with what you said to me about the amount of time you been involved with the person who dies that can have an impact. We've been together for well over thirty five years and living as we do we have been very, very reliant on one another so the impact on him will be huge. And Cat's a big softy underneath that tough exterior and I'm sure that some of her life experiences, about which I'm sure she has not told you, will make her ability to deal with bereavement a lot more difficult.

I'm glad we've had this wee chat, but more importantly I would like to ask you to help them both, if and when my time comes. I know that Alistair likes you, and given what you told me about the need for somebody to have a focus in their life, then maybe you could find something for Alistair to focus on, not just the croft, but a bit more than that. And then as far as Cat's concerned I cannot ask too much of you but it would be really nice for me to think that you could give her some help too. She's already had more than one major, awful, experience in her life and I'm afraid she has not really got over that yet, so my going will only make that worse for her. She doesn't seem to have any good friends locally, because she left here to go to school in Dornoch when she was only just over eleven years old and she only fully came back a few years ago.

You didn't come here today to hear all this, and I had no intention really of telling you all that I have done. It's been helpful for me to feel that I've got some of these things off my chest, but I do implore you not to say anything to Alistair or Cat."

"I promise to do my best to be discreet. But I feel I ought to add a sort of condition to my agreement about saying nothing to your two. It's more of a request than a condition, but it is said to try to be helpful. I would really like to ask you to consider going and seeing the doctor and I'll tell you why. My father's death was a sudden one so far as I was concerned and so was the death of Linda and Carole. My mother's death, however, was a bit different and we had time together once we knew how serious her condition was and during that period we could talk. I felt that at the end of the process when she did die we left one another with a better understanding of each other. I think that may have helped her, but it certainly helped me cope with her passing.

If you went to the doctor you would not be forced to accept any treatment he proposed, but on the other hand you may begin to understand timescales and the likely progress of any loss of faculties. Once you know these things, and if they are as bad as you suspect, I would urge you to talk to Alistair and Cat and engage them in the process of coming to terms with your departure. I am only asking you please to make an appointment, get to know where you stand and then all your family and friends can be part of the process of whatever is likely to be forthcoming. For the time being I thank you for feeling able to confide in me and I will keep my council, for a week or two, whilst you have chance to see the doctor."

She looked at me, and after a long, long pause she said.

"Thank you for listening and whilst I was against the idea of confirming my worst suspicions, I suppose you may be right and I will make an appointment in the next couple of weeks or so."

Part 3   Reverberation

New perspective

Then came lambing. Had I been without the assistance of Alistair and Cat my eventual healthy crop of lambs would have been a third less than was actually achieved. These two experienced 'lambers' saved many a little life. Towards the end, with teaching and encouragement, I just about learnt to cope with reaching and pulling little legs and wiping away membrane from little mouths and noses and getting, in most cases, a satisfying tiny 'baa' for my efforts.

By early May most of the lambing was complete and I had a healthy sized crop of lambs which would certainly go a long way towards a decent income in due course. My little venture with Dougie was also going well and whilst we were not ever going to make our fortunes, I could see that I was on the road to financial survival. The lambing experience had kept me very busy and my thoughts, following the return from the south, had been pushed towards the back of my mind and, I suppose, I was very content to let them stay there.

The anniversary of my arrival in Clackmore had come and gone without being marked because by now we were into preparations for haymaking and I was helping Dougie to service and repair a variety of equipment which would be needed for this important work. The days were again long and my work was spread out over a twelve to fourteen hour period. One would not necessarily be hard at it all that time, but you would be on your feet for much of it. One day I was helping Dougie who was mending a baler. He had called me to request that, when he had fixed a broken bracket he needed my help to lift and hold the heavy metal arm, whilst he put bolts in the underneath side of it. Standing there holding a heavy piece of metal, as Dougie did his work, my mind did run to that anniversary of my arrival.

What a long way I had come in these last twelve months. I had acquired a dog, my constant companion, always there, as now laying full stretch, chin on legs tongue out, eyes watching me. I had acquired not only a friend in Dougie but a business partner in a very small enterprise but nevertheless one that would, together with my crofting and little bits of accounts work for other people, sustain my way of life for the foreseeable future. I was part of a living, working community and I was becoming accepted into it. My other neighbours Alistair, Morag and Cat were my good friends. With the Inquest and other events of 20th March behind me I could look forward slightly more often than dwelling in the past.

One day I was out working on a bit of broken fencing, up on the ridge, towards the main road end of the valley. At some point I heard a sheep calling, as though lambing or otherwise in trouble, so I went to investigate. It was an old ewe whom I may have thought was not in lamb, but who must have been because she showed all the signs of being about to give birth. So I prepared to give a hand if necessary. Whilst I was so engaged I didn't notice a horse and rider approach along the top of the ridge. Whilst I was busy locating a couple of legs to pull the lamb out, I was conscious of the sound of a horse cropping grass nearby and glanced up to see Sally standing there watching me whilst holding her horse. I muttered a brief hello and carried on with what I was doing. Eventually with one last tug a lovely little lamb came into view covered, as usual, in mucus. I scraped some away from its face and it began to breathe and I put it in front of its mother so that she could begin the cleaning and bonding process. I wiped my hands on a nearby tuft of grass and then stood up

"Wow that was amazing. I bet you could do a job as a midwife." Sally said.

"I'll let you into a secret," I replied, "given the same situation two months ago I would have run a mile to avoid getting involved."

She laughed.

"Anyway," she said, looking around, "I'm not supposed to talk to you. But I just wanted to say thank you for what you did for me a couple months back. This old horse means a lot to me and as you can see he has fully recovered now and so I really am ever so grateful for your kindness, it was much appreciated."

I assured her that I had only done what anybody would have done and it had been my great pleasure to help.

"Hmm. Great pleasure eh! I thought so, I saw you looking at my tits whilst you were putting on the TCP."

Flustered and no doubt blushing at her directness I stuttered.

"Sorry, I live on my own and don't have much to do with girls these days".

"Don't worry," she said with a little laugh, "I used to be a model and I am used to men looking at my chest not my eyes when they talk to me. But thank you anyway for your kindness, as you will have noticed I'm not used to that. I don't suppose I'll be able to call on you again as I'm under strict orders not to ride on the beach and not to come anywhere near your house. Just seeing you here, out of sight of the road, meant I felt I could stop and just say thank you."

"I thought your husband's actions and attitude were a little bit over the top, but having said that it's nothing to do with me how you and him carry on."

"Humph!" She said. "I don't carry on, but he bloody well does."

"It's as bad as that is it?"

"No." She said, "it's worse."

"Why don't you leave then?" I said.

"Now, you know I shouldn't be having this conversation and I'd better get off."

"You can't say what you just said and leave me dangling," I said, "particularly, if as you say, you are not going to be able to come by my croft and tell me on another day. I live on my own, and I have no reason to tell anybody else anything, but obviously you have a tough time. I have had a tough time myself and it's good to be able to talk about it; only if you want to of course."

"How tough?" She asked. So I briefly told her the outline of what had happened to my girls, omitting the location of the incident.

"Oh! That is awful. I am so sorry for your loss." she said.

"Look;" she went on after a brief hesitation, "you were a stranger to me and yet you are the first man who has shown me any kindness in the better part of the last 10 years, and actually since long before that. The men in my life have been bastards. It started with me drunken father who beat me mother kept us in poverty because of his boozing and when I got older he wasn't afraid of touching me up. So I ran away, and when you run off when you're fifteen and a bit, life is going to be hard. You run from what you know to be bad but at that age you assume that people will help you, but not me, I ran into more badness. I dossed down wiv some mates and then got in with a wrong crowd and got into being teamed up with a load of men who were after some fresh meat.

I had various jobs offered to me in modelling, now that's a laugh, modelling usually means walking around in different dresses, in my case it was walking around without any dresses. Do you know I got my picture in the magazines; but not 'Women's Weekly', most of mine was in 'Spic and Span'. All those photographers came up to you and said stuff like 'you make the most marvellous model with your lovely face', what they really meant was you look to have big tits. One of my girlfriends of the time used to say we were 'Humpty Dumpty girls', all we ever got was humped and dumped.

Then, me life changes, along comes this older man who seems to really enjoy shagging me and wants to keep me for his own. At first that life were wonderful, I could have anything I wanted, new clothes, going out to smart places and he even buys me a pony. All right he only ever wants rough sex, but I'm used to that so I put up with it, and even when I fall pregnant by him and I'm terrified that he is gonna chuck me out I'm amazed when he doesn't. We have little Henry and to start with he is the proud father, but then gradually it wears off and I think he was getting a bit tired of me, and I almost wondered if I was coming to the end of the road wiv him. Then he decides to come up here and wants me to come with him. I often wonder why, because he hasn't got a sentimental bone in his body, but nevertheless he says I were coming.

Since we got up here it's like being under house arrest, I aren't allowed out other than to ride me horse, which is limited now to a ride along this ridge and down to the bay with the jetty in it, or the other way up into the hills past the peat diggings. I can take Henry to and from school but only if one of those two drivers takes me. Franco and Mario, the two hard men who drive around in a Commer van, you've probably seen?" I nodded.

"They're hard as nails and thick as puddings and they're terrified of the boss, as he likes to be called. But they're hired hands who'll do their jobs as long as they are getting paid. There's no loyalty to him, but he's daft enough not to see that, because he thinks he has everyone under control.

I hate my bloody life but for Henry's sake there's nothing much I can do about it. I need to look after Henry and so I have to put up wiv this miserable life. Meantime the Boss hardly ever bothers shagging me any more cos he's onto his new business and all he thinks about is making money. But we have had a couple of 'important visitors' and if required I have to turn a trick wiv them. Apart from him and Henry and the two drivers we have dear Marge, who is the theoretical housekeeper, and whose cooking is shit, mainly because she's pissed half the bleedin' time. But she's smart enough to keep sober enough so as to keep an eye on me, especially when the boys aren't around. More recently we got the silent Scotsman, who must owe the boss some money and is paying for his troubles by bringing his trawler around here and doing as he is told.

So yeah! Before you ask; life's a breeze. Trouble is, I really want a hurricane to blow four particular people out my life and leave me and Henry to get on with ours. But it will never happen.

Oh my God what have I said! You were so kind to me but I shouldn't have given you this little story, because if he finds out that I said what I just said he is such a bloody nutcase that he could end up coming and doing for you. Take my advice and please, please, don't utter a word of this to anybody. It will probably not be good for you; but it will certainly be curtains for me."

"I've no reason to say a word," I said, "and I won't. I am so very sorry that you are in this desperate position and I only wish I could help you. If there is ever anything I can do for you then feel free to contact me at any time or if you can't do it yourself send a message and I'll do what I can."

"How on earth could I send a message?" She asked, "I am watched day and night and apart from on these rides I couldn't expect to see you."

"Well, in absolute emergency you could trust Callum the postman to bring a message or if you gave your little boy a note to give to Jeannie, the schoolteacher, she would give it to my friend Cat, who drives the school bus, and who in turn is her friend. It would then get to me."

"I doubt I'll need to do that, I've put up with it all these years and I'm sure I'll go on doing that for Henry's sake."

She went back to her horse and swung deftly up into the saddle and turned.

"I am really sorry for your tragic loss;" she said, "I had just assumed you were unmarried, because your house seemed a bit like a bachelor flat."

I laughed and said.

"You're quite correct I live there alone."

"Well, find somebody." She said, "you'd make a good husband; women like to be shown kindness. So, if ever hisself throws hisself off a cliff, just look out, because I might come knocking at your door. And I will let you have a proper look then!"

With that she rode off, leaving me completely depressed by her story and the thoughts of this vulnerable young woman living in such oppressive circumstances, which seemed hard to believe could really happen, in the modern era of 1964. What an awful person she was married to and what an awful life to have to lead, but I admired the fact that she was so responsible as to want to be sure to care for her little boy, despite all she had to endure.

Less than half an hour ago I had brought an innocent life into the world. By the law of averages, since its mother had not rejected it in the time since its birth, it was likely to grow up like its brethren. An early life of being mothered in still fairly harsh but improving weather conditions, a chance to go off gambling in little packs as lambs are wont to do, enjoying youth and early adolescence. It would then move on to an independent existence of grazing in beautiful fresh, clean air. I hadn't checked its gender when I delivered it, because Sally had interrupted me, but if it was a female it may go on to spend many happy years in this lovely place with only having to endure an annual bothering from a ram and the subsequent production of offspring. If it was a male it may have somewhat of a shorter existence, it's fair to say, but in that case it would have had a happy life and a quick death.

What of this little boy Henry, by the sound of things he did not have a very happy time because of the difficulties his mother experienced. In fact he sounded to have a rather difficult life and who knows what the many apparently negative influences that were around him just now would have on him as he grew up.

Somewhat in a mood of melancholy I finished my bit of fencing and returned to do some jobs around the croft house and perhaps get a bite of something to eat for lunch. I was surprised to see Cat's horse tethered outside and I went in expecting to find her in the house but she was not there. I went out and found her helping Dougie, who was down in the pit, by holding one end of a new exhaust in place whilst he fitted a bracket to hold the other end.

"Hello." Said Cat. "I was looking for you and then Dougie persuaded me to give him a hand on this job."

"What a soft touch you are," I said, "how do you think he manages when some gullible person like you is not around?"

"But, he said he couldn't be holding this end whilst he is five feet away under the car screwing a bracket to fix the other end."

"Now, that is absolutely true, but if you were not here he would have got those two beer crates which you can see one either side of the inspection pit and put them in the right position, then put that lath of wood between them to hold the other end roughly level, whilst he did that bracket. It's just that he is too lazy." She addressed Dougie.

"Would you have done that if I hadn't been here?"

To which, after a long pause, he sheepishly replied.

"Maybe"

"You're a terrible man, Dougie," said Cat "you told me you couldn't possibly do it without me!"

Dougie looked at her for a moment.

"Whell, I certainly couldn't possibly have done it as quickly, without you."

Having fixed the forward bracket Dougie walked back in the inspection pit and took the other end from Cat's hand.

"I'm going to make a piece for my lunch," I said, "you want to join me Cat?" and she nodded.

"Dougie. I'll make a piece for you, come in when you're ready." He grunted in reply.

As we walked back to the croft Cat explained the reason for her visit.

"I've come to say a big thank you because mum says that whilst dad and I were off in Inverness getting his eye done she had a long talk with you as a result of which she realised that, for a number of reasons, she ought to go and see the doctor about feeling so sleepy and achy. There isn't any clear news yet the doctor says he wants her to go to Inverness to have a number of tests. He said that she could be there for several days, even up to a week. She was reluctant to go and, from what I can tell, she told the doctor that she didn't see any point if it was something so bad that she would have to have a load of treatment and not necessarily get anywhere.

Her brother Jim got stomach cancer and they decided to operate. When they opened him up it was so extensive that they just sewed him up again and said there was nothing more they could do. Whilst there is no way of being certain about this, she felt sure that the experience of the operation shortened his life, albeit for a few months and at the same time the operation hampered his normal living just whilst he was trying to recover from it, never mind what the cancer was doing.

Our doctor then said that there was nothing on or off the table but her symptoms did not immediately suggest cancer to him. He said he had some idea and he would send a note of that through to Inverness but if he was right he was hopeful that the condition could be dealt with through medication."

Cat told me that, shortly after seeing the doctor, Morag had received a letter to say that she was required to attend in Inverness for a period of inpatient assessment at the start of August. However after consultation with the doctor, where Cat accompanied her and pointed out that her mother's propensity to sleep was getting worse she asked if anything could be done sooner and he agreed to make enquiries. A few days later another letter set the date for the hospital investigation for the first week in June and she was to present herself on Sunday, 1st June with a view to tests beginning the following day. It was arranged that Cat would drive her down to Inverness on the Sunday and return, as she was still needed to work transporting schoolchildren for a couple more weeks thereafter, because the summer holidays did not begin till early July. Alistair would then go down on the Tuesday or

Wednesday following and stay with some friends, until the results were known.

"Mum says that she would like you to come up for your supper tonight, so that she can say thank you for persuading her to go to the doctor and I can't tell you how happy dad and I feel, firstly that you have helped her to face going to seek treatment and, secondly, for the hope that it's not as bad as we had at first expected."

My afternoon was spent finishing hoeing up my potatoes, which were coming on apace, the seed potatoes had in fact come in part payment for the use of the tractor by another local crofter in lieu of cash. Another bit of new life, I thought, that's the second lot today. I reflected upon the fact that my new life was so much easier to deal with, because in essence it was a blank page upon which anything could be written. Once one gets older, life becomes more complex. Issues with which one has to engage multiply and you come to the realisation that it's very hard to sort out the complexities of your own life, never mind even beginning to consider the complexities of other people's.

In a very peculiar sort of way Linda and Carole will never become more complex for me than they were on the day that they died. On the other hand, had they lived, every day and every year would have made them and our relationships more complex. Perhaps, I thought, it may be easier to lead the single life but on the other hand loneliness can lead to increasing internal complexity which may, or may not, make life happier.

On that note of profundity, and with hoeing duties completed I went to wash my hands, round up my dog, find my bike and set off for a supper with friends.

In due course the date for Morag to go to the hospital arrived and Cat took her, delivered her and returned home. Alistair had been very worried about being away from the croft for any length of time, in this busy period of the year but Cat, Dougie and I together with a number of other neighbours, who might be said to be in our loose cooperative, all assured him that we would pitch in to help out.

Two days later Alistair set off for Inverness and we all kept our fingers crossed for a good outcome.

Significant night

On the Wednesday evening Cat's minibus pulled up outside the croft just as Dougie was walking away from his workshop *en route* to go home.

"Great news!" She shouted to us both as I came out of the door.

"I just rang dad at his friend's house and they have found out what is wrong with mum. She has got a serious thyroid deficiency and they have already started treatment, but they will release her to come home tomorrow. She will be on to a drug called Thyroxine for the rest of her life, but it will mean she lives quite normally. Isn't that great news?"

"Aye." Said Dougie, in his usual laconic style.

As for me I have to admit I was far more effusive.

"That is wonderful news it would be great to have Morag back and feeling healthy again, I'm so pleased for you and your dad as well."

Just then Mr. Roy got up and stared across the valley. As a good sheep dog he was not greatly prone to much barking but he did give two short 'woof, woofs'.

"Mr Roy says a car is coming." I interpreted.

"Speak doggie language then now do you?" Cat teased.

"No, but he does just that when any vehicle approaches and I call it his car coming message."

Sure enough a vehicle could be seen dropping down the valley towards the stream. It was the Commer van and it passed us with the three front seat occupants staring straight ahead as usual.

"What a miserable lot," I said, "they must be going fishing tonight."

"Well," said Cat, "let's have something to eat. I will rustle us up something at home if you two would care to come up and join me."

Dougie declined.

"I'll be awa hame wi' that lot nearby. Not sure about them going fishing but they are a fishy lot so I'll mind my wee hoose." And with that he trudged off.

"Stay here, I have too many eggs, plenty bread and some baked beans; if that will do for you." I said to Cat.

She chatted on whilst we busied ourselves, me setting about our meal, using some of the many eggs my chickens had presented to me whilst she, in elated mood, chatted about how this would raise a big grey cloud from over their household. Whilst we made our meal of omelette, toast and baked beans she carried on chatting on about her mother and all Morag meant to her. She had clearly, and understandably, been very worried about her mother's condition and what it would mean, not just for her, but particularly to Alistair if anything were to have been seriously wrong. How she should perhaps, as a nurse, have realised what Morag's condition might have been. For my part I tried to get her to realise that she was probably too close to the matter to be objective about it and anyway the real thing was that her mum could be treated and would regain her health.

We took our mugs of tea and moved through into my improved sitting room which I had managed to furnish with some second-hand chairs and a settee. After a while she asked me again about my visit south, apologising if she had seemed disinterested when she first asked me, before Morag's first visit to the doctor. I chatted for a while about seeing Tommy and Daisy and the rest of Linda's family and how seeing them had brought back a lot of memories. I said that I had experienced a moment of extreme emotion standing at the spot where they had fallen and I explained how Freddie had helped me move on from that. Whilst I had managed to cope with seeing Tommy, Daisy and Win and attending the Inquest, I had felt unable to return to look at the house at Boundaries Road, as I felt that would have been too much. Indeed, just talking about it made me feel emotional, as I suppose I had not let emotion come to the fore whilst I was down there, but on reflection I realised what I had enjoyed about my earlier life and equally what I had lost.

I guess a tear must have rolled down my cheek for suddenly Cat put down her mug, shuffled across the sofa and wiped the tear away with a finger and sat there looking at me. I knew in that moment that I wanted to hold her, to have some tactile contact with another human being, something I had now missed for over a year. Equally I was constrained by the realisation that I had developed some feelings for Cat and, was I to express those feelings, my guilt would increase and life could become most awfully complicated. I turned my face to look at her and looked into her eyes, she stared back into mine and in that moment we were two human beings in need of mutual comfort and so very slowly, almost waiting for rejection, she moved towards me until at last our lips met.

Everything went from my mind as I sank into the warmth of a human embrace. What a relief and release from all the pressures and tensions of the past few months. I felt it should stop but I was unable to help myself and Cat seemed eager for that human contact too, so arms were put about bodies as the kisses continued. Then a hand began to explore, her hand not mine, sexual arousal had started. I returned the compliment as my hand wandered to seek out her breast and suddenly Cat became very forcefully involved in foreplay to the point where a warning light flashed and I tried to call a halt. Perhaps an emotional argument reminding ourselves of the consequences of starting a relationship would have been effective, but I didn't use that argument I used a mechanical one, pointing out that I didn't believe I had any Durex at which she breathlessly laughed and said that I didn't need one.

My upbringing was very strict in terms of the lessons about sex. When I got to a certain age, and in the absence of a father, it had been my mother who was brave enough to outline some of the issues relating to the birds and the bees. Not that she went into the detailed descriptions of the mechanics, but she was extremely strong, amazingly for that day and age, on the issue of the importance of men using contraceptives. Both from her own nursing career and, I think, from a close friend who had had an unwanted pregnancy, she had developed a strong view about the responsibility of the male. However, I had obviously not paid sufficient attention to her strictures given that a couple of months before my planned wedding to Linda I had somewhat recklessly neglected to use a condom and the result was Carole. Thereafter, Linda and I, not wishing to have another child, because we felt we could not afford it, always used condoms and I suppose I was spurred on in this by realising that if Linda could become pregnant the first time I'd never used a condom then perhaps failing to use one would mean that I could create another pregnancy.

"Please Ewan believe me, there's no fear you will get me pregnant."

From this I assumed that she had some sort of female device fitted and my mechanical objection was therefore dismissed. And so she came at me again lips, tongues, and hands working hard and the gradual dispensation with various items of clothing. Soon it was apparent that she was urgently seeking coitus. It was all going too fast for me, not because I didn't want it to happen but because I was not used to this urgent, almost aggressive, sexual behaviour. I managed to slow her down by taking her hand and leading her up to my bed. On the way I asked her not to rush and to be more gentle, so that we could enjoy each other less frantically. She was compliant with that request and we did take our time and in the end we did join together slowly, and then more quickly, then shudderingly urgently, and ultimately noisily.

    I have always been able to sleep and have always felt very sorry for those who struggle to get enough of it, either by failing to get to sleep or by sleeping and then waking too early. This tendency to sleep deeply had only been increased by my new life, which made me physically tired as well. During the summer months I went to bed at ten in the evening, sometimes it was still light. I was usually awake not long after five most mornings having hardly turned over in the interim. So after these sexual exertions I might have been out for the count for some time but in fact in the early hours, about three o'clock, I jerked awake partially because the light was still on but mainly because Cat had just turned over and in my single bed this movement was obvious. It was a movement that I was not used to. Added to this the already dishevelled covers had been taken from me and were now only half covering Cat.

    I turned my head to glimpse a bare back and, wondering how to regain some of the covers for I felt quite chilly, I raised myself onto an elbow and looked at the sheet to see how I could extricate it from her clutched, as it was, to her breasts with the rest on the floor on her side. My eyes were drawn to her lower half and I caught sight of the end of a scar, very low on her tummy, just above the hip and going down towards her other hip. She must have sensed me moving because she turned back and saw where I was looking.

"Oh." She said, almost instantly awake.

"Scar on my belly and another on my face. What's it all about you're thinking. I ought to have told you about that before we did what we just did. But, can I tell you that I really like you and that ever since I returned to Clackmore a few years ago I have lived like a nun and I so desperately needed that shag. Whilst I hadn't planned this I feel so much better now and I would like to hope that we can do it again."

Pulling on the bedclothes we snuggled together face-to-face.

"Do I sense you have issues about whether or not you should be involving yourself with anybody else, so soon after your wife's death?" She asked, "I do hope that what just happened will not come between us because, as I said, I really like you. I realise that if we are seen to be getting together some people may have problems with that, but there's no reason why they should, because I'm a free agent and, sadly for you, and I know it's not what you would have wanted, so too are you.

However there are things you need to know about me which may affect whether or not events of this evening end up being a very enjoyable shag, which, as I said I for one was in some need of, but which we can agree to leave behind and be forgotten. Or, on the other hand, whether it might be the start of a real relationship. The decision is yours, I am not asking for a commitment from you because I am guessing that you are still in a bad place from your bereavement. As I say, I needed that bit of human contact because I have purposely avoided relationships ever since I came back. These last few years have been my convalescence from a nasty life experience. It has been easy to work on the croft and to slip back into being a member of this community, where I grew up, but I have purposely not engaged in relationship forming because I was keeping my options open as to whether or not I would decide to stay.

You know that I went nursing in Glasgow and I was there for five years and then I came back. Well the coming back was not entirely voluntary; I was in fact running away from a man who, I can now cheerfully tell you, pretty well ruined my life.

When I was growing up I led a very sheltered life until, as required by the education system here, I had to go to boarding school on the other side of the country, living in the Girls Hostel in Dornoch, from the age of just over 11 years. It was an eye-opener to come face-to-face with other young people, some of whom had very different values to those which had been instilled in me. My education was then interrupted by the polio episode and that, together with being away at school, led me to want to see more of this big wide world and nursing training seemed an acceptable reason for moving away. For my first year or two I lived in the nurse's home, but you need to know that even then I enjoyed male company. In about the third year of my five years away I met a young doctor in training and after a few dates I totally fell for him.

Unfortunately for me I started to live with him, as he was full of promises about a life to come, together. What started as a happy relationship eventually soon began to turn sour especially when his true colours were revealed when I became pregnant. Now you are the only person who knows about this scar, except the doctor and my mum. So irrespective of what happens to this relationship you need to know the truth, but if there is no future to 'us' then fine, but I implore you to never tell this bit of my story, as in this community it may brand me as a bad one, and then I may not feel I have any other option other than to move away and that may be devastating for my mum and dad.

The doctor I had teamed up with was called James and at the start of our relationship he was very gentle, both generally and in bed. He talked about our future together and about the fact that he was keen to go to America and what a wonderful life we would have, because doctors over there earn so much more money. I was totally besotted with him and only in hindsight could I see the change in our relationship over a period of time. He'd made it clear that, for the purposes of his career, a child was not something to embark upon at this stage, and he was very careful to use a condom. Remember this is all before 1962 and the advent of the pill.

As time went by his gentleness in bed gradually changed and he became rougher and I suppose I got used to his ways. Then he persuaded me to have a cervical cap fitted, something which you may have heard of, sometimes it is called a Dutch Cap. This then meant he could dispense with his own need to fumble about and take precautions which seemed even more exciting to him and his demands on me became more rough and excessive. Eventually there was an accident and this led to my pregnancy. To say that he was not best suited is a complete understatement, he was raging angry and almost without any consideration of my views, he made some enquiries amongst his doctor mates to effectively procure an abortion.

Despite his anger about the pregnancy he still seemed to want me around. Looking back he seems to have seen me as his possession and as such I was still part of his plans for America. He made out that this termination was for the best, because it was for our future together. Although his attitude to the pregnancy had disappointed me I was still stupid enough to believe that we could have a life and a family together once we got on our feet in America, but at the moment having a child was not the best timing. Cutting a long story short, and the story does involve cutting, I had what might be described as a backstreet abortion and there were complications. I developed a severe infection internally and, to put no finer point on it, I had to have a complete hysterectomy to resolve the botched abortion. Clearly the surgeon who did my operation was aware of what had happened, but I think James managed to get across that it was me who had wanted to get rid of the child, and had gone off on my own to try and achieve that end. In any event, there was no comeback and after recuperating at the home of a friend of his in Perth, I returned to him and to work. Again he had managed to smooth things over at work; it was obviously known that I had had a hysterectomy but not the reason why.

So far as mum and dad were concerned I was working on a secondment in Perth and when I wrote home I just made it sound as though I was enjoying a bit of a change. After a couple of months I returned from Perth to live with James, until I started work again. Initially he was very gentle and caring but I did notice, what I should have noticed before, namely that he remained very possessive. Then as, at least temporarily, he could not indulge in sexual aggressiveness that began to take other forms and, on occasion when he was angry, he would hit me. I knew from the very first smack I got that I had made a mistake by teaming up with this man but I guess, like many other women do, I tried to excuse it as a mistake on his part one that hopefully would not be repeated.

But it was.

Eventually his possessiveness and his violence became too much and so I told him I was leaving and he went mad and after a blazing row he completely lost it and smashed a bottle and deliberately glassed me, hence the scar on my face. I threatened him with the police and he realised that he had gone too far and I also said that I would inform the consultant under whom he was working. He suddenly realised that by overstepping the mark he had put himself in a very vulnerable position and like all possessive bullies he was suddenly scared for himself. So I got him to agree that he would let me go and not pursue me and in return I would say nothing. Of course he quickly agreed to that but I was not so foolish as to think that he would let me go so easily, possessive people do not easily surrender what they possess.

So I told him that I would go straightaway that night and see a very close friend, whom I could trust, and I would tell her about what he had done to me, of his possessiveness and his violence and in particular the injury to my face. I said I would put all his violence to me including the glassing in writing and I would get her to sign and date it as a witness. Then I would get a solicitor to keep the letter and, if he were ever to approach me again, I would ensure that the letter got to all relevant authorities. I did exactly that and then got myself stitched up, offered my resignation, worked my notice and decided to come home to Clackmore, to put distance between us and to allow myself some support whilst recovering from my wounds, both physical and mental. Hearing what has happened to other women I think I was lucky and he has never come near me again.

When I got home I gave as the reason for my resignation as being related to the scar on my face, which was so obvious. My cover story was that I'd been working in the accident and emergency department which, in Glasgow in those days was often plagued by drunks, and my story was that one of these had glassed me and run off when he realised what he had done and could not be traced. I told people that this really upset me and I felt I needed a break before I could return to nursing. As a cover story this was brilliant, as it not only worked for all the people I knew it also worked for dad and I had thought worked for mum too.

Unfortunately one day she walked in on me when I was half dressed and she saw the same scar that you saw today. I told her the whole story and we cried together for a long time, but we managed to get ourselves together before dad returned home that evening and up until today she's the only one that knows the real full story.

Then I suppose that I got lucky, because after some months of just working on the croft, the school transport part time job came up and that was really great. More recently the locum district nurse work has become available to me. But I was only ever going to stay for a while. I have stayed that bit longer because I have been worried about mum, but now my options are open again.

So you can see that what you are dealing with here is some seriously damaged goods and I wanted you to know that. I've enjoyed tonight, and if you want we could do it again, but at this stage you need to know what you are in danger of taking on and I will quite understand if you decide it's all far too complicated."

"Poor you," I said, pulling her close, "sometimes I feel very sorry for myself, especially when people take a sort of pitying line about the loss of my two girls. And, if indeed I am wounded, then it is a wound relating to my having to deal with the suffering of others, albeit ones I cared about, whereas your wound is related to your own physical and mental suffering and so much harder to bear I would imagine.

I would like us to continue to get to know one another, and I think maybe there is the potential for a future for us together, but I feel that I just don't want to rush into something that either of us would subsequently regret. I was thinking just the other day that I knew you as a work colleague and seeing all that you could do made me admire you very much and to value what was, at that time, a happy working relationship. Like you, I am glad that last night happened and I want to know more about you and to spend more time with you."

"Even though now you've heard I'm damaged goods?" She asked.

"I am damaged too, just damaged in a different way and because we've both been damaged we need to go slowly. I couldn't bear it if I fully committed myself to you only to find that you felt, after all, that this was not what you wanted. Equally I suspect that if you……."

'Car coming', or rather 'woof, woof.' Barked Mr Roy, who must've stolen upstairs at some point and gone to sleep on the landing instead of his usual kennel in the porch.

"Oh!" I said, "I must've forgotten to put the ruddy dog out last night."

Cat giggled.

"I wonder if he sees his master in a new light this morning?"

At that point there was a bang outside and moments later the sound of a revving engine and men's voices. There is no window at the back of the house, for it faces onto the weather side of the bay, so there was no way we could see what might be happening on the road. After a while with much clashing of gears and revving, eventually doors slammed and sounds of a vehicle being driven off could be heard.

"The Commer boys?" Said Cat, "well according to my watch its three thirty seven in the morning and we have a good hour or so until we have to get up. The choices seem to be to get up and get a good early start for the day, or, see if we can improve on our last night's performance with some more practice."

She looked at me with a huge grin on her face.

"Come on Mr Roy," I ordered, jumping out of bed, "you need to go out."

"Then what?" Cat asked.

As I grabbed the dog and took him towards the stairs.

"More practice."

I shouted over my shoulder.

Potential repercussions

A moment of sexual intimacy between two persons who are not in an established relationship, irrespective of the fact that the act is consensual and in private, is rarely inconsequential. If either, or both, of the parties is in another relationship there is the question of how to manage this infidelity. If the sex has been paid for then that may limit the consequences, unless like Cabinet Minister Mr Profumo just the year before, the liaison is discovered and one of his contacts other clients was a Russian spy. But for ordinary folk, like you and me, there are consequences on a number of minor levels for even if we are not otherwise encumbered the expectations of one party may differ from another.

For Linda and I our coming together, albeit in the 1950s when sex before marriage was still frowned upon, only became inconsequential because we were, and remained, completely in love and the planned wedding went ahead. The consequences given that Linda became pregnant might have been horrendous if, for whatever reason, either she, or I, had changed our minds. For Cat the opposite was true and she had fallen for this James but then he had ill-used her and she was now wrestling with the aftermath of that. But in those early days of a relationship it is all too easy to start without giving sufficient attention to potential consequences. If you are not careful the cat can truly be out of the bag once the (whatever you call it) is out of the trousers.

The process of beginning and going on to consummate a relationship may engender a drug like effect on the behaviour and demeanour of the parties. For me the physical consequences of this most wonderful coming together were personally very satisfying and it was quite difficult to wipe the smile off my face. It is not hard for those around you to notice this changed behaviour and so it was when Dougie arrived for work the following morning to find Cat's minibus just driving away and me standing watching.

To his credit, Dougie made no comment in relation to what he had observed but instead beckoned me to follow him down the sloping rough driveway towards the tarmacked road.

"Look at this." He said, indicating a lot of churned up sand at the edge of the road which was also spilling onto the road itself.

"Looks like them eejits in the van have run off the road here."

I could see what he meant, the vehicle had got too close to the edge of the road dropped off into the sandy ground beside it. It had operated like those sand traps on the lower parts of steep hills to slow a vehicle whose brakes had failed and had made it hard for the van to gain traction.

"Well," I said, "I heard some noise last night about three, some voices, revving engine and some doors banging I guess it must have been them." Dougie nodded.

"They were away from the moorings about nine or so last evening and I thought I heard them back of one. Then there was noise and sounds of loading the van which seemed to go on for ages, but there was quite a swell coming into the bay and maybe they had trouble landing their catch. I have to say Ewan that I feel there is something funny going on here. How many months is it that the trawler has been here? And it only goes out every three or four weeks and then only for a few hours. I've asked about in Lochinver but nobody is seeing them land fish. So what's it all about?"

After the exertions and interruptions of the night I was not desperately motivated, as I normally would have been, to start work. So I suggested to Dougie that we went up to the house made a brew and talk about the case of the mystery trawler.

"Well," I said when we had brewed up, "let's consider what we know, although it's fairly limited. The trawler only arrived shortly after the new residents came to Newton Lodge. Since then we know the telephone has been connected up there because we found that out from Callum who knew the Post Office lads who were at work installing the line. We know that the men with the Commer van live at the Lodge and that they and all the residents there seem to keep themselves to themselves. None of them have made any attempt to become part of the community. We also know that the trawler skipper too stays at the Lodge."

"Well according to Callum," Dougie added, "originally the skipper stayed there all the time and got letters postmarked Macduff, but more recently, from what he says, it may be that he leaves the Lodge for a while and I have worked out that is probably not long after the trawler has done a trip."

I told Dougie of my experience with the Commer driver on the evening I was returning from Lochinver with Cat. Their aggressive and rude behaviour on that occasion, was mirrored in the way they drove around with set looking faces and never offering thanks to anyone who gave way to them. Finally, and respecting the confidence which had been entrusted to me on the day I was spoken to by Sally, I simply said to Dougie that after I had rescued her, subsequent to her fall from the horse, her husband had come to collect her and was a most obnoxious and aggressive man.

For all of this we agreed that perhaps we should find out a little more about the trawler itself. As Dougie had already explained he'd been asking around in Lochinver, they'd not been landing or selling any fish and nobody had seen the skipper. So he had talked to the other skippers about the boat itself which apparently was named Deveronvale 36. The letters and number on the side indicated that it was registered as a fishing vessel in Peterhead, but one of the skippers knew that it had been bought by someone who had been previously fishing out of Macduff. That of course tied in with the postmark on letters that Callum reported having delivered to the Lodge. We thought that the best way forward was to make some more enquiries and the logic was that one of us needed to go to Macduff.

If somebody was writing to him it would likely be a wife or parent and maybe we could get some information by contacting them. The problem was that the trawler had been out last night and, according to Callum, the skipper seemed to go on a week's leave before returning.

By now it was high summer, the first crop of hay had been gathered and sheep shearing was over. Animal husbandry was at a fairly slack time and aside from peat cutting and a second crop of hay, to be gathered in due course, things were not too hectic about the croft. So we thought the best way forward was for me to wait for about two weeks and then make a trip to Macduff, to see what I could discover that would either add to, or take away from, our concerns. Provisionally I set Tuesday 23rd June for my departure.

I got up to take the empty mugs to the kitchen and I heard Dougie's chair push back and I assumed that he would have gone out of the door and up to the barn but when I turned after rinsing the mugs he was stood by the door looking at me.

"Yon lassie needs looking after. By my reckoning she's had enough hurt in her life to not need any more."

This brought me up short, and no doubt I went red in the face, but I gave back.

"I have no intention of hurting 'yon lassie' as you call her."

"No, maybe no intention but be sure you din'na let it happen. When Roddy died I was very unhappy because I'd lost a friend. Then you came along and even just after a year I have a better going on with you than I did with Roddy. I want that to stay as it is, but my first loyalty is to Alistair and Morag, as they have been my only other friends and we've been close since I moved here. They would do anything to make sure that Catriona was happy and they'd be fierce to anyone who made her unhappy. If you make her unhappy then all your work for this year or so will not be enough to save you.

My life has no been straightforward. Once upon a time I spent several months in an asylum, how I got there I don't remember because I was out of my heid after my mother died. One day Dr Rennison, who was the psychiatrist who admitted me there in the first place and who was in charge overall, called me into his office to ask me what plans I would have if he was to let me out. I told him that I could come here and he said that was good, because a man with my problems would do better with solitude, if he could get it. He told' me that I had something of a personality disorder which I would have forever and that superimposed on top of that, and what brought me to the hospital, was a reactive depression due to my mother's death.

He said that when he admitted me and looked into my eyes he had seen a lost soul, but in recent weeks my eyes had told him a different story, not necessarily a happy ending, because I would still have problems for the rest of my life unless I could find solitude and a small circle of good friends.

And when that lassie came home from Glasgow I looked into her eyes and I knew, in the same way as Dr Rennison when he first saw me, that she was a troubled soul. Maybes it was the glassing but maybe it was more. It seems to me that as time has gone by, those eyes have shown her to recover. I will keep looking at her eyes and if I see any hurt at all coming into them, then I will be knocking on your door."

With that he turned and stomped off.

To say I was stunned doesn't even approach the way I felt as he departed. This was the longest speech I had ever heard Dougie make. I recognised straightaway that he had made it because he needed just a few friends and it was critical to him that they were all okay. Realising that Cat had probably spent the night at my croft house he was giving me a very severe warning about all that I might lose if I were to cause her any hurt. His perception of Cat's state of mind, when she returned home, suggested that he was of the view that the one incident of glassing during the course of her work may not have been enough to account for the state in which he felt her to be.

It also told me very forcibly that I was treading on very dangerous ground in getting mixed up emotionally with another member of this very tight knit, interdependent working community.

The smile had most certainly been wiped off my face and in its place there came feelings of acute anxiety that I had done the wrong thing. On top of that there returned the feelings of guilt about having been unfaithful to Linda. But, on the other hand, over a year had passed since we had laid her in the ground and how long was it proper for me to have to honour her by remaining chaste? I had not planned to seduce Cat, and in fact if there was any seduction it was more on her part the mine, but I should have shown greater resolve and not responded.

Guilt.

Guilt.

Guilt.

And more guilt.

Would it go away?

Should it go away?

Confused?

You bet.

Ask me what I did that day and, like the time immediately after I'd learnt of Linda's death, I would have no recollection, but somehow I got through to the early evening and Dougie departed homeward with a nondescript nod.

I decided that I had to face into Cat's family, as the longer I left it the more difficult it would be, so I decided to cycle up and see if Morag had got home. Alistair's car was outside and in fact he saw me arrive and came out to greet me. As he approached I fought back the thought of how differently he might have approached me if he was aware that just twelve or so hours ago I was in bed with his daughter.

"Isn't it wonderful news!" He beamed. I shook him warmly by his proffered hand and enthusiastically concurred.

"It's such a relief," he said, "of course I don't want her to be ill at all, but to know that it's something that can be treated and that effectively it should not make any difference to her life once she is recovered a little bit more, is wonderful. Anyway, come away in."

We went in and Morag was sitting at the table and clearly a meal had just been completed. Alistair said he would take the cases upstairs and Cat was in the kitchen, but put her head round the door and broadly smiled and mouthed a 'Hello Ewan' and, given that her mother had her back to her, she blew me a little kiss and then returned to the kitchen. I smiled and turned to Morag who looked at me and indicated a chair opposite her and waited till the other two were about their tasks.

"Whilst they are busy I just wanted to say thank you for that conversation we had and for not saying any of the stuff that I told you."

"That's quite all right," I said, "I'm so pleased that things have turned out the way they have."

After Alistair came back in carrying some mugs of tea and Cat completed the washing up we sat for a while over our brews and Morag told the tale of how she had gone on at the hospital.

She said how worried she'd been on the journey down, although she'd slept a good bit of the way and even more worried in the hospital itself wondering what the outcome was going to be. From the outset though, the doctor she saw was fairly confident that this was not a matter that she needed to worry too much about. But he said that he did need to complete some tests, in order to be certain of what the G.P. in Lochinver had already suggested might be the issue. It only took to the end of the second day for the diagnosis to be confirmed and for her to be started on some treatment. She said she'd noticed a difference already but that the doctor had suggested that it would take a month or two before she felt fully up to her old self again. She would have to return for some more tests in a few weeks to ensure that the level of the medication was correct, but other than that they hoped it would all be plain sailing.

It was a very happy household and I was quite content to enjoy the mood. However, I had to stop myself from looking at Cat too frequently, for fear that a Cheshire cat grin might appear on my face. By about nine o'clock I felt it was time for me to make a move and having said my 'cheerio's' I moved to the door to go outside to collect my bike and my dog to go home. Cat followed me on the pretext of having to get something from the minibus.

"Are you still okay after last night?" She asked.

"I'm all right, by and large, but I have to tell you that Dougie must have put two and two together when he saw your mini bus leaving this morning and he has issued me with a dire warning about the consequences of my hurting you, in any shape or form. I know he was serious because he made what, I suspect, must have been the longest speech that he has ever made this last twenty years or more. I should also tell you that he thought you looked so devastated when you came home and that he was surprised that just a Glasgow glassing was all that was involved. I said nothing of course, but it shows how perceptive he must be. Anyway, what about you?"

"I'm absolutely fine," she said, "and I'm sorry about Dougie, but he really is great friends with mum and dad and, thinking back on it, when I came home he was forever fussing me like an old hen. Encouraging me in all sorts of ways, like taking me out on his boat and the like. I am sorry that at such an early stage he's noticed our friendship and said what he has to you, so maybe it's important we have a talk. How about if I tell mum and dad that there's a band down in Lochinver on Saturday night, which there may be anyway although I don't know that, and we could use it as an opportunity to spend some time together."

I nodded, and the date was fixed.

On the Saturday I collected Cat and we drove off towards Lochinver, on the way there we decided that we were not that bothered about a drink, but a chance to be together and talk would be really nice so I turned off and we drove down the road to Achmelvich beach. We got there about half past eight and it was a beautiful evening and the sun would not be setting until well gone ten o'clock. After sitting in the van for a while talking and engaging in an occasional bit of hand holding and necking, we went for a walk on the beautiful sands with a benign sea rippling gently onto the shore.

"Do you think Dougie was implying that he would be saying something to mum and dad?" She asked me.

"Oh no, nothing of the sort," I replied, "it was a man-to-man warning telling me to be responsible and treat you kindly or there would be consequences. The implication was that he would withdraw from our working together and would then set about telling local people that I had misused you, which of course would presumably mean my life here would be untenable."

"Wow," she replied, "that's pretty heavy stuff."

"Yes, but it shows how much he cares about your mum and dad and you and I can understand that. But it's also set me back a bit, I have to confess, because I guess I have a big guilt complex and that part of me keeps telling me that what we did the other night was disloyal to Linda. Now I know that's not true, but perhaps my distance from Linda is of a much shorter span than your distance from James. Equally you were no doubt glad to see the back of James, whereas that was not true for me so far as Linda was concerned."

"So do you want to put us on hold then?" She asked.

"Oh heavens no!" I replied, "I did not plan for the other night to happen but from my perspective it came about in two ways. You were tremendously relieved and delighted that your mother's health was going to be restored, whereas you had worried that her symptoms were signalling her demise. For my part, I have to tell you, that I am very fond of your mum and that she and I have talked about a lot of things, especially at the time she thought she was very ill and so on one level I shared your delight and I still do. But also I had come to enjoy the company of this tall Amazonian-like creature who was part of my working and social life. I hesitate to say that my feelings were developed enough to make a move but I guess, looking back, they were beginning down that road. The celebration of your mother's reprieve fuelled my elation as well."

I turned to her and saw tears falling from her eyes.

"I'm sorry," I said, "I didn't mean to upset you."

"Well you have," she replied, "but it's upset of a nice kind because you are telling me that you had some feelings, however limited, for me and whilst I'm big and brash and was ready to live with a one-night stand, as I told you the other night, I guess there was some hope that maybe there could be more of a connection between us.

Before your uncle Roddy died I was thinking it was getting towards time for me to move on again, although I never said that to mum and dad. I felt that James was behind me but I couldn't see anybody around here who could offer me what I was looking for. All the lads around my age are locals, I know them, all their abilities and their indiscretions and there was nobody who sparked my interest in any way. I was careful, therefore, not to encourage any of them. Yet on the other hand I recognise in myself that despite, or is it even because, I can now not have children, that I do have a need for a relationship which involves sex as well as companionship.

I was on the verge of considering returning to nursing, by joining one of the Armed Forces on the basis that maybe I would be able to get home more often than in an ordinary nursing job. Just as I was about to announce this decision, and put it in train, the locum district nurse job came up and I saw that as a sign that perhaps I should stay a little longer.

Then you came into our lives and to start with it was just interesting to watch some silly young man who knew nothing about crofting try to pick up the mantle of the amazing Roddy Mathieson. And yes, before you ask, there was a degree of pity for your situation as well as your ignorance of all things crofting and country. But, a bit like you, working together brought me to understand a little bit more about this funny Englishman and again like you, more recently I had wondered if, and how, a relationship between us might work. Even so the events of the other night were spontaneous in the way that you suggested."

    We walked in silence for a while just holding hands. I guess each of us had said a little bit about the fact that there had been outline thoughts of the possibility of a relationship, even before the events of a few nights ago.

    "So where do we go from here?" I said at last and the words hung in the air for quite some time before I said.

    "Do you think we should go quite slowly with this?"

    "Well the obvious answer is yes, in terms of anyone apart from your guard dog and Dougie knowing, but in a community like this, the coincidental change in both of our moods will not go unnoticed. So for that reason I suspect it's better for us to say that we are, to use that old-fashioned term 'walking out' and then we could take more opportunities to have evenings like this."

    "Yes." I said, "I agree, but how do you think your mum and dad will take it?"

    "Dad I'm not sure about, like all fathers he is bound to be a bit protective and whilst he is not up to the sort of hard word delivery that Dougie was able to impart to you this morning, he will no doubt say something to suggest that you keep your zipper up." She laughed and then went on, "but mum will be delighted she thinks the sun shines from your proverbial and if dad has any qualms at all she will talk him round."

"Okay," I said, "so we take it very gently both for the right reasons and the reason that it is the correct thing for us to do and certainly as far as our family and friends are concerned."

"Yes," she said, "we must take things nice and slowly; but there is one condition."

"What's that?" I asked.

"Well I am desperate, and I use that word advisedly, that albeit we're going slowly with the relationship overall, that we must find the odd occasion to involve ourselves in what I believe we called some of those practice sessions, the other night."

I grinned and shook my head.

"I'm glad you agree." She said with a wide smile.

In order to move to other things, I decided to say something about the other subject that Dougie and I had discussed.

"You know the other night there was that noise from the road in the early morning?" I said and she nodded, "and do you remember that van, the one we had the confrontation with the evening we'd been into Lochinver? Well Dougie and I feel that there is something funny going on."

I went on to share with her the concern Dougie and I had about the unusual arrangements for the trawler and its infrequency of putting to sea. I also explained that its arrival occurred not long after Newton Lodge was in receipt of its new residents, which included the idiots with the van. I also mentioned my meeting with the horse rider and the arrogant and aggressive husband who came to retrieve her. Finally, I told her that Dougie and I had decided we would find out a little more about this trawler and its ownership. So I asked her if she would mind looking after Mr Roy for a couple of days, as she had done when I made my big trip south.

"I don't mind that," she said, "I would offer to come with you, but school is still on and I do not like to have to ask for time off."

I said I thought it was probably best, in any event, that I go alone as I was only thinking of a quick trip, no more than a couple of days. Also, if we went away together now, that would sort of suggest that we were becoming more than just friends and I thought we'd agreed that we would keep it quiet until we both knew more about where we wanted to go.

"You're right," she said, "but maybe you should have a cover story for your trip."

I thought for a minute and then suggested that I could say that my friend Billy was coming to Glasgow for work and I was making a quick trip down to see him as he was hoping to emigrate soon and the chances of our meeting again would be limited. She thought that would be sufficient. It was passed ten o'clock by now and we thought we had better get on home even though it was still daylight and the sinking sun still had another few minutes to run before it disappeared below the horizon.

She suggested that I should also have a cover story for my journey as to why I might be asking about this trawler when I got to Macduff, if I didn't want the enquiries linked back to here. We agreed that I would travel, under an alias, in my work old suit with my small suitcase and given my previous work, I could say I was an accountant working for a big firm and I was on my way to do a surprise audit. If asked where, I could say I cannot say or it would not be a surprise, and perhaps suggest that the business in question was in the locality and that could cover either Macduff itself, or allude to Banff just across the river.

Two weeks later Cat took me to the main road out of Lochinver fairly early in the morning and waited until she saw me get a lift. Arriving in Lairg I bought a ticket to Banff. I was in Inverness by early afternoon and then I took an Aberdeen bound train, alighting at Elgin to take the local service to Banff. In the mid-afternoon we left Elgin in a fairly quiet three carriage train. We quickly got out into the countryside and I was approached by the guard who, after inspecting my ticket, was happy to get into conversation.

"Is this your first journey on this line he asked?" In an accent that I could not quickly identify I only knew that it was not Scottish accent, and I told him it was.

"Well please enjoy it because only a few months ago, in March, the government decided that stupid man, Dr. Beeching, was right and lots of smaller lines are to be closed including this one. In fact the last bit of the line from Tillynaught to Banff will close to passengers in just over a week, so you are going to be one of the last to do the whole trip. I am not a native of these parts, but my wife is, and I moved up here from Wales a few years ago and it is the most beautiful part of the world, and this line is really lovely."

By this time we were out into some fairly undulating farming countryside.

"Over to your right there is the town of Llanbryde which, as a Welshman, I always find quite funny with the double 'L' it almost ought to be Welsh. Some say it could be of Pictish origin as that could be translated as the Church Place of St Bride. Now I find it even more amusing since I originate in Porthcawl and my uncle lived in a nearby village called St Brides Major. And that little hamlet we are just passing across the fields is Muir of Lochs where my in-laws live, look!" He said pointing, "that first cottage with the little windmill."

"Why a windmill" I asked.

"It's over a little well," he replied, and went on, "Anyway, soon we will be stopping in Garmouth. As soon as we leave there, look out, because we'll be crossing the River Spey which is quite wide at this point because it's only a mile or so from entering the sea. Then it's on across a lovely flat area, until we come to Port Gordon and on to Buckie. We then go inland a little ways before you will need to move to the other side of the carriage and look out on the left hand side at the splendid view as we cross the Cullen viaduct. Don't miss it, it's a wonderful view. We lose the sea for a bit but you will see it again as we come into Banff station, which is the end of the line. Anyway I do hope you enjoy this trip, as I say savour it, you may not have another chance and that is a great shame."

He was right; the view as we came into Cullen was breath-taking, particularly over the viaduct, which straddles the main street of the town which is on one side with the sea and harbour on the other. I enjoyed the whole journey, the more so because I knew what to look out for. But eventually we chugged into Banff about four o'clock in the afternoon.

I asked at the ticket barrier for directions for MacDuff and the elderly porter shook his head and said that I should not be going there.

"Why not?" I asked.

"It's just ma wee joke," he said, "there was a great rivalry between the toons in days gone by and as you go you will see that there is a big kirk tower on the hill, wi' a clock in it. After one of they squabbles between the toons the clock face pointing towards Banff was removed, so that we over here coulda'na use their clock to tell the time from it. It's just ma silly joke. Anyways, follow round the sea passing the harbour and up the side of the river Deveron. Go over across the river bridge and down beside the river and in about twenty five minutes to half an hour walking you will be there."

I thanked him for his directions and after a leisurely stroll, noticing the clock tower, with its missing face on the Banff side, as I passed, I walked into the little port of MacDuff. Despite the sunny day, there was a very stiff breeze blowing, and unusually for the summer it was coming from the north, and the tide was well in. I stopped to watch a trawler which was heading for the narrow harbour entrance and for about 20 minutes was mesmerised by the incredible skill of the master of the vessel.

The waves were coming in towards me as I stood looking straight down the harbour entrance and the vessel was pitching as it approached the narrow harbour breakwaters. I was facing that entrance and to my left was a small amount of harbour leading to a boatyard; to my right the seawall came in towards me and then stopped, offering an entrance to an inner harbour. In fact, from the first inner harbour you could go through to another beyond. The width of both the outer and inner harbour entrances was only about three or four times the width of the incoming vessel itself, yet on it came straight towards me. Pitching wildly in the rough sea it came in between the outer walls and when it got to the correct point, still pitching but also moving quite fast, suddenly, as the helm went up, the vessel spun to the left and smoothly moved into the first inner harbour and toward what looked to be a fish dock area.

An older man had come to join me as the vessel approached this point and we had watched together for a few minutes, in companionable silence, but as the boat went into the inner harbour he turned to me.

"Marvellous seamanship don't you think." To which I could do none other than heartily agree.

"Just visiting?" He questioned, looking at my suitcase, and I nodded, "and will you be needing some lodgings for the night?"

He looked at me, assessing my likely socio-economic status and obviously decided not to refer me to the hotel, which was behind us, or indeed to any other, but said that a Mrs Campbell, whom he knew, took in lodgers at a very reasonable rate. I said that I would be very pleased if he could direct me there, to which he replied that he would be happy to take me there himself as his house was that way. First, however, he indicated that he was just going to call in across the road, indicating a fisherman's hostelry which, I rightly suspected, might have sawdust on the floor, and I took this is as his none too subtle suggestion that for his advising me about cheap lodgings he might be rewarded with a dram. And he was.

One dram led to another, although I stuck to beer, and in due course, after work, a number of fishermen and shipwrights from the local shipyard came in and after a while I felt I was able to ask about Deveronvale 36. By great good fortune a man called Stuart, who had helped the skipper sail the trawler round to our inlet and help establish its moorings, was there and, as I was buying, he was talking. It seems that the skipper was a Graham Thompson, who came originally from Hull and had worked out of that port as a deckhand on trawlers. He moved to Arbroath for a while and married a local lass and they had two young children, girl twins. But he had a gambling problem, it seems, and things were not going well for him, then all of a sudden, here he was buying a trawler from a skipper who was retiring. His wife and kids came to join him and they lived in Clergy Street, in the only house with a green door.

Stuart, the deckhand who had helped Graham Thompson, went on to say that he said that although he needed the money, because the boat he usually worked on was in for a refit, he could not get off the Deveronvale quick enough. To get from Macduff to its present moorings required going north up the east coast of Scotland, around the north coast via the Pentland Firth and then turning south at Cape Wrath and then down our west coast. It took three days to get round to its present mooring because there was a bit of engine trouble, which necessitated a stop in Wick. Throughout the trip Graham hardly said a word and looked like an unhappy man, which Stuart thought was a surprise, given he had just got his own boat. Stuart had asked Graham what he was going to do for a crew, but the latter had said he had some old mates, from Arbroath, who would join him in a few days. Asked why he was laying moorings in this inlet he basically told Stuart to mind his own business. When they had got all safely done they were picked up by a van and Stuart had to ride in the back till they got to some big house. There he was paid in cash and one of the van men drove him to get the post bus in Lochinver. On that journey the van driver was pretty silent and made it clear that conversation was not encouraged.

 The tale had come out fairly easily and it did not seem sensible to ask too many questions and, to their reasonable request as to why I had any interest in the matter, I said a work colleague had been on a cycling holiday on the west coast and taken a wrong turning onto a dead end and was surprised to see a trawler moored in a narrow inlet and had just made a mental note of the name. Conversation moved on and my guide took me in due course to my lodgings, a small house run by his widowed sister. I signed her little book as James Brown. She also wanted my address. Something I had not planned for, so I made up a fictitious address in Richmond.

In my Spartan room I considered what I had learned and thought I had probably got enough information and could leave first thing in the morning. The man Thompson had fishing experience but he was also a man with a possible gambling problem. Then suddenly he is the proud owner of a trawler. So if our man at Newton Lodge was really into something less than legal then it was quite possible that he had need of a trawler and someone to sail it but that someone would need to be a person over whom he could hold sway. The trawler could have been bought for Thompson on that basis. But as I thought on, I had in my mind's eye the face of a man, sat between two minders in the front of the van, looking straight ahead and also looking quite disconsolate.

My recollection was that at the beginning, Thompson did not seem to have been allowed home, but now he was getting short home leaves and in the early days a lot of mail had come to him presumably from his family. If indeed Thompson was a reluctant employee, then he might be a source of information in due course. But in order to get that information, given that it would appear that nobody at Newton Lodge was supposed to speak to anybody local, then maybe I would need some more personal information, as a reason for making contact with him.

I had arranged an early call for the following day and by eight was bidding farewell to my hostess. My somewhat battered suit and tie did give me the vague appearance of some minor official and so I proceeded to Clergy Street and sought out the only front door painted in green, out of about 30 houses; I recognised the shade of green as the same as the boot topping on the trawler at home. I knew from experience that people treated officialdom with great caution and so, before knocking on the door, I went to a local shop and purchased a bottle of milk and a girls magazine called 'Jackie' which, only after I had purchased it, did the shopkeeper reveal that this was a new magazine which only came out the year before and was for teenage girls, so perhaps a bit too old for the girls I was going to see. I stowed my purchases carefully inside my suitcase, so that the bottom of the bottle would be at the lower part of the case when I was carrying it.

Returning to the green door I knocked and in due course it was opened by a fairly careworn young woman and I could hear the voices of some small children in the background.

"Mrs. Thompson?" I enquired.

"Yes." she said with suspicion.

"I'm from the Council Education Department and records say that you have two children and that you moved here from Arbroath." She nodded and I went on, "I've come to see why they're not at school."

She replied that her children were twins and only three years of age and not yet old enough for school. I pretended to be flustered at this point.

"Oh dear the information must be wrong. But as luck would have it we have also got a scheme of providing some fresh milk to children under school age and I think I've got the last bottle in my bag."

I rummaged and produced the bottle, which looked as though it would be quite welcome. Her continuing suspicion was temporarily assuaged by the production of this gift and, as I had hoped, she dropped her guard a bit, and soon I was able to discover that she was Mary and the children were Jenny and Jess. At this I said I would amend council records, with that I turned and left. I did not look back before I reached the corner of the street, but I sensed that this lady was now quite confused and her suspicions were beginning to resurface. I still hoped the bottle of milk would mollify her, but I could almost feel that, after some discussions about free milk with her neighbours, the Council Education Department may be getting a visit later.

But I was off to catch a train.

What now?

My return journey was fairly straightforward, retracing my steps on the train and then, via a couple of lifts, I was deposited at the junction of the road down to my croft. It was late afternoon and I called in to collect Mr Roy. Cat offered me a lift in the minibus for the last bit of the journey and, having had to walk quite a bit between my lifts on the way back, I was glad to accept. I managed to dodge some of the more detailed enquiries from Alistair and Morag about my so called 'visit to Glasgow to meet my old friend Billy', but said that it had only been brief but it was good to be able to say goodbye to somebody who had been a friend for many years and who was soon to emigrate.

Cat was eager to know about my trip, but I said I thought Dougie would be at work in the garage, so I suggested waiting so that I could tell them both together. On arrival at my house Dougie emerged and we all went into the house on the promise of some tea.

"I'll tell you the story when I have got the kettle on," I said to them both, as Dougie wiped his hands on an oily rag. As we sat round my kitchen table, waiting for the kettle to boil, I related the story of my visit and the information I had garnered. I then went to make the tea whilst they discussed what I had told them.

"Certainly looks like yon trawler skipper is here under sufferance." Dougie said, as I returned with the drinks.

"Okay," said Cat, "he might owe the man at Newton Lodge some money, or a favour, and he may be working that off somewhat reluctantly that's not really a crime."

"No," replied Dougie, "but if somebody had bought, or helped him to buy a boat, so that he could repay a former debt, given the value of the boat he would surely be working very hard at the fishing; but, as we have seen, he is not."

"Well," I said, "sitting on that train I've had a lot of time to think and three previously unconnected bits of information have sort of converged in my mind. The first thing is, and this must stay just between the three of us, that I have learnt something of the nature of your man at the Lodge. When his wife, Sally, had a riding accident down on the beach she walked up to my house with her lame horse and I attended to her."

"Did you now," said Cat in a mock stern voice, "would you care to expand on your concept of 'attending' to a rather striking young woman!"

"I told you before, she had grazed her arm and I put some TCP on it whilst we waited for her husband to come."

"I hope it was just her arm," said Cat with a broad grin on her face," I've only seen her out riding or collecting her lad from school and she always has plenty of war paint on, and, as one of my former nursing friends would say she looks 'all tits, teeth and toenails', but then she was married to a sailor and they have sayings for everything."

"As I was saying," ignoring her wind up, "her husband turned up and was pretty nasty to her and dragged her off in a very threatening manner. I just thought him a pig or idiot and gave relatively little thought to it until some weeks later she made it in her way to approach me, when I was mending some fences, to say thank you for my efforts. From that, in course of what I think may have been a somewhat careless conversation on her part, I learnt that she seems to be trapped in a most unhappy relationship and were it not for her little boy, Henry, she would have been long gone."

"You canny interfere between a man and his missus." Said Dougie.

After this exchange I noticed Cat's face muscles tighten but she said nothing so I hurried on.

"My sentiments also and I don't want to. But what it does say is that this man is probably a nasty piece of work, and quite recently I was told about another nasty piece of work. When I went down to the Inquest in March I met my old friend Billy, who had got himself into some trouble that he was just about to extricate himself from. His dad had been a spiv during the war and, when Billy was working for him, he was just an ordinary run-of-the-mill wheeler and dealer. However, he ended up working for somebody who seems to be something more like a gangster and the business turned from more than ordinary wheeling and dealing into one which also engaged in the supply of pep pills, LSD and other drugs to the punters using this stuff in London. Eventually this included hard drugs and it was at this point that my friend wanted out.

Billy said that he did not wish to go on being involved in this aspect of the business, into which he had been gradually dragged, but that he was terrified to leave what he was doing because effectively he had come to learn a lot about how the operation worked and who was running it. To just leave would put him in danger as it seemed those in the know who had left before him seemed, and I use his word, to 'disappear'. To the best of my knowledge he has emigrated, but the day before he left he told me about this man, Knuckles, who had moved from being a bad boy running a local business, to taking over a large scale drug import business. Billy said he'd moved nearer the coast. I assumed the south coast, although when I heard that the drug supply was coming from Holland, I revised that to the possibility it was Essex or Suffolk.

But what if it was Clackmore?

I was wondering if our trawler, which as Dougie points out, cannot be making much of a living from fishing, has something to do with it. So do you think that seagoing vessels that have come from Holland could be coming into Lochinver or any other port nearby and handing some drugs over before they dock?"

"Well," Dougie said, "if we assume that your idea is correct how far would our trawler have got to go find a port on this coast that would be able to cater for, say, a small coaster. There is only Lochinver and Kinlochbervie or I suppose over to Stornaway on the Isle of Lewis. Or I suppose you might find a sheltered bay in which a coaster could anchor, whilst meeting up with the trawler. But in either case there would be questions asked because we do not get many coasters coming into our local fishing ports, though Stornaway is more likely to have coasters going in. If one was anchored off somebody would see it. You know how the jungle drums work up here, anything out of the ordinary is a talking point and others would have said something and we would have heard."

Cat had been looking thoughtful.

"Let's suppose for a minute," she said, "that your idea that this man is the drugs man your friend Billy talked about. Lots of people look at a map and see our coast, from Ullapool northwards, as the real back of beyond. A small and sparsely scattered population, cut off to some degree by single track roads and hostile weather on occasion. A city person might be tempted to think that it was the ideal place for an illegal enterprise to go on in secret, away from places like London with a high police presence. But, as Dougie has just pointed out, anything out of the ordinary up here is, ironically, more visible. Just a couple of summers ago two English criminals on the run, whose descriptions had been circulated, came up here and pitched tent up the Lochinver river. I guess that they thought that driving up an unmade track and turning off at a fishing bothy with no soul in sight meant they could lie low successfully."

"I heard they did lie low, they cut the legs off their camp beds." Said Dougie, with a twinkle in his eye.

Pause.

"Be serious, Dougie." Cat admonished, as belatedly we caught up with Dougie's little schoolboy joke.

"Anyway, the presence of the tent was noted by a ghilly and, when they went for supplies, a local shopkeeper felt that they were unlikely tourists. Both these folk independently alerted the local police and they were captured within a few days of their arrival."

"John Buchan." Said Dougie.

Cat and I looked at one another trying to see if this was yet another of Dougie's jokes, but if it was, it evaded us. Seeing our confusion Dougie explained.

"John Buchan wrote 'The Thirty Nine Steps'. A man in trouble living in London needs to get away from a problem he's landed in and he goes off and catches a train to Scotland. True, he doesa'na get any further than Clackmannanshire, which is a long way south of here, but he gets away…..for a while. So ever since that book, yer London types probably think that Scotland is such an unpopulated backwater full of illiterate Picts, that it is just the place to go when you are in a bit of bother with the local polis or others. They think that nobody will notice them"

"So I think," said Cat, "what we are both saying is that people think that by coming up here they will be invisible even if what they are wanting to do is to carry on something illegal because they won't be noticed." Dougie nodded and went on.

"But really this is the worst place in the world for that because people here are generally inquisitive about their neighbours, not out of badness you understand, mainly because there are relatively few neighbours and also because a community needs people to play a part in its wider life. Really the only way to achieve the peace and quiet you need to carry on some criminal enterprise up here, is to be like Ewan and fit into the life so nobody thinks you are in any way out of the ordinary." After a pause I said.

"There is another piece of the story which I haven't told you and it's somewhere in here……. ," I said, rummaging in the table drawer for the envelope Billy had given me. I retrieved it, opened the envelope and showed them the message that had baffled me the first time I had looked at it.

"Any ideas?"

I asked and the other two stared at it silently, just as I had done originally.

Deliverer = PACCO gives Date and time then
Channel 16/8. Receiver = GAEKP
Spiro - PD355 201063 del to Boyo Richmond 231063
25,000

"What on earth is that?" I asked.

Cat shook her head but Dougie looked thoughtful and then after a while he said.

"Well on my boat I have a marine VHF radio just in case of emergency, and I know that channel 16 is the one I am tuned to, as it is the international distress channel and also the international call up channel. Once you have made contact you often switch to another channel for talking ship to ship communication, and one of those channels is channel 8, so that could relate to VHF communication. Then maybe the two codenames, like

'Deliverer', will be used rather than the normal ship names to avoid identification."

"So could you monitor that channel when the trawler goes out, so that we could see where a ship carrying the stuff from Holland might berth or anchor?" I said.

"Well, first you would have to know when it was going out and be ready, but second with an aerial on a little boat like mine you probably only have a range of five or so miles, so if they went beyond that you may not hear them. Also they are unlikely to say where they are and I have no radar or other direction finding equipment."

"Have all the trawler trips been at night?" Cat asked, "the ones which you have talked about seem to have been."

I looked at Dougie and first he shrugged his shoulders but then said.

"That's the only time I've seen the trawler go out, in the night."

"So," I said, "they could rendezvous with a coaster and transfer, whatever it has brought, on to the trawler which could then bring it ashore."

"Yes," agreed Dougie, "that's possible but it would take a pretty good seaman to transfer cargo at sea, in all weathers, in darkness out in the Minch. On the other hand, I suppose they could come inshore and do it somewhere nearby that's a bit more sheltered, but, if they are not wanting to be seen, then that would not be ideal. Going back to your man Billy's note, by the way, I have no idea about the other stuff in it except that you will have noted that PD355 is the fishing registration number on our trawler here"

"You know," said Cat, "we could just be adding two and two together here and making seventeen. It is all wild speculation. We need to know a lot more before we can even be confident that we know what is going on and then, when we do, we need to inform the authorities. However, at this stage we have no evidence whatsoever and we could end up accusing people of something which is a figment of our imaginations. It may be nothing to do with this man here, nasty or not. As you said a little earlier, even if he is the boss man he could have folk on the south or east coasts plying his trade on his behalf."

"I take that point," I said, "but you have got to admit that the very fact of berthing a trawler in a most isolated and unusual place, albeit sheltered from the worst elements, and it only goes out every month or so, is very suspicious. What we know about the skipper is also suspicious, as it seems as though he is here involuntarily. Then the new arrivals at the Lodge are clearly unsavoury types and you must have to think that something is wrong. However I do agree that there is nothing to say at this stage that they are linked to my friend Billy's story, but let's at least find out what is happening in this operation here and then we can tell the police what we know and they can take it from there."

"Well why don't we go to the police now," asked Cat, "and say what we know and let them deal with it?"

I looked at her for quite a while and then I turned and looked at Dougie and both of them watched me, no doubt wondering why I was silent. But the silence was a hesitation. Hesitation borne of the fact that the further we'd gone into this issue the more the possibility grew that this could be Billy's Mr Knuckles. That in itself was not a problem, but as things had developed the more I got the idea that this was the drug baron to whom Billy had referred. I also knew at the back of my mind that Billy had told me two stories. The first was of a drug dealer, but the second was potentially a much more personal story.

My silence and hesitation was about weighing up whether or not to refer to this second part of Billy's story and whilst I was tempted to, I decided that perhaps at this stage it was better left out.

"Because," I replied, "we have already gone down the road of looking into the matter and perhaps you could indulge me to dig a little further, just to see if there is a link to Billy's story. If we tell the police and if they act and there is something amiss they will deal with that crime, and that alone."

A mistake.

Cat did not notice it.

Dougie did.

Looking at me steadily he repeated the words.

"'That crime and that alone' what did you mean by that crime alone, what other crime could be worse than trafficking drugs?"

He had got me. I'd slipped up badly and under that steady gaze I realised that untruths, or to be fair half-truths, were unacceptable. So with a sigh I said.

"Well there were two parts to Billy's story, but before I tell you about the second part can I first explain that in the beginning in my mind I made absolutely no connection between the funny goings-on at Newton Lodge and the story Billy told me. The issues were both literally and metaphorically miles apart.

Billy told me about a man who is engaged in importing illegal drugs from Holland for sale in the London area of England. Up here, some six hundred and more miles away, I experience an incident of road rage from a couple of newly arrived English, thuggish looking, men and I help a young woman who's had a fall from a horse and discover, in doing so, that her husband is not a nice man. Neither Hercule Poirot nor Miss Marple would have made any connection.

But my second contact with Sally, as I came to know her, gave me more information about the nature of her husband and also it located both her and him as being from the area where Billy worked and I used to live. Very gradually it has been dawning on me that now there is a possibility that the man who is currently living at Newton Lodge is possibly the same Knuckles character from Billy's south-west London patch.

If it was just that, then may be even with the limited information we have I might've accepted going to the police, although I'm still not so sure, because as it is there is not a lot of actual evidence that the police could use. Even if they were interested it would be quite difficult to set up any form of surveillance around here.

But Billy did tell me something else and this gives me a much more personal interest in the potential Mr Knuckles. It may be, and it only comes from hearsay evidence, that he might be the man who was driving the car that killed Linda and Carole."

Cat gasped. Dougie's eyes remained firmly on mine. I went on.

"The police and the Inquest were broadly satisfied that a man who apparently died as a result of a suicide jump into the river Thames was the one responsible for the deaths of Linda and Carole because he had in his pocket a suicide note stating this. Billy's take however, just from word-of-mouth of other associates of this man Knuckles, suggests that the suicide was staged because he, Knuckles, was worried that the police may be getting closer to the fact that he himself was the actual driver. Because of this suicide, or according to Billy a murder made to look like suicide, again no evidence, the police and the courts cleared up a crime and cause of death respectively and at the same time Mr Knuckles was freed from any suspicion in the matter.

The further things have gone on the more I think the likelihood increases that our man up at Newton Lodge is indeed in the drug smuggling business and potentially is the killer of my wife and daughter. That is why I said a little earlier that he would be got for this crime alone, because as sure as eggs is eggs he is not going to confess to a crime which has already been cleared up."

"So what is 'Our Hero' going to do then, grab him by the throat and beat him within an inch of his life till he confesses?" Asked Dougie.

"Dougie I don't know what I'm going to do, I have no plans beyond what we have all just discussed. However, it is possible that I could get some small satisfaction and revenge, by establishing and reporting his illegal activities and by providing enough evidence to get him sent to jail for a long time."

"Ewan," Cat said, "don't get your hopes up that this man is ever going to confess, as you say, why should he? If you even begin to think it could happen you are only going to be disappointed. As you say, even if he was responsible, why would he ever admit it now? However, given what you say, there is an added personal dimension and whether or not he ever admits or is convicted for the murder of your wife and daughter you can at least make him pay for this awful drug smuggling, if that's what it is. I think we should take our little investigation a bit further, the question is how do we go forward?"

"Well," I said, "perhaps there are some weak links in his chain. For instance there is the abused wife and the reluctant skipper. On the other hand the former is held by fear, not fear for herself particularly, but certainly fear for her little boy. I suspect too that the other one is under some threat as to what might happen, not just to him but to his wife and twin girls, if he were to step out of line."

"Well you've got me really fired up." Said Dougie; and just looking at him I noticed a zeal and animation that was unique in my observation of his demeanour and I realised that his normally terse communication was getting more fulsome by the minute. He hurried on.

"Just for a wee while leave to one side any of the more personal issues which may or may not relate to you, Ewan, and just think about a man who is a rude and aggressive bully and who appears to have come up here, no doubt thinking we are a bunch of stupid yokels, to carry on an awful business that could be ruining lots of people's lives through the illegal importation of drugs.

So we need to get together some of this evidence that Ewan keeps talking about. It seems to me that I haven't really got myself involved in thinking about these stupid people, beyond making the odd grumble about their rudeness and the way that they have, in a wee way, upset my normal carry on by mooring their trawler in ma bay and then sometimes disturbing ma shuteye. But now I start to think about it there are a number of practical things that they will have to have done in relation to the trawler.

You may not realise it but when I go to my fishing I only go in the daylight. If I was based in Lochinver, with its big wide bay, there are lights on the houses and navigation lights including on the fish pier, so I could go out at night and still safely get back. But I cannot leave the mooring in my little inlet between the mainland and the island in darkness because I wouldn't be able to see where I was going, let alone being able to regain my moorings when I returned. So that first of all raises the point, which I should have thought about before, as to how they are navigating that much bigger vessel to and from its moorings at night.

So perhaps the first thing we can do is to take a better look at the trawler and also have a look around down by the jetty. They don't seem to come down all on any regular basis, although maybe once or twice a week they seem to bring the skipper down and he probably goes out and does some maintenance and then they come back for him later in the day. So we could wait for them to come on one of those maintenance days and then, the day afterwards, when they will probably not be there, we could have a much closer look see."

We basically all agreed that this was a practical first step in trying to build some substance onto our suppositions and, Cat counselled, we should take things slowly and try to build up a picture which we could write down. Then in due course, if we did conclude there was something wrong going on, we could show our notes to the police. So, we were all to keep an eye out for them coming down to the jetty and then the following day we could have a look around.

I purposely avoided mentioning the letter lodged with Mr McKay, as we had still not formally linked Billy's Mr. Knuckles to the Newton Lodge man. Also, I was loathe to refer to it at all since he had given it to me as a sort of insurance against any threats from Knuckles or his men. In so far as was humanly possible I wanted that letter to stay secret.

After this conversation of honesty and openness with my two friends I felt a weight lifted from my shoulders, not just due to the fact that things I'd kept bottled up inside at the back of my mind were now out there with two people whom I knew would keep my confidence, but also because there was a plan of action. It was invigorating and exciting and very different to the normal sort of July. There were lots of things to do on the croft, but it was not a period of extreme activity. Planting and lambing were over and apart from the peat digging and sheep shearing there were no major jobs to be done until the second hay cutting and the harvesting of vegetables later in the year. General maintenance was the order of the day and this could always be put to one side for the odd day, or half day, here and there in order to begin our detective work.

Look out if you're a baddie, I thought.

Sixty percent of Clackmore's Famous Five were on the case.

Garnering information

A few days after our council of war the van appeared in the morning and delivered the trawler skipper to his maintenance duties. It made a return trip in the afternoon to collect him. The following day Mr Roy and I cycled over to Dougie's, well I cycled and Mr Roy ran.

We went down to the jetty and the crumbling boat shed and I helped Dougie to launch his dinghy and we rowed out in the direction of his fishing boat. Dougie was rowing and had his back to the direction of travel and I pointed out that he needed to go left a bit, to get to the trawler, as he was heading straight for his own boat.

"That's the idea," said Dougie, "I doubt anyone would be looking, but if they are, then they are just going to see us going out to my boat. We clambered aboard his boat and as the tide was ebbing both vessels were lying with their bows pointing away from the sea. Thus, we were able to study the trawler, which was to seaward of us, from the shelter of the overhang behind Dougie's cabin. He took out a battered pair of binoculars and just looked. After a while he said.

"You see that white metal thing on his wheelhouse roof, well that's one of these new-fangled radar scanners and by the looks of it I bet its cost a pretty penny. So that will mean that he will be able to see the shoreline either side of the inlet, both the mainland and the island, so that will help him in general terms when approaching the coast from seaward. But a good sailor would not want to rely on just the radar entering a narrow inlet like this and even if he was daft enough to try that, picking up his mooring buoy, despite it's a very big one I notice, would not be easy in the dark."

He then went into his little cabin and looked forward, using his binoculars, he seemed to be scanning the hillside at the end of the inlet. He spent some time looking and then, with an air of disappointment, removed the binoculars from his eyes. Before his hands holding the binoculars had even fallen to his side he swiftly raised them up again and this time was staring at a point much nearer the rocks that were just above high water level. He made a grunt of satisfaction and replaced the binoculars on the little ledge in his wheelhouse where they usually lived.

"We're off for another wee row." He announced.

Without further ado he closed up his cabin and moved to the dinghy indicating that I should get in. This time there was no pretence, we rowed straight towards the trawler as we were passing it I stared at the bright white lettering on the side, not the much smaller lettering of the name of the boat, the great big letters read PD355.

"Dougie, that's the number in the note." I said.

"Some of us," he said, "were aware of this fact some days ago and indeed even mentioned it out loud in company and were perhaps foolish in making an assumption that others had bothered to listen to what they were told. If our lives depended on your powers of observation and listening then we would stand little hope."

We reached the stern of the vessel and resting on his oars he pointed out that, although there was a net hanging on one of the stanchions on one side of the low-lying transom of the vessel, the whole of the working area was clear and where the fish would have been hauled aboard there was no sign of any remnants of bits of fish.

We proceeded up the other side of the trawler to their large mooring buoy and Dougie pointed.

"Aha! Since they arrived they have welded that small cage on top of it he said. If you see that canvas covered thing inside the cage I am willing to bet that that's a car battery. Do you see the wires leading from that to the wee light on the top? This is how he picks up his buoy in the night, because when they tie the dinghy to the buoy to release the trawler he will switch the little light on. It doesn't need to be very powerful it just needs to be enough for you to see it when you know you're in the vicinity of it. But he will not see that from very far out, so after the radar approach to the inlet, this light will still not be visible."

Dougie again began to row and we sped back to the jetty and hauled his dinghy out and returned it to its normal place of residence. We were welcomed back by Mr Roy who had obviously been disappointed not to have been allowed another sea voyage on this occasion. Dougie fondled the dog's ears and told him it was time for 'walkies' and set off at a brisk pace along a path that took us towards the head of the inlet. He kept stopping and looking towards the trawler and the distant sea. After about a quarter of an hour Dougie turned off from the path and went down towards the rocks near the shore and a few minutes later he beckoned me to join him.

When I arrived beside him he was standing next to another wrapped battery with leads going towards a little stand with a domed head which was obviously some home-made arrangement. Dougie showed me that this was in fact a more substantial and powerful light and that it was enclosed within its casing in the dome which meant that the light would only be visible towards the sea and would not be visible to the side or rear.

"Now, you stand just here." He instructed and immediately went off, striking up the hillside. As he walked up he kept turning and looking at me and then looking beyond me until eventually he stopped, by an outcrop of rock and, after a moment or two of looking around, he turned waved at me and raised both his thumbs in the air. A series of gestures followed indicating that we should head back towards the jetty. Dougie had to negotiate more difficult terrain than had I, and so I was back at the jetty before him. As he approached he had a big smile on his face.

"Now if only I had paid attention before, or even given the matter any serious thought, I should have realised that navigating in and out in the dark was impossible but what they have done is quite clever. The light that they have on top of the buoy is no too bright because it's just for the very last part of their approach. The first part is achieved by using the radar but the other two lights they've installed, one higher up the brae than the other, are called 'leading lights'. Once they have reached the edge of the inlet then they can pick up the two brighter lights and, provided they keep one directly above the other, they know they are running on a safe course to lead them in, until they see the little light on top of the buoy.

That has taken a good bit of thinking out as well as installing. The Northern Lighthouse Board are responsible for lights and navigation marks all around the Scottish coast and I did'na think it was even legal to install your own, but I don't actually ken that. The fact that they have shaded the leading lights also means that they do not want the casual walker to notice them. So, what we have here is a fishing boat that doesn't seem to catch fish, firstly because we don't know where it is landing them if it's catching them and, secondly, because the working area at the stern of the trawler hasn't seen fish for ages. We also know that they hardly ever go out. So everything points to some sort of hush-hush activity. So now let's go and have a look in the old boat shed by the jetty."

The old building revealed very little. Clearly it had been used by animals, probably in the winter, but there were no real signs of anything else since the time Dougie's father had used it to keep lobster pots and store cattle feed. However, on the rocky area to the far side of the jetty there was an unusual amount of cut rope. Items like this often end up on the shore having drifted in on the tide, you can find things like this on most beaches and in rocks nearby. But here there was a much greater profusion. We both agreed this was unusual but there was no immediate explanation for it.

We went back up to Dougie's croft and over a mug of tea we discussed our findings. Albeit the trawler was equipped to fish, at least in part, it was clear that it wasn't really engaged in that activity. Nevertheless, a great deal of trouble had been taken for it to be able to be moored in the inlet and given the wherewithal to navigate to and from its mooring buoy in darkness.

"What we really need," said Dougie, "is to have an idea of which direction they head when they're going out on one of their trips. To find this out we really need advance warning or, at the very least, to be able to set off at the drop of a hat as soon as they've left the bay."

"Would we be able to follow them out?" I asked, to which Dougie replied that that was most unlikely, as his vessel was not fitted with any radar and the trawler was much faster than his little boat.

"If we had advanced warning of them going out," Dougie said, "we could go out ourselves and wait and see which direction they took, because it's just occurred to me that at this time of the year, on a trip that ends up with them getting back at two or three in the morning, they would probably be setting off well before the last of the daylight. We could be out at the edge of the inlet, pretending to lift lobster pots, and we could note the direction in which they were going. If it became dark we could use their leading lights to get back in and once we passed the light on their buoy and if we took a good torch we could probably see our mooring because it's not far ahead."

After rummaging in my pocket I suggested that we had another look at the note Billy had given me.

Deliverer = PACCO gives Date and time then
Channel 16/8. Receiver = GAEKP
Spiro - PD355 201063 del to Boyo Richmond 231063
25,000

"I've been thinking about this," said Dougie, "and as you managed to catch up earlier when we were out in the dinghy 'PD 355' surely must be our friend the trawler. Again as I told you Channel 16 is the VHF call-up and emergency channel and then Channel 8 is one of the two channels you could switch over to, in order to continue your conversation. I've been thinking about these other letters and I spoke to an old merchant navy 'sparks' or radio officer who lives up the back of Lochinver, whom I know vaguely. He told me that a ship's call signs are four letters, but that amateur radio operators, or 'radio hams,' use five letters for their call signs. Going on in the conversation it came out that the prefix GA is the start of a UK radio ham call sign. I didn't like to say too much so I couldn't be asking about the other thing, that 'PACCO'."

"What are the chances that you could ask him about that one without giving anything away?" I asked.

"I could ask," said Dougie, "but it might cost me a few more whiskeys than I can afford."

"Don't worry," I replied, "I'll lend you some money. Okay, let's call it a day for now and maybe tomorrow we can tell Cat what we found out and think about where to go from here."

"Agreed," said Dougie, "but all that we've learnt today only increases my thinking that the likelihood is that they are definitely up to no good."

The following day Cat called in and I went to get Dougie from the garage so that we could convene a council of war. Dougie and I filled her in on all that we discovered, such as it was, and we discussed the options for moving forward. Having listened to all that we had to say, Cat summarised.

"So apart from the possibility of talking to this amateur radio man about the other item that might be a call sign, you seem to think that the best way would be to assess which direction the trawler was going the next time it set off." We nodded.

"Dougie suggested," I said, "we may stay out there a little while and see if we can pick up his VHF transmissions."

"But how would you get back if it was dark?" she asked.

"By using their leading marks." said Dougie.

"But in order to do that you have to know when they going out and in turn you need to have that information in advance. So how are we going to do that?" Asked Cat.

"Well I will leave you two young ones to ponder on that and I'll awa hame for an early tea and then I have some pots to check on this fine evening." Said Dougie. And with that he rose and went to the door and any other person would there have put on their hat, except Dougie never took off his oil stained bobble hat; even in bed I suspected.

"I'm sure you'll let me know what you come up with tomorrow." He said and with that he left.

"Well," said Cat, "after all the heavy-handed 'be very sure that ye behave yourselves' warnings he's gone off and left us alone."

She walked to the door and went outside was gone for a couple of minutes, as she returned she said.

"Yes he's off up the road on his way home and my mum is not making the tea at our house for at least another hour and a half. She came to me and planted a big kiss on my lips and pulling me to my feet whispered in my ear.

"Now, enough of this serious stuff it's practice time."

A little later after emotions had subsided, blood pressure returned to something approaching normal and dissipated strength came back into our bodies as we lay comfortably naked and very close together due to the confines of the single bed I turned to Cat.

"It may be a longshot you know but I wonder if that lass Sally would be able to tip us off."

"Why would she?"

"Well, I don't know this, but clearly she is here under sufferance really because she cares a great deal for the little boy Henry, otherwise I think she would have been long gone, she strikes me as a survivor and would have risked leaving her husband if there was only herself to consider. She clearly felt that her husband was all right in the beginning, but as time has gone by she has been badly used and often abused. Of course she may be so terrified of him and the consequences of giving anything away that she would be unwilling to give us that sort of information. But I feel that if I asked her then even though she may not be prepared to actually take any action against him, neither would she tell him that I'd asked the question."

"How do you suggest we contact her?" Cat asked

"Well do you think we could pass a note through Jeannie at the school, if you asked her?"

"I don't think that would be fair and we don't want to involve anybody else. But on the other hand I am around when the children are going to and coming out of school and maybe I could contrive a meeting with her, even though she always appears with one or two of her minders present. The only problem is that school breaks up in less than a couple of weeks and if she doesn't know when the next trip will be and, even if she is agreeable, it will be very difficult for her to get a message to us." I nodded.

"Yes but the last trip was at least a couple of weeks ago and so chances are that the next one could well be within the next fortnight and we would just have to risk it."

"Okay, what should I tell her because I thought she said she wasn't supposed to come down near your croft anymore?"

"Well, you could say that for the next couple of days after you give her the message, I would be working just on the other side of the ridge from the road where she saw me helping that ewe to lamb."

"Okay," said Cat, "I'll see what I can do and if I am able to pass the message I'll let you know as soon as possible."

"Now that's settled," she said, climbing on top of me, "I do think there is just enough time for another quick practice before I have to set off home for tea."

Just two days later I was in the barn helping Dougie to set up a small compressor which he had managed to source, second-hand, and which had been delivered the previous day. This would be extremely helpful to him in mending tyres and also in removing wheel nuts and obviously with inflating tyres as well. Cat arrived in the morning having completed her school run and, although we heard her arrive, I could only yell for her to come round to the barn, because at that point we were in the middle of a delicate operation lifting the heavy compressor into the space we had cleared for it. After we'd completed locating it we turned to Cat who had a broad smile on her face somewhat akin to her Cheshire cousin.

"Gentleman, you are looking at the Cat who may not have got the cream but she certainly deserves it. I know I said I was willing to try to pass a message to your Sally girl, but when it came to it this morning, I was as nervous as a kitten. No joke intended. She arrived in the big car, with one of the minders and she got out of the front seat, went to the back door and got the boy Henry out and walked towards school.

She was a bit taken aback when I walked towards them and squatted down and said to Henry 'hello Henry it's nice to see you. Going to have a good day at school today?' And then I looked up to his mother from my squatting position and said, 'you can tell your driver that I spoke to Henry because I thought he was a bit upset, but he wasn't. My real purpose is to say Ewan, your friend from the croft by the sea, would like to see you about an urgent matter and if you could possibly ride over the top of the ridge to where you saw him helping the ewe give birth, he will be there for the next two or three mornings.' Then I stood up and took Henry's hand, he knows me quite well as I have often looked after him on trips out from school, and said 'we'll look after him, see you at school coming out time.'

She said to me, 'yes okay I'll see you at school coming out time but' and here she slightly changed her tone of voice, 'more likely tomorrow.' To be fair to her she didn't turn a hair and walked off back to her car and at least she had a story to tell the minder if asked.

So I assume from this that she was indicating that she was likely to be able to ride out tomorrow and so I should be sure to be up there by ten o'clock tomorrow morning at the latest. Anyway," she ended, "must go, as I promised to take dad to Lochinver. Say a nice good bye to your modern day Mata Hari."

And with that she left us to get on with our work.

The following morning I started walking up the road as though I was going towards Dougie's croft and once I had crested the hill I turned off and went cross country, behind the ridge that would shield me from our valley and it also shielded me from the main road, although you would need a good pair of binoculars to see anybody moving at that distance from there. Mr Roy was his usual eager bounding self, rushing back and forth and no doubt anticipating some good sport in putting the wind up some of those dumb white woolly beasts that it was his pleasure to be Lord over. I was far too early and it was over an hour before Mr Roy, who had been sitting beside me wondering at my unusual inactivity, and wanting the fun to start with the woolly beasts, suddenly pricked his ears up and got up 'Lie down', I commanded, in the gruff voice necessary for that command and with a look of disappointment he did as he was bid. A short while later Sally arrived in her usual immaculate riding out costume, heavily made up and with no hair out of place under her riding hat.

She dismounted.

"Where's the blanket then? She said, "I don't mind doing it outdoors but it'll cost you extra if my bum gets all green from the grass, unless, that is, you had something other than the missionary position in mind of course."

I could not immediately call a reply to mind.

"God you're so bloody serious," she said, "you should see your face! Anyway I got you wrong the first time, I thought you were a big tit man but I see you girlfriend is much slimmer."

"Sally," I said, "this is serious."

"I assumed that it must be serious," she replied and her face showed that this time she meant it, "I didn't really think you'd invited me up here for a shag, although I must confess a nice bit of gentleness and loving wouldn't go amiss in my life at the moment, but I am guessing you're going to ask me to do something that possibly I might not want to do. All the men I have known recently are like that."

There was no point in my beating about the bush.

"Rightly or wrongly I make the assumption that your husband is up to no good and from enquiries that I've made I believe he is importing drugs and using the trawler to do that, I think he bought the house at Newton Lodge......"

"......... He didn't buy it." She interjected, He's told everybody that but he's just renting it actually….."

"Oh! I suppose that makes sense for him not to have wasted a lot of money. Anyway I make the assumption from what you told me last time that you are just trying to have an easy life with your little boy Henry and that you wouldn't want to be the person who gave his little game away. I respect that, but I also have my own reasons for wanting to put an end to this drug smuggling and in order to do that I have been gathering some evidence that I hope will be sufficient for the authorities to take a look at him.

I want to make sure that you are in no way blamed and so all I'm asking for is one simple piece of information which would be really helpful. That is advance warning of the next time the trawler is going to be going out on one of its regular three or four weekly trips."

"Are you really just a local yokel?" She asked. "I've already established that you come from London, so you could just be part of one of his bloody competitor's gangs and you can use this information to drop him in it and then take over yourself."

"I'd not thought of that." I said. "So I am gonna have to tell you something that will perhaps make you understand that, in addition to being against the supply of things that ruin people's lives, I have a personal agenda that means I want to give him his comeuppance. So, Harry Evans." I said and paused.

I looked at her face and I could see that this was a name she recognised.

"Poor old Harry found drowned in the Thames after jumping off a bridge, with a convenient suicide note in which he confesses that he has suddenly developed a guilt complex about an event that has taken place a year before. It's apparently affected him so badly that he's got to take his own life. He wants the world to know that he was the driver of a getaway car which killed a woman and a child."

"Your woman? Your child?"

"My lovely Linda and my darling Carole."

There was a long pause.

"So what's the plan," she said, "because if your idea is that you are going to get some evidence of his drug trade and then come up and face him wiv it and try to get him to confess, not only will you fail to get a confession, but you'll probably get a bullet in your head as well. And then, no doubt, end up buried up in some of those peat workings."

"Funny you should say that, one of my friends has told me the same thing, but no that's not the idea, what I want is to get enough evidence to be able to go to the police and get him done for this. Supplying drugs won't get him life in jail, like murder, but it should get him a good long time and that will be revenge enough for me."

She thought for a while.

"Well, you're right I don't want to tell you a lot of stuff because I'm afraid you don't really know who you're dealing with. This man won't hesitate to use intimidation, threats, violence and even murder to save his very lucrative business, not to mention his own skin and you know that I'm right because of what happened to Harry Evans. So I don't want to be drawn into saying anything, because if he got hold of you, I'll tell you now, he would get information out of you and however much you wanted to keep me out of it you wouldn't succeed.

But, whilst I am never told when these things are going to happen it's not hard to work out that there's gonna be a run on a particular day. There's the telephone call and then a load of activity, usually two days before. And by complete coincidence there was a call this morning, early, so I am assuming that tomorrow night they will be off on their trip because there was lots of things being done round the Lodge today. In fact that helped me to get out on the horse, because no doubt they were happy to see me going out of their way. Now if I am wrong I can pass a message, when I pick up Henry tonight, via your friend......."

"......... Cat."

"……..Cat, so tell her that if I do not try to speak to her tonight then it's on for tomorrow. If I have to pass a message tell her I will walk over to her and ask if Henry has been alright today as I was a bit worried he was off colour this morning and, at the same time, I will tell her whatever I know about a change of plans."

"Thank you." I said.

"I only hope you realise what a very dangerous path you are treading, but at least I now understand why you are treading it and I wish you all the best. If it doesn't work out he can't blame me for too much, you see I owe it to Henry not to be found to be a grass, but I hope to God it does work out and that he gets nicked and then, who knows, my life and Henry's might take a huge turn for the better."

She returned to her grazing horse, put one foot in the stirrup and heaved herself up.

"You and this Cat an item then?" She asked.

I hesitated

"Good," she said, "you obviously need some loving after what it sounds like you must have been through."

She turned the horse's head, clicked her tongue and it began to walk away. Then she turned and said over her shoulder.

"Hope it all works out for you and her. If not, and if I'm free then just let me know, because without Knuckles around I could quite enjoy the life up here."

As I made my way back I reflected on her amazingly direct style, it was something that I had never come across before. Her life experience was completely at odds with anything I had ever known and I supposed that one would have to develop a very hard exterior to cope with all the abuse she had suffered in the past and, by the sound of things, still did. Yet it was so admirable that, for the sake of this little boy, she was willing to endure the hardships just to try to ensure that he had as decent a life as possible. If her husband was not on the scene in her life and Cat was not on the scene in mine, I could see that it would not be beyond the realms of possibility that we could have a go of making a life together.

I made a mental note to say to Cat that if we were successful in getting her husband jailed that we ought to offer to help her to settle in the area, if she wanted, as it would be a good life for Henry. But then, I thought, with a husband not on the scene, she would probably want to go back to the big city.

All conjecture.
Forget it.
What next?

Final preparations

Later, having passed a message to Cat about a possible contact from Sally at school coming-out time, she reported that in fact Sally had completely ignored her and so we made the assumption that the trawler was going out as planned. The following day I broke off work about four o'clock and called Dougie from the barn for some scrambled eggs on toast, as our pre-evening meal. Then we prepared a sandwich, or a 'piece' as Dougie would have it, for supper later on, together with a flask of hot water and a couple of tea bags. Not long after five we both set off and Mr Roy was disappointed when, somewhat unusually, I tied him to a long length of rope that I had placed there to the purpose and which was anchored to a heavy duty nail, inside the porch.

"You stay there Mr Roy," I said, "I have fetched you some water and you'll be all right till the morning if that's what it takes."

"Pah," said Dougie, "talking to animals at last. You must have become a crofter. Roddy used to do that, both to this one and his previous dog, Rob."

We trudged up the road, on over the hill and down past Dougie's cottage to the jetty. We launched his little dinghy and with our food and a flask we set off to his boat. It was only about half past six when we cast off the moorings and Dougie remarked that we were far too early and so it proved. We were fortunate in that it was a reasonable summer's day, there was quite a breeze which Dougie said a real fisherman had told him indicated about force three on the Beaufort wind scale, as that was when the tops of some waves were just beginning to show flecks of white; there was also quite a swell.

Bits of white outside the boat and, as far as my face was concerned, an awful lot of white inside too. Dougie had taken us out of our bit of the inlet, round the seaward part of the island and into the bit of inlet on its other side. The bit out in the sea was only half a mile or so but it was the only way to access the inlet on the father side of the island, as its landward side was almost joined to the mainland by a ridge of rocks. These were submerged an hour or so each side of high tide but were otherwise visible and therefore a bar to the passage of boats. There was relatively little shelter on the inlet on the other side of the island and we had to say stay near its seaward end in order to get a view of the trawler when it emerged.

Dougie was used to the motion of the boat but even he, after three hours of it, was, I suspected, getting a little bit less than happy. As with any discomfiture or illness, you can be driven in on yourself and so it was with us, in terms of noticing the appearance of the trawler.

We were beginning to be worried that they were not, after all, going out that night and Dougie had set a limit on our staying out until ten o'clock, that being the latest we could set off to make it back to his mooring, before it went completely dark. His tide and sunset tables told him that the sun would go down officially at about a quarter past nine. So, our increasing anxiety was allayed when, at a little after nine o'clock, the trawler appeared round the end of the island.

"Get down!" Said Dougie, failing to notice that, in my queasy state, I had already sunk to the deck and was sitting with my back to the wheelhouse with my knees drawn up, wishing to be onshore as soon as possible. Immediately Dougie set to work hauling up a pot which, if he had hauled it up once, he had hauled up twenty times. When it surfaced he pretended to take something out of it and throw it back into the sea, pretended to re-bait it and then lowered the pot over the side. Then glanced up and lifted a laconic hand in the direction of the trawler.

"Did they see you?" I asked.

"I canna tell you that as they are all in the wheelhouse," said Dougie, "but if they were looking this way then the skipper at least will have been satisfied that I had observed the usual niceties and he probably waved back, even if I did'na see him. It's the done thing in the circumstances to give a friendly wave even if it's to unfriendly people."

Dougie motored over to a nearby lobster pot marker, floating on the surface, and he hauled again. We continued this by visiting different buoys marking the location of different pots for quite a while until the trawler was fast disappearing out into the Minch.

"Right," said Dougie, "they can't see what I'm doing any more so let's head back to our bit of the inlet as we want to be sure that they set those lights up, otherwise we will never get back in ourselves and it's now beginning to get dark. Also I want to get a sort of bearing of the direction she's travelling in."

We passed the outside of the island and regained the opening of our bit of the inlet and Dougie put the engine to idle. His boat was fitted with the mandatory little compass of the magnetic variety and it was something that he never used so far as I'm aware.

"Stand-up and point where you can see the trawler just disappearing, it's all right they can't see you at this distance, keep your arm out long enough for me to get some rough idea of their heading. Difficult to say................. it's north of west but how much north of west I'm not sure, maybe as far as north-west."

"What does that tell us?" I asked, being completely ignorant of seagoing and navigational matters.

"Don't know yet, but there's a silly old soak down in Lochinver who used to be in what the local trawler folk call the 'Grey Funnel Line', or to you and me the Royal Navy because they all have grey funnels. He's forever banging on about the principles of navigation which has, as far as I could ever understand, something to do with speed, time, distance and course, though not necessarily in that order. So I noted that he left the inlet at quarter past nine, or 2115 in nautical time and we will see what time he returns."

"Good man Dougie," I said, "where would I be without you. Now; do you awfully mind getting this rocking beast back to its moorings and allow this humble landsman to rediscover his land legs."

"Not just yet, I've been keeping an ear out on channel 16 and I'm turning the sound up now because I am hoping it won't be too long till they get where they are going if they are gonna be back in again by about two in the morning. But first, as its getting dark, let's be sure that they have lit the leading lights, otherwise we will have to go in now."

It was twilight and as we looked landward up the inlet there, twinkling away at the head of it, we saw the two distant little leading lights. Dougie kept using the engine to vaguely keep the lights one above the other as we also listened to the VHF radio. Meanwhile my face got whiter and whiter with my queasiness. Then at 2252, as Dougie noted down, we heard an accented voice over the airwaves.

"Deliverer to receiver, do you read me over." It was followed by a silence. Was there no reply? Then after a pause the same voice came again.

"Copy that. Channel 8."

Dougie fiddled with the dials on his set and retuned to channel 8.

"We can hear the other one but not our trawler." He explained and, as he did so the voice came again.

"Yes I have you to points on my port bow. No near traffic."

There was then a pause which seemed to go on for ages and indeed was six or seven minutes before the voice came again.

"Two packages for you. Lights are working on both do you see?"

A further short silence and then.

"Good. See you next time. Happy fishing."

Switching off the radio Dougie engaged the engine and, keeping the two leading marks one above the other, we negotiated the darkened inlet. After a few minutes we saw the much less bright light on top of their mooring buoy and we felt our way forward of that. By using a torch I scanned the surface of the water and eventually saw our buoy and we moored to it. Then we rowed the dinghy ashore, where we returned it to its normal station upside down beside the old boat shed.

We went up to Dougie's croft and made a new brew which, when it was cool enough I drank thirstily, to replace some of the liquid I'd lost during the latter part of our little voyage.

"Well, I think I have it now," said Dougie, "yon trawler went straight out into the Minch on a course somewhere between west and north-west. She probably manages about ten or twelve knots and so in an hour and a half she would be over fifteen miles offshore. I only have a road map of this whole part of the coast, from Cape Wrath to Skye, but drawing a line between Cape Wrath and the top of the Isle of Skye then about fifteen to twenty miles out from here would allow you to be close to the main shipping route passing between those two points. The delivery ship told them he left two packages under lights, or something to that effect. So I'm guessing that they slow down, put these packages with lights on into the water and then set off again. After that the trawler goes in and picks the packages up from the water, and brings them back in.

All we need to do now is see what happens when they come ashore, but that's not gonna be easy because it's pretty black out there and although they must have a flashlight or two it may be near impossible to see what they're doing."

It was nearly one thirty in the morning when the trawler regained her moorings and with the benefit of Dougie's binoculars, brought ashore from his own boat to the purpose, he gave me a running commentary on what was happening.

"I can see the working lights on the trawler come on and them busying themselves with that oversized rowboat they call a dinghy that they have, …………….. and, ……yes, I can see they're lowering a biggish package into it."

He described two people bringing the first package ashore then both going back for the second. When the second was ashore one man returned in the dinghy whilst the one who stayed ashore appeared to be starting work on the packages. In due course the second man returned with the skipper who went off, presumably to douse the leading lights, whilst the other two busied themselves apparently continuing cutting open the packages which they must have retrieved from the water. After that they began loading whatever they had got from the packages into the van. It was a fairly lengthy process and towards the end they appeared to be clearing up by the looks of things and also stuffing the remnants of the packaging into the van as well. So it was going on to about three in the morning when the van roared into life and they set up off up the hill, passing us unseen watchers in Dougie's croft, and away.

The following morning I was in my bed till gone nine and fortunately there was nothing that needed early morning attention at this time of the year, other than releasing the hens from their overnight confinement and providing them fresh water and food. Dougie did not appear till the afternoon. Cat called to enquire after us both and saw two red eyed zombies. We gave her a quick run-down of events but I suggested that maybe we should leave it a while for us to get back to normal after our missing night's sleep. Thus it was agreed that we meet after Cat had done her school run the following day.

So it was that the following morning we were all gathered in my kitchen with a cup of tea discussing what we had learned from our spying exercise. We all felt that we now had something to really set down in writing.

"It's a good job that yon lassie was able to give us a warning as to when the trawler was going out." Said Dougie.

"Yes. And to be fair she took a big risk after what she told me about the ruthlessness of her husband," I replied, "were he ever to know what she had done then her life may not be worth living, or, she may not even have one to live. He certainly seems a bad lot giving her beatings and even making her sleep with other men."

"Did she tell you that he really has made her do things like that?" Cat burst out somewhat emotionally, and when I nodded she went on, "these controlling and abusive men absolutely ruin so many women's lives and they need punishment far more than they ever get from the law. Many's the time I thought that I would be perfectly capable of taking a large sharp knife to a part of James's anatomy."

There was a pause during which my brain said something about the possibility that Cat's outburst had possibly revealed something she might not ordinarily have done. I was thinking that maybe her emotions had overtaken her judgement. So it proved as Dougie said.

"And I would have helped you to cut his balls off too if only you'd said."

Cat stared at him.

"I tolt young Ewan here that there was more to your homecoming than a Glasgow glassing, for a strong young woman like you. I tolt him I'd looked into your eyes and all that hurt went much deeper than a one-off incident, nasty or not. I have seen you recover from those darkest days when you first came back home. I saw you move forward and a little light began to return to those eyes, but about a year ago I thought some dullness was coming back into them again. Nothing so awful as when you were first back here, but a dullness nonetheless. And then more recently those eyes have begun to twinkle, even sparkle. So I had a word with this young man here and told him, not quite in so many words, that if he was ever to be the cause of putting that sparkle out of your eyes his life would not be worth living in these parts."

"Dougie you are a lovely man and thank you for being my friend and for being mum and dad's friend too." She said with tears falling gently from her eyes.

"And yes, I was abused in Glasgow and not just by a drunk with a glass, in fact, not even by a drunk with a glass. And I did come here as a bolthole. And yes, a year ago I could cheerfully have gone away again. But then Ewan came along and having him around has made my life so much better. But whatever you do Dougie, and whatever happens either way, don't blame Ewan. It was me that made the first moves, just like it was me who had recovered first from being in some dark days and making a play for Ewan, whilst he was still vulnerable and not fully recovered from some very dark days of his own. I don't know where our relationship is going, although from my point of view I hope it keeps going, I want it to keep going but if it doesn't; please don't blame him."

Dougie nodded his head, just once, but he did nod it.

"Well," I said, "as it seems to be confession time then I want to say that Cat's description of how our relationship started accords with mine. And I think it's very perceptive of her to say that she was further out of her dark place than I was out of mine. And yes, I've had a lot of guilt about loving somebody new, when the girl I thought was the love of my life has only been in the cemetery for just over a year. But maybe," I said looking at Cat, "I should say that despite the short time we have been together I, for one, know that I want us to go on being together, forever."

"Ewan Mathieson! I do hope that was a marriage proposal," said Cat, "because the 29th February in this leap year had passed before I felt able to make that suggestion and I couldn't possibly have asked you again for another four years." She looked at me and we both smiled and joined hands across the table.

"Well I think you two young people should go and talk to Alistair and Morag." Said Dougie, "but before you do, we ought to decide what to do next about our trawler friends."

"Well," I said, "reflecting on what happened last night, I did wonder if we could get a sample of whatever is in the packages." They both looked at me with some scepticism.

"If we were able to get notice of the next trip from Sally, I could hide at the back of the old shed and when the first package is ashore and they are off for the second, I could cut into it find out what's inside and get a sample.

Then we could all drive into Lochinver and give the police hard evidence, as well as all the circumstantial stuff which we can write down in advance."

"Too risky and unnecessary," said Cat, "surely we have enough already without taking that risk?"

Dougie drew in his breath.

"Your man Ewan wants to nail this bastard for this crime because he canna get him for the crime he really wants him punished for and, I am guessin', that this is his second best. I think that if we go to the cops their interest will be raised, but equally there may be some 'discussions' about whether our local lot have to sort it out, or the polis from London, or even the Customs and Excise. The whole matter would then drift around and they maybe not even be able to link Mr Big into it at all. So, whilst sharing your concern, Cat, I tend to agree with Ewan."

"What if you get a sample and its baked beans or cigarettes?" Cat asked.

"Baked beans tins or even bottles of booze would be too heavy to be worth trying to transfer but cigarettes are a possibility," I replied, "however, all the information and circumstantial evidence that we have found so far, together with and the original information from Billy suggests that this is a smuggling operation and it relates to drugs and I, for one, am pretty convinced it is."

Dougie nodded and suggested that we at least try to find out if we could get the date of the next trip.

Cat looked thoughtfully at both Dougie and me in turn.

"I can see that I might be outnumbered if I asked for a vote on this. So alright I'll have another word with your friend Sally before school ends as obviously the next trip is going to be while school is out. And I'll see what she suggests as to how she might be able to communicate with us."

We all agreed and as I didn't feel very much like work that day Cat and I agreed to go and talk to her mum and dad and Dougie said he was just going to potter in the barn.

Our announcement to Alistair and Morag that we were wanting them to know that we were seriously walking out delighted them both. It turned out that they had obviously realised that we two were becoming closer together, given the amount of time we were spending with each other. Perhaps they did not realise quite how close becoming closer together meant! But leaving that to one side it was a very happy meeting. Immediately they wanted to know when we were thinking of getting married and what our plans were.

"We have not talked this through," I said, "and Cat and I need to think about it some more. Certainly from my point of view, and unless she is desperately against this, I would prefer something small. A big wedding with lots of family and friends does not feel right in my circumstances and frankly I'm not completely looking forward to phoning my former in-laws to tell them about this development so relatively soon after the death of their daughter. So can we keep it all between ourselves, for a month or two, so that we can think about both what we want and what would be best."

And, I thought, get the next trawler trip out of the way.

It was agreed that nothing would be said until such times as Cat and I had considered all the implications and in the meantime nobody, apart from the four of us, would know, although we did admit that Dougie had guessed and so was aware too.

During the next few weeks life went on much as usual but certain things about our investigation were progressed.

Cat managed a quick conversation with Sally one day before the end of term and Sally's reply had been that she would do her best to find out and also would think about how to make contact when she had the information. She had apparently also said to Cat that she ought to look after me, as she 'had a good one there'.

Dougie discovered from the sparks in Lochinver that PACCO was probably a call sign from a radio ham station registered in the Netherlands

I had told Cat and Dougie that in due course I would write a note and then that I would be the one who dealt with the police, as I did not want them to be involved, not for their sakes particularly but mainly because so far as possible I needed to ensure that Billy was never mentioned. So one evening, early in the school holidays, when Cat came down to make me some tea, we sat after the meal with a piece of paper and I wrote a little note for the police.

Ewan Mathieson,
Shore Croft,
Clackmore,
Sutherland.

29th July 1964

To whom it may concern,
I the undersigned wish you to investigate what I believe may be a smuggling operation which is being done through the hamlet of Clackmore, Sutherland. My interest in the matter started when in the autumn of 1963 I became aware that a small trawler 'Deveronvale 36' registered as PD 355 had set up moorings in the channel at the end of

Clackmore Bay road, a dead end road terminating at a jetty.

This was unusual and as time went on things became more unusual in that this vessel only rarely went to sea and when it did it was often at night and only for short periods of a few hours. Added to this a black Commer van registration number APO 514 B seemed to service the trawler and the two men usually driving it were aggressive and rude and annoyed not just me, but many other local people with their actions and attitude. So as a result I decided to make further personal enquiries, to satisfy my own interest. I give below some of the other information which I have got as a result of these enquiries.

The trawler may be registered to a Graham Thompson whose home address may be in Clergy Street, Macduff. It is clear from my observations that whatever he is doing it is unlikely to be normal fishing, since he only puts to sea about once every month for a few hours. There seems little evidence on the working area of the trawler of fish being recently caught and no apparent landing of fish at the jetty or, so far as I can tell, at local fish docks.

I visited Macduff and spoke to a fisherman, Stuart, surname not known, who said to me that he had helped Thompson, by sailing as crew from Macduff when the trawler was brought round here and he helped him to lay the present moorings. He said that Thompson had recently acquired the vessel and, despite this, he seemed quiet and unhappy on the trip round. I wonder if Thompson is under some form of duress in relation to his ownership or operation of the vessel.

I observed one of the trips that the trawler made on 1st July 1964; at that time I had access to a VHF radio receiver. The vessel left its moorings at approximately 2130 and proceeded straight out into the Minch in vaguely a north westerly direction. At about 2300 I heard a call up on Channel 16 VHF stating that the caller was 'Deliverer' and asking for 'Receiver'. I was unable to hear any reply but there was one, I must assume, since they changed to Channel 8. My understanding of the one-sided conversation was that 'Deliverer' had put two lighted packages overboard for the other vessel; I believe the trawler, to collect.

It may be that the 'Deliverer' is a vessel called 'Spiro' and it may have links to a radio station with a call sign of PACCO or be related to that call sign. I understand that call sign may be registered in the Netherlands and I also believe that the vessel has links with that country. Similarly PD 355 may have some relation to the UK radio call sign GAEKP.

I observed two packages to be removed from the trawler and brought ashore when it returned at about 0130 on 2nd July and the contents were unpacked and loaded into the Commer van. All packaging was also removed. The van normally stays at Newton Lodge.

Some of the above facts, especially relating to the trip I monitored I can confirm on oath, the other things are just my guesses. One other practical point of fact is that two leading lights have been unofficially installed at the end of the bay to aid the trawler's night time navigation. These are battery operated so must be activated by the trawler crew when it intends going out. So far as I know nobody has permission to install these lights.

I believe that a person named Eric Porter who has recently been living at Newton Lodge may be involved in this operation, even if he does not participate personally in the trawler trips.

I have set down these facts in advance as I am proposing to attempt to obtain some further physical evidence as to the nature of what, I suspect, is some illegal

importation scheme on the next occasion the trawler goes out and then I will immediately bring that evidence to you along with this letter.
Ewan Mathieson

    When I put down the pen I turned to Cat.

    "Do you think that reads OK? In the sense that it says all the facts and conjecture are mine? The last thing I want to do is to drop Billy in it in any way."

    "No, you have made it sound that you were being a real nosey parker." She replied.

    "Well when we either get, or fail to get, a result from the next trip," I said, "I will take it to the police and I will be the one who gives the evidence in the main, although sadly I guess you and Dougie could possibly be dragged into it, but hopefully I can try to avoid that. But there is one final piece of information that you do not know and I am only telling you, and you alone, for the purposes of what Billy referred to as insurance. You see as well as the note Billy also gave me a letter which was sealed in the presence of some official and it sets out his own information. I want to avoid this being brought up, but if, at the end of the day I or you or Dougie get into any trouble then we will have to make reference to the letter, which is in the hands of Mr McKay my solicitor in Inverness. I only want it referred to as a last resort, since it will incriminate Billy and drag him back from whatever life he is making for himself."

    Cat nodded.

    After that it was life as normal until one day Sally rode down to Alistair and Morag's house but both Alistair and Cat were out

    She asked Morag to be sure to tell Cat 'tomorrow night'. Morag relayed the message to Cat and she passed it on to me and I to Dougie.

Tomorrow night.
Thursday, 13 August 1964.
Unlucky for some?

Tragic Coincidence

It occurred to me, that August Thursday morning, walking towards Dougie's croft, that I had been fortunate in having fair weather days on many of the significant occasions in my life at Clackmore. It had been a nice day when I drew up in my van and studied the croft house on my first day. Then again my day of remembrance at Achmelvich was fine and so, relatively speaking, was the weather on the day we had spied upon the trawler. Today was different, a misty drizzle wetted me as I walked, and upon my arrival at Dougie's house he greeted me, in a return to his monosyllabic ways of our early days, with single the word. "Dreich."

"Very." I replied, mirroring his loquaciousness.

He had been awaiting my arrival and so without further ado, or indeed conversation, we headed off down towards the jetty. We had agreed the previous evening that we needed to reconnoitre a suitable hiding place for me to be used when the trawler was returning, as I had volunteered to be the one to try to collect a sample of the cargo. Dougie had suggested that it was not sufficient just to lurk at the back of the old shed because, although it would be dark, it was just possible that I could be noticed as the trawler came in, if they studied the shoreline at all.

After about half an hour of poking about, through bits of heather and long grass and the odd bit of gorse, we were agreed that a group of rocks twenty yards from the shed would be the ideal location. I could shelter there and when they rowed ashore with the first package and set off to return to the trawler for the next, I could then quickly cover the distance to the shed. After peek around the corner to see when the tender had arrived at the trawler and they were busy starting to unload the second package, I could move forward and cut into the first one, try to obtain a sample of what was inside and then make a quick retreat.

Shortly afterwards the minibus came over the brow of the hill and, as arranged, Cat collected us and we went back to my croft for a welcome cup of tea and, in the case of Dougie and myself, an opportunity to dry out. We then rehearsed our plan which broadly went like this.

In the late afternoon, Cat was to tell Alistair and Morag that we were suspicious about what the trawler was up to and that we had thought it unwise to worry them by mentioning our concerns to them before this. She would also tell them that we were planning on observing what they were doing tonight and, having done so, we were going to share our suspicions with the police. She would be explaining that she was not involved, it was just Dougie and I, but that she was coming down to make me some tea, because it was probably going to be an all-night operation since the trawler seemed to not get back in until two or three in the morning. She would remain in my croft with me and Dougie until the men in the van went down to the trawler, sometime in the mid-evening. She would then return to their house until Dougie and I called and we would then all set off for a visit to the local constable.

For our part Dougie, Cat and I planned to have our meal and once the van had gone by we would wave Cat off back home, so that her parents would not be worried; for undoubtedly they would note the passing of the van too. Dougie and I would remain at my place for a good two hours and then we would go to his house and keep watch for the lights of the trawler, on its return journey. As soon as the lights became visible I would nip down the road to the boat shed and traverse the twenty yards to my rocky hiding place, to await time for action. Finally it was agreed that if there was any sign of danger of our being seen, or if they changed arrangements and did not leave the first package unattended, then we would abort the exercise and go to the police anyway.

Despite this detailed rehearsal of our plan we found it was only mid-morning and there were probably twelve or so hours until the action could begin. After the animation of discussing the plans conversation gradually dried up, as I suppose each of us began to reflect upon what lay ahead. Eventually it was decided that Dougie had some work he could do in the garage and Cat could take her mother shopping into Lochinver and so those two went about their business leaving me to my own devices. I felt very much at a loose end and given the weather I wasn't much motivated to start any outside job, so I turned my attention to some outstanding paperwork in relation to invoices and bills for Dougie's garage repairs. That took me through till an early lunch when I made a piece and mug of tea for both myself and Dougie but he took his outside, so that he could carry on with some job that he was in the middle of in the barn.

I have no memory of the afternoon beyond the fact that it was interminable and I was greatly relieved when, about five o'clock, Cat arrived and with that began preparation of our evening meal. Conversation during the meal and during the clearing and washing up was desultory to say the least, there was clear anxiety in all of us, but nobody wanted to be the first to admit it. Not long after eight o'clock Mr Roy, who had been allowed in out of the continuing drizzle rose up with his 'woof, woof' to indicate the approach of a vehicle. I immediately went to the door and outside and I walked away from the croft house with Mr Roy running excitedly around me, no doubt in the mistaken belief that after a boring day of inactivity at last I was going out to do something. I needed to check that all looked in order with the Commer van. So busy was I looking towards them that I inadvertently didn't see Mr Roy passing in front of me and almost tripped right over him. For this reason my usual clear view of the front of the van as it passed over the bridge across the stream was interrupted and delayed slightly. But, before the van was passed me completely, I was able to look up and, whilst my quick glance did not enable me to confirm the identity of the people, it did confirm that there were two passengers beside the driver. So the normal arrangement was being followed.

About half an hour later I walked Cat out to the minibus and gave her a kiss and she hugged me.

"Now just be careful," she said and with that she got in and drove off.

The next hour and a half went so slowly. I was reminded of a song, I think it was from a musical and whether I had the words right I do not know but in my memory what had stuck in my head was 'the minutes go like hours and the hours go so slowly' and I thought how apt those words were to my present situation. I envied Dougie who had taken himself off to an armchair and looked to be sound asleep. Eventually, painfully, the big hand on Uncle Roddy's ticking mantelpiece clock got to the twelve and the little hand pointed to the eleven and I felt able to wake him.

"Okay Dougie let's make a start."

Once again Mr Roy was disappointed to find that I provided him with a bowl of water, he much preferred his regular trips to the stream, and fastened him up to the rope to leave him outside. He followed Dougie and I out into the rain.

"Go back in your silly dog. Sit in the porch it's nice and dry." With several looks over his doggie shoulder and head hanging, he went slowly back into the porch turned and the last I saw of him he was sitting and watching us.

We crested the rise and looked down in the darkness and from what we could make out there was no trawler in the inlet. The mist in the air from the continuing drizzle made visibility less than usual, a factor which had not occurred to us in our plans. After a brief discussion we felt it worthwhile walking down to the jetty, to make sure that the trawler was definitely gone and also to check that there was nobody about. The Commer van had been turned in the small area near the jetty and had been reversed with its back doors towards the jetty itself, ready for loading.

"Looks like they're all organised", I said to Dougie and he agreed.

"I'm a bit bothered about the visibility," said Dougie, "we had assumed that, watching from my croft, we would be able to see the trawler's lights long before she reached the inlet and this would have given you plenty of time to get down to your hiding spot. But now I'm not so sure. From up there on the hill we may not see the trawler's lights until she's well into the inlet and if we wait till then they might see you scurrying down."

"That's okay," I said, "I'll come down in good time we just have to estimate what time she's going to be back."

Bearing in mind what had happened on the previous occasion, we felt that they could not be back before about one in the morning, so I could come down and hide in the rocks about twelve thirty. With this in mind we retreated out of the weather into Dougie's croft house for another long wait.

Frustration, or anxiety, or whatever, led me to become so impatient that at just after midnight I said I thought I would l go down to hide, and although Dougie tried to put me off I was leaving his home just ten minutes later. In the meantime I had made a quick toilet trip and then double checked that I had all I needed to cut open the packages. In a small holdall I had already gathered in advance a sharply honed kitchen knife, a Stanley knife and just in case they were insufficient I also had packed a hand held axe as well.

Within twenty minutes of hiding amongst the rocks I was already feeling wet and cold and realising that Dougie had been right about not setting off too early. An hour or more later I was utterly miserable, frozen and fast losing the will to continue with this operation. So it was with inordinate relief that at about one twenty in the morning I thought I heard the sound of an engine. Moments later I caught a glimpse of the trawler's white masthead light and also its green navigation light as it proceeded slowly up the inlet. Despite the drizzle there was little in the way of wind and voices could be heard presumably in general discussion and with orders relating to picking up the mooring buoy.

After some time, with occasional distant shouting, things went quiet and in a while I heard the boat bumping alongside the jetty. I dared not look but conversation started again and some of it was angry. There was sound of canvas being dragged along the ground, some indistinct conversation, and then the sound of the van door being opened and then shut. Shortly after that the sound of the boat setting off again and, as I had rehearsed in my mind, I counted slowly to fifty to give good time for the boat to be on its way back to the trawler. Then I risked a peek and sure enough it was over half way there. I felt for the holdall and stooping low I ran for the boat shed and crouched beside it. Twenty yards away the van was parked in darkness, facing uphill away from me, with its rear doors opened ready for loading.

I rose, ready to make my attempt on the package, when my heart nearly jumped out of my chest as a crouching figure was running towards me and I was paralysed with fear.

"Leave it Ewan and come away!" Said a breathless Dougie.

I was a million miles away from recovering my 'sang' and the 'froid' stood not one chance in a million of being found, so, instead of obeying the clear command, I dithered in a mentally uncomprehending state.

"Bloody come on Ewan," Dougie insisted, but seeing that I needed to be given some understanding or reason, he blurted out.

"Cat and Sally are up at my croft. Sally says that your man got a tip off today that the cops are onto his little operation and he went mad. He got so mad that the drunken cook upset him and Sally thinks he shot her. He came down here in the front with the minders and the skipper must have been in the back of the van. They are taking this load and getting out."

As my heart began to resume its normal place in my chest and my disorientated brain began to comprehend what he was saying, Dougie made another attempt to engender some action from me.

"Ewan! He's apparently gone mad and he has got a gun: so come on!"

We just had time to take about half a dozen paces when the headlights of the van snapped on and the driver's door was flung open and the angry aggressive husband, of that visit to my house to collect Sally, appeared. The interior light of the van showed that there was a black looking item in his right hand. He commanded us to stay where we were and calmly addressed us in a voice that was hard, firm and steady, no trace of the emotion or anger. Or, if it was there, it was well controlled.

"What a good job I decided to stay in the van, after bringing the first load and let those tosser's do the rest of the hard work. So I was on hand to see two idiots who appear daft enough to take me on. Are you coppers? Move over a bit more into the headlights and let's see who we are dealing with."

He waved the arm attached to the hand that held the black thing, motioning us to move nearer the centre of the road where the headlights were illuminating the aged crumbling wet tarmac.

"Well, well, well the bloody pig farmer from the cottage near the sea and a mate. You had me worried there for a while, I thought you might have been a real threat. What are you yokels up to then, yer Scots scum?"

Having recovered a bit from my paralysis I found my tongue was a bit more in control than my bowels.

"Sheep." I said.

"Ha," he laughed, "trying to make me believe that you are rounding up sheep at this time of night don't be stupid."

"No. I am a sheep farmer; I don't keep pigs in fact, after your visit to my house, I realised that you were the first pig ever to come onto my croft. What is more I know what you have been up to with your trawler and it is not fishing. You are a drug smuggler."

"So, was it you that talked to the cops?" He said his tone hardening

What, my mind asked, was it that Sally had said about his belief that he was untouchable and whenever anybody threatened him he became very angry? Perhaps now, if I could upset his current apparent personal equilibrium, he might get angry and that might offer an opportunity for getting out of this awful situation. Revealing that a lot was known about him and his operation might upset him enough to make him angry.

"You mean telling them a few helpful truths like the short wave radio connection between a station in the Netherlands and one in the UK. About the 'deliverer' and the 'receiver' and the 'Spiro' and this fishing trawler and the fact that one of your early deliveries went to Boyo in Richmond." I was here remembering the contents of Billy's note.

He was obviously surprised but spoke in a level tone.

"I suppose next you're going to tell me how much Boyo paid me for that little lot."

"Twenty five grand, I believe." I said, guessing.

I suspect that, if I had been able to see his face, his bottom jaw may just have slackened a little bit in surprise.

"So," I hurried on, "I told them that I would try to get some evidence for them tonight, by ripping open the first package when, if things had been normal, your lads dumped it and went back for the next. But fair enough, you have nabbed us so what about we let you get all the stuff in the van and set off. We will promise not to tell the cops till the morning and you and your two can get off and sell your stuff and then hide."

"How did you contact the cops?" He asked.

Good question.

"Well, I know a policemen in Inverness and I told him and he passed it on."

"For a while there I was starting to believe you, but you see today I had a little call from a copper in London over whom I have a little, what shall we say, 'influence', and he told me that some anonymous written evidence had arrived with the drugs squad in London and so it obviously was not a telephone call from some plod in Inverness.

So I do not think your suggestion is going to be the way forward. I shall be sticking to my plan and just in case you may be interested I have always succeeded because I am good at snooker. When you are a good snooker player you learn the art of planning your next shot, of thinking ahead, and I have always been good at that. So this lot goes in the van and me and my boys go south, cash in more than double what I got for that first lot and, with false passports all ready, we are off to get some sunshine in a nice little place I have been preparing, which doesn't have any extradition arrangements with dear 'Old Blighty'. As well as thinking ahead, you sometimes need to be able to make tough, ruthless decisions in life, and most people I have ever dealt with are too weak, but not me. If people stand in my way they fall."

"Like Harry Evans?" I asked.

Again he was thrown a bit.

"Well Harry was bringing trouble to my door so he needed to make an exit"

"No!" I said. "You had been the cause of the trouble and Harry was a way for you to throw the cops off your scent. You had been the one to kill that woman and child when you were driving Harry away from that jewellery robbery in Hounslow. You and your arrogant disregard for anybody who, heaven forbid, would dare to try to get in the way of Mr Bloody Knuckles Porter and what he wanted."

"So what? Two people were in my way and I could have avoided them. But if I had I could well have lost control of the car again and I would have been caught. Didn't mean them any harm; wrong place for them to be at the wrong time. Simple equation, succeed or fail. I always succeed whatever it takes. Anyway what is that to do with you?"

"Only that they were my wife and only daughter, which is probably of no consequence to you but it changed my life. I came up here to escape from the memory of that loss that you caused and then by amazing coincidence you turn up on my doorstep."

"Well, there's a coincidence indeed," he said, "just the one problem for you is, it's a tragic and fatal coincidence"

And after letting the words hang in the air for a while he continued.

"Because you and your hillbilly mate here," he said waving the black object in his hand at Dougie, "are just gonna have to go bye bye's, in order for us to be sure that nobody is going to set the cops on us before we have got ourselves our money and then got off to the sun."

During this bit of conversation the two thugs and trawler skipper, having heard the initial commotion ashore, had come hurriedly back to support their boss and at this point the boat bumped alongside the jetty and the men got out and came towards the little tableau in the headlights of their van.

Without taking his eyes from us, Knuckles addressed these three newcomers over his right shoulder in a very cold and calculating level voice.

"So, these two local yokels seem to have been a bit more active than I'd realised and they certainly know a lot about our operation. But it doesn't matter since we were finishing today anyway and this nice little earner of an operation has to be put to one side, all because of these two bastards and some other meddling person down in the smoke. They are, sadly for them, probably in a position to be star witnesses as far as I can see and I don't like star witnesses, especially those who think they're gonna star against me. So here's what we are gonna do.

I am gonna get rid of these two in a moment and you, Thommo," he said addressing the trawler skipper, "are going to take the bodies, tie a couple of rocks to them and when you get far enough offshore, you're gonna throw them over the side and your payment for this will be that you can return to your fishing and keep the trawler."

"Graham Thompson," I said, "don't believe a word of it, you and Mary and Jess and Jenny may not remain under his direct control, but he will sell the debt on to somebody else and you will never escape."

Speaking to me the skipper said.

"So it was you giving Mary some milk and a cock and bull story about being with the Education Department."

"Yes," I said, "and whatever you do don't believe any promises this man makes you."

During these exchanges I had been conscious that Dougie, who, when we had first been stopped was only about three paces away from me, to my left, had been inching further away from me and at this point he burst into a run back towards the boat shed.

Immediately Knuckles brought his arm up and swinging it to his right fired twice at Dougie, dispelling any possible doubt that the black object, in his hand, was indeed a firearm.

"You stay where you are." he commanded me.

"You two," he addressed the thugs, "find him! One of you each side of that shed; when you get him kill him."

Returning to look in my direction he began an advance in my direction.

"Goodbye Mr Busybody it's time to say your prayers if you are that way inclined."

"Do not do it! You bastard." Screamed a female voice from somewhere behind me, back up the road. I glanced over my shoulder and there on the edge of the beam of the van's lights were two women. The speaker had been Sally, and then beside her, was Cat.

Sally went on.

"You can't kill everybody in the world just to cover up all your crimes," she said to her husband, "it's time to realise that too many people know about what you've done."

"You girls go away," I shouted, "one of you go to the left and the other right and run into the darkness, they can't deal with me and Dougie and come looking for you as well. Just hide and let him go away and get on his boat or plane and disappear to whatever hidey-hole he has planned. I just want to know you are both safe."

"Good advice," said Knuckles, "and I will give him this, it's a good plan but you are not going to run for two reasons. The first is that it will be light in a couple of hours and, believe me we would find you but more important, Sally, you slag, is that if you do not behave I will find that precious brat of yours and get rid of him. So you'll do what you have always done and that is to do like I tells yer so he can survive. Anyway, we're wasting time and this one," indicating me, "has annoyed me and I don't like people who annoy me. His arm came up again, this time in a more measured way and directed towards me, but, just at this moment there was a scream from by the shed.

"Bastard's got an axe and has nearly chopped me bloody arm off." Screamed one of the men.

The scream caused Knuckles to glance away from me momentarily and I realised this was my chance and I'd covered the three paces, well actually two and a half of them, before he realised his mistake in looking away from me. The raised arm which had turned over ninety degrees to face the direction of the shed now swung back towards me. At that point I experienced another moment of excessively high emotion, similar but different to the occasion when that policeman had come to do his death knock at my office door.

A confusion of sounds shattered the still wet, night.

There was the screaming from the man who had discovered, far too late, that Dougie had retrieved the axe in my holdall. There were shouts of warning and anguish from the trawler skipper, Sally and Cat. There was somewhere in the very back of my mind a wailing sound, which I knew was familiar from my days in Feltham, yet which, my mind elsewhere, I could not quite place. Then, there was a sort of plop sound, as Knuckles fired his gun too early with the upswing of his arm and almost at once a searing pain in my left hip. Then I was onto him grappling for my life. Adrenaline raced through my body as I concentrated on grabbing at his arm and I successfully did so, but as I pushed it away from me he managed to pull the trigger yet again.

And I heard a scream from behind me.

No time to deal with all those things buzzing round in my head, my life was on the line. So I fought and I kicked and I scratched and I bit and despite the fact that Knuckles was a strong man he had made the mistake of letting others do too much of his physical dirty work over the last few years. On the other hand I was a crofter, I carried bales of hay, animal feed and sometimes even animals themselves, and so I was fit. My wound was just above the thigh, as it turned out, but even with that flesh wound he was no match for me, given the two factors of my current strength and fitness levels, on the one hand and the imperative that I did not wish to die on the other.

Towards the end of the struggle I was conscious of hearing the sound of running boots approaching, but my mind-set was clear, to get the gun and turn its business end away from me. I believe he discharged it once more, during the struggle and no doubt he was planning to fire again, but, as I ripped his arm across his body, the gun went off and fairly quickly the strength seemed to go away from him.

I was hauled to my feet by a huge man in the uniform of the Ross and Cromarty Police force, commonly the 'Big Heilan Polis' to local folk, I'm sure they had to be over six feet tall to be accepted in that force in those days, and I turned to an amazing scene.

There were at least three sets of vehicle headlights shining down the road and one of the cars had been exited so quickly that the wailing siren noise was still sounding, until somebody turned it off, and in its place were shouts and scuffles A few of the men around were dressed in police uniforms and others were not, but those not engaged in grappling with prisoners, or attending to the wounded, were all looking somewhat shocked at the scene they found themselves amongst.

I felt disorientated standing there in the continuing drizzle, beginning to regain breath as the towering constable knelt beside me doing something with, or to, the slumped figure of Knuckles.

Then I heard a cry.

"Help me, help me," in a voice I immediately recognised as belonging to Cat.

It was her voice, but it was strained and breathless.

I looked up the road and there, in the midst of it all, between the newly arrived vehicles and me I could see Dougie.

Our eyes met and he looked at me and shook his head.

Just beside him I could just see Cat, doubled over, head facing away from me.

In the vehicle's headlights I could see, trickling slowly down the wet road beside her in my direction, a spreading and ever-increasing pool of blood.

Post Script

I have been writing this tale from the very nice Highland Council sheltered accommodation in which I have lived these past couple of years. At the age of seventy eight in 2013, I eventually surrendered to what had for some time been the inevitable. For the first year and a bit after moving here I was quite able to get out with my sticks and walk the fifty or so yards to the main road where it runs beside the sea. There I could occupy myself for hours, just sitting on a bench and watching the fishing boats in the bay and the traffic on the road. Occasional passers-by would stop to pass the time of day, as is the Highland custom. Such a very civilised custom, I think.

In the summer months when tourists invaded and there were more people about, ironically, meaningful contact was less frequent, since many of my regular local contacts became busier in their seasonal jobs servicing the needs of those very visitors. Then again, most visitors, who have more time than usual in their busy lives, are still unlikely to approach a curmudgeonly looking old guy, with a couple of sticks, sat on a bench. Children sometimes approach and will say a word or two until they are called away by their city-minded parents who are so hidebound by the 'don't talk to strangers' message, that they intercede with a 'I hope s/he has not been bothering you'.

Over time, from my original suburban roots, I had transmogrified into the highlander approach to life with an insatiable interest in all around me, and especially my fellow man and woman. Never losing a chance to 'have a blether' with anyone who came my way. Also, over time since my arrival, I had become a real crofter, of whom my benefactor, Uncle Roddy, as well as my own father, would have been proud. To have to surrender to the ravages of health and not to make it to the blissful prospect of a death on the croft, which had come to mean so much to me, in emulation of Uncle Roddy, was one of my great disappointments in life. But the alleged benefits of our wonderful health system are not, in my opinion, necessarily a good thing. Animals, I had come to recognise, go when their time comes. The Vet may be called occasionally but by and large we let the animals go and I am sorry that in this brave new world they would not let me go as I would have wished, on the croft. But I have tried not to be too disappointed and to make the best of things.

In my case a slight stroke robbed me of some movement on my left side and affected my leg more than my hand. It made it impossible for me to continue crofting in the way to which I had become accustomed. At first I resisted, but not only was I assailed by these health problems, there was the changed nature of the place I had so come to love. After 1976 crofters could buy their crofts and then, of course, they could go on to sell them and gradually the crofting community became the holiday home location. Nothing at all like the community which had so enveloped me when I first moved there in 1963. Furthermore, there was nobody left there to help me. Dougie, Alistair, Morag and my dear wife all left me in the ten years up to 2005. Every death, of each of these wonderful friends, felt like a nail in my own coffin as I make my inexorable way to that which awaits us all. But for those responsible for providing health care to the elderly in a sparsely populated area, with limited resources, I presented a problem which would be better and more economically managed by admission to sheltered accommodation.

Their arguments were strong and I could see that. As with Roddy, my bed was back downstairs and I could not do everything for myself; toenails were the most frustrating challenge. I hung on for a while but when my last dog died, I succumbed to what I had realised for some time was the inevitable.

About six months ago even my simple pleasure of independently walking, albeit slowly and with a pair of sticks, to my favourite seat near the sea, was denied to me and any option for going outside required a wheelchair. My wonderful, wonderful, carers chatter to me, bringing all the local gossip and news and get me from bed to wheelchair in the mornings and reverse the process at night. When that first happened they would station me, after my breakfast in the morning, facing the little driveway outside my flat. There were the occasional passers-by, though not many and the days were long, even with my old friend, the radio, to help me.

My carers understood my great desire to go outside but they had not the time in their busy schedules to help me. They did, however, arrange for some local volunteers from the Kirk to come, on days when it was not raining or exceedingly cold, and push me over to beside my favourite seat. To start with, whichever one came thought they were doing me a favour by sitting on the seat beside me and chatting. After a while I managed to persuade them that, whilst I appreciated it and all they did for me, it would be nice also to be left alone for an hour or so. I think a bit reluctantly and with disappointment they spoke together and agreed if that's what I wanted, then that's what they should do and as a result a few old friends did stop by, when they saw me sitting in the chair alone, and that was rather nice.

One day staring out watching a trawler making its way towards the open sea, my mind went back to the events of 1964 and my second summer at Clackmore. It was an autumn day and it occurred to me that my visits to this favourite vantage point would soon begin to diminish, as increasingly my twice weekly assistants would deem the weather too wet or too cold and forgetting, of course, that being out in the elements was part of my life. Watching that trawler then made me wonder if I could pass some of the winter months by writing down all that happened in those very early days up here. My army days had taught me to type and so I mentioned to one of my carers about sourcing me a typewriter. She laughed and told me she could do better than that.

That was how I became the proud possessor of somebody's cast off computer, complete with tower, screen and keyboard. One of my wheelchair pushers also sourced me a trainer to teach me how to write things on the screen and to save what I had written. In fact this trainer turned out to be a spotty faced 14-year-old young man who did manage to train me in the simple skills of what I suppose you might call word processing, but it was not without frustration for him, as I ponderously had to write down every step to be taken in accessing my file and saving it. Nevertheless I got there and it's most significant product is the tale that you have just waded through – unless you got so bored you skipped to the end.

My son Roddy read the story and complained that I had ended it at the epilogue. He said I needed to round it off by saying what happened afterwards. I was against it initially because I thought that it was better to have an enigmatic ending, and anyway anybody reading it would just have to talk to him and he could explain. The matter was left unresolved and I would have left it there but I found that I missed filling my days with my one-handed tapping of the keys. It's hard-working with just one hand

and certainly trying to do 'shift' and make a letter into a capital is a right pain.

Roddy, I suppose the Americans would say Roddy Jr, has turned out a fine young man. I'm so glad that he came into my life as a result of those awful events of 1964 and I'm also glad that, in the fullness of time, I was able to adopt him, it was always planned but it took ages before it could happen. There was all the rigmarole of the police investigation, complicated by the legal differences between Scotland and England. My role in causing the death of Eric Porter was months under consideration by the Police and the Procurator Fiscal. I was not charged with any offence at the end of it all. Only then could the authorities begin to look at my desire to adopt which led to a period of enquiry by the Social Work Department and moved on to several visits from a Curator ad Litem, the independent reporter to the Courts. But finally, two years later, I got there.

When he was adopted he was given the middle name of Roderick as a nod to what would have been his late uncle by adoption and almost immediately I began to call him Roddy, as a way of trying to distance him from that fearful, silent and oppressed little boy who had lived at Newton Lodge. I believe it was helpful to him to continue to go to the same school and to begin to be accepted by the other local children. His happiness appeared to increase exponentially over the next years and he loved the life on the croft, with his great friend Mr Roy and with his absolutely greatest friend, uncle Dougie.

That dear man taught him practical engineering from a very early age, almost to the point where it upset me sometimes that little Roddy would far prefer to have his head stuck in a vehicle engine than be out doing crofting work. Neither of them were great talkers, Dougie through his experience of mental illness and Roddy through the repression of his early years, but they became almost inseparable and, working together, Roddy learnt how to fix anything and everything. Fortunately, by the time he was due to go to secondary school in 1971, he was a much more rounded individual than might have been the case had he continued in his former life. He was loved in his new home by us, his adoptive grandparents, his special friend Dougie, by Mr Roy and by the 'extended family' of various the crofters around. Through all this he became a secure child and one able to go forward into the world confident that he knew who he was and being comfortable with that.

Eventually, and inevitably, he went off to study engineering and became highly qualified and is now managing an engineering firm in Glasgow. He is living up in Helensburgh with his lovely Polish wife Dorota, which she tells me means 'God's gift'. She has certainly been God's gift to him, because I know he is very happy with her and they have two lovely children, my grandchildren. Their son is called Peter, but on his birth certificate it is spelt Piotr, after his maternal grandfather of that name, who had been part of the First Independent Parachute Brigade of Poland. This was formed in the Second World War, based initially in Scotland, and after the war Piotr settled in Glasgow. Roddy and Dorota's daughter, and apple of my eye, I must confess, is named for her paternal grandmother.

Linda.

They used to come up once or twice a year, when the kids were younger, and help out round the croft at hay time and they loved to come in 'tattie' week. As time went on and the children got a bit older, and Roddy became more successful at work, they took to staying in one of the hotels in Lochinver, because the croft was very basic still and they could easily afford it, given Roddy's employment. They also came back to bury friends and relatives. Roddy was clearly moved at the death of his mother but the emotion was equally as high when his mentor Dougie died. He gave a eulogy at the funeral in a packed Kirk in which he told Dougie's life tale, warts and all, and ended with this wonderful tribute. I have the note he made for himself on a dog eared bit of paper still.

'My mum and dad gave me so much and I am most grateful to them for all their love and help. But, I first met Dougie when I was only about six years old and I had come from what, nowadays, people would call a very 'dark place'. He let me work alongside him and over many years I learned to fix any, and every, mechanical thing. He was there most days of my childhood; just there listening, teaching and never judging. When I was going to college he said to me how happy he was and how he was sure I would do well. He looked me in the face and said 'I know it will be fine because I looked into your eyes when you first came to work with me and I saw a very troubled soul. Now your eyes tell me that your darkness has gone' and I knew he was right.'

Now, I thought, where did I hear that before?

Before I return to that dark day in 1964, there is one other subsequent event which may help you understand the nature of the happenings on that fateful day.

There was a knock on my door at the croft in about 2006, not long after my wife had died, a middle-aged man who looked somewhat familiar stood there and asked if I was Ewan Mathieson. I did not get many callers whom I did not know and who asked for me by name, so I was somewhat cautious and said 'who wants to know?' This somewhat flustered the young man, whom I now realised, spoke with an American accent. He told me that he was sorry but that he was on a mission to pass on something that his father had requested him to let Ewan Mathieson, of Shore Croft, Clackmore, Scotland, have, after his death. Apparently his father had died the previous year, and the young man explained that as a Canadian, (so I got the accent wrong then) he had a number of friends who were descended from Scots and who said how 'pretty' (his word not mine) the country was here, so he thought he would deliver the letter in person.

He indicated that his hire car contained his wife and two teenage children and I invited them all to come away in. The adults exchanged glances and after negotiation including explanations involving, a long trip, non-stop from Ullapool, lunch time, nice beach, picnic stuff in the car, etc., it was agreed that his wife and kids would go to the beach. That left dad to do the business with the scruffy old man in the run down croft house. Anyway, it turned out he was William Edwards, son of Billy, yes, he turned out to be the son of my erstwhile friend Billy Johnson. His mission, entrusted to him by his dying father, was to bring me a photograph and a story. We did the story first.

It was simple. Billy had gone to Canada, as I had suspected, where his friend set him up with accommodation and a job working in his host's business as a carpenter and joiner; a skill which, unbeknown to me, had been a hobby of Billy's in his secondary school days, when we were out of touch. Initially he was working for his friend around Vancouver, where very quickly he became involved with a young woman and they decided to set up home together.

Not wanting another life of looking over his shoulder, he was honest with his girlfriend and he told her his whole story. She absolved him from significant blame, but said that they ought to try and regularise things and that one way would be to give the police in London information about Knuckles Porter, without revealing Billy's identity. She helped him by typing an anonymous letter containing the details from his original letter which he had taken with him. The letter from which the copy he had handed to me at the Red Lion had been made and which I had later lodged with Mr McKay my solicitor. She arranged for a friend, who was a merchant seaman, to post the letter at his next port, which in fact turned out to be San Diego, in California. The letter was addressed to the police at 'New Scotland Yard, London, England' and was posted air mail in the middle of June.

Subsequently he was made aware of the death of Porter and supported by his fiancée he made a clean breast of things to the Canadian authorities. Over a couple of years, which included contact between the British and Canadian authorities, his story was checked and eventually he was able to apply for Canadian citizenship. During this time the man before me was born and was given the surname Edwards, as that was his mother's name and the couple were not at that stage married. In fact Billy subsequently changed his name to Edwards as part of moving to his new life. William told me his father and mother had a happy marriage and indeed his mother was still alive. He, himself, had enjoyed a happy childhood and he felt that at the end his father had been proud of all he had achieved for his family.

Before my visitor went to join his wife and kids he handed me a colour photograph showing a family group, Billy, beside a rather cheerful looking big woman whom I presumed to be his wife, because beside her was a much younger version of the young man now before me and tall young woman.

"Mum and dad and me and," he said pointing to the very attractive tall blonde girl beside him, "that is my sister; Carole."

He noticed my emotions coming to the fore and making his excuses he went off to re-join his family; duty done.

After he left I stayed for a long time looking at the photo, thinking of Billy and being pleased that it had all worked out for him. Just out of curiosity I turned it over and read.

"Have often thought of my first real friend, but never wanted to lift any rocks in the old country, in case what came out did not suit. I just wanted you to know.
  Billy"

After the event at the jetty, and during the subsequent investigation and my questioning, it became clear that police concern about the dealings of Eric Porter had been of longstanding interest to them. Then several weeks prior to the fatal night, and out of the blue, a letter had been received post marked 'San Diego, California' offering a vast array of information about Porter's operations. It explained that contact was made between two radio hams, one working for Porter in London and the other working for his supplier in Rotterdam. This set the date and time for the 'drop' of the packages in the Minch and the ship adjusted its speed to ensure to be in the right location at the right time, always at night to ensure nobody could see what was happening.

Most information was historic, but very helpful nonetheless. It detailed certain alleged former deals, between Porter and known criminals and it all seemed to tie in with their own investigations. But it did not produce clear evidence sufficient to arrest and charge him with anything significant.

It had obviously, I deduced from what they said, included the information which Billy had given to me.

They described how they had been able to monitor the two short wave radio stations and to link the ship, which was indeed the 'Spiro', to the smuggling of drugs, which they suspected. They obtained this intelligence in respect of the previous trip, the one which Dougie and I had witnessed from his fishing boat. Enquiries with the coastguard and police in Rotterdam and Greenock showed that the 'Spiro', a little coaster, was not a hard worked vessel. She was based in a small port on the river Maas, in Holland, and seemed to make about one voyage a month, usually with very small cargoes bound for Greenock, Belfast or Dublin. Always on her three day outward journey she went north about mainland Britain, via the Pentland Firth, even though to get to Dublin in particular, it would have been shorter to go through the Straits of Dover and down the English Channel before turning up the Irish Sea.

Then they made further enquiries about Porter himself, as he had clearly left his old haunts in West London, and they discovered that he had moved to Newton Lodge. The local police had made discrete general enquiries and, of course, had already been led to understand, by local people, that the Newton Lodge residents were unpopular because of their general demeanour and behaviour. Also the peculiar location of the trawler was well known to local fishermen and they deduced that it was likely to be the scene of the landing of the drugs from the Spiro. So, they planned with the Ross and Cromarty Constabulary to mount an operation to catch the gang in the act, just as soon as any radio communication was intercepted specifying the date of the next trip. This meant that they became belatedly aware of the proposed trip on the 13th August. As the information only came to hand two days in advance, officers were dispatched from London to liaise with the local force and make plans to intercept the gang.

On the afternoon of the appointed day an officer, dressed in civilian clothes and posing as an ornithologist, approached the island from the opposite side, in a hired dinghy. He spent a miserable wet afternoon until he was able to report, by radio, that the trawler had left and gone out to sea. At this point the main force of officers, about seven I think, left Lochinver and drove to Stoer, about four miles from our jetty, where they waited for the lookout to report the trawler's return. The plan was that when the lookout reported that the gang were all ashore and could not escape out to sea again, then he would signal and the main group would move in. When the lookout saw that there was trouble by the jetty and then the trawler was vacated by all the remaining three hurrying to shore, he radioed to the main group to set off, warning sirens sounding.

There, I have done what young Roddy asked and tied up the loose ends.

I had been against my son's request to run the story to this conclusion, because the tale about the evening of the scattering the ashes mentioned in the prologue stands alone as an event which marked the termination of a transition period in my life. A period bookended by two significant sets of sudden deaths, both of which changed my life's course. Eighteen months on a roller coaster; from low to high to low again. By the greatest of good fortune the highs were to remain for many years until, as is the nature of life, things begin to decline to one's nadir.

Throughout my subsequent life, germinating the seed planted by uncle Roddy in his letter to me, I have lived by the sea and so most days, I have been able to look at it and call to mind the people whose memories it evokes. Not just the person whose ashes we scattered that day, but also my father, who's resting place it is and his brother Roddy, who saw that same sea as giving him memories of his much loved brother, lost to that element. For me it also brings to mind the new friends I made beside that sea, who have all gone before me, like Dougie, Alistair and Morag and my original Mr Roy and several of his successors.

But the sea has never been the catalyst for my remembrance of Linda and Carole, because their ethereal presence has always existed with me, and always will.

Those figures that returned to the cottage from the scattering of the ashes included young Henry, later to become Roddy my adopted son, with his then greatest friend, Mr Roy. In those early dark days he had little to say he just communicated silently, no doubt by osmosis, with that apparently understanding animal. Later on, when the old dog died, he transferred his affection to his new and lasting good friend; his Uncle Dougie.

Eventually, much later in that sombre, ashes scattering autumn evening, long after Henry was in bed and asleep, I looked at my wife, sitting by the fire and reflected on the tragic co-incidence which had caused the death of the woman we were that day mourning.

"There," I said, "hopefully we have set her free, and when I look at the sea on any day, but especially a calm one, I will think of her. Let's always remember that brave young woman that a billion to one chance random shot struck in the neck shattering her carotid artery. There was absolutely nothing anybody could have done to save her."

"I know, but it was awful that night with all the blood gushing out, with me bending over her trying to staunch the spurting artery and her looking at me, with pleading eyes and whispering to me, 'please, please look after Henry,'" said Cat.

"And we will." I replied.

And we did.

Acknowledgements

My first visit to the Assynt area of north west Scotland was in 1967 and I was so impressed with the beautiful scenery that I persuaded my wife to spend our honeymoon in the Culag Hotel, Lochinver in 1970. Six nights on full board and change from fifty pounds. We also returned to the area to camp in the first years of our marriage, until the children came along and then the long journey north was less appealing during their early years; especially after they ended the wonderful 'Motorail' service from York to Inverness. On one of these early holidays we were told the story, which appears in the book, about English criminals who attempted to hide from the law by wild camping in a tent in this 'remote' area where they believed they would never be found. Indeed, they were almost instantly noticed and arrested very quickly. Whether the story was true or apocryphal I do not know, but it became the long gestating germ for this tale.

There are several people who deserve thanks for bringing this tale to any reader. My first venture into print was to produce a snapshot of my work as a Probation Officer when I first took up that employment in the mid 1960s. With the help of Publish Nation, *"The Heydays for the Independent Probation Officer in England and Wales – 1950s to 1970s'* was self-published in 2018. They made getting into print such an easy exercise that I decided to use their servces again on this occasion.

Reading, re-reading and correcting is quite a chore I am grateful to Kathy, my wife, who was a long suffering helper in this task, but any remaining errors and omissions are of course mine. Throughout the project Kathy gave me support and encouragement and I particularly valued her patience and willingness to discuss themes and issues as I went along.

Then my friend from merchant navy days, Ian Brown, deserves the credit for introducing me to the Assynt area, where he grew up, in the first place. Then more recently for sending me some personal memories of his early life as background before I started writing. He also was kind enough to read a draft and comment on issues relating to the authenticity of a way of life which he experienced in his own childhood in both that area and era.

Perhaps here I should make clear that Clackmore does not exist, but I did have in mind the general land and seascape between Lochinver and Drumbeg as I constructed the tale, but Clackmore Bay is just a figment of my imagination.

Finally another long standing friend, Richard Alred, an established and successful landscape artist, agreed to paint an original cover picture for me. His professional work has often taken in views of Perthshire but he has visited Assynt and he also studied Kathy's photograhs of the general area I had in mind before producing this brilliant imaginary depiction of my fictitiuos location.

Baildon, West Yorkshire.   2020

www.ingramcontent.com/pod-product-compliance
Ingram Content Group UK Ltd.
Pitfield, Milton Keynes, MK11 3LW, UK
UKHW022021310325
456929UK00006B/477